I0703536

The Secret Within

C. J. Mellberg

Disclaimer

Warning for sensitive readers.

This book is suitable for eighteen years of age and over only. It contains chapters that can be hard to read for some readers, having the following triggers: It contains blood violence, rape, explicit sex, and war. Some are more described than others places. So be aware.

This is Book One of a series.

Contents

Dedications

For my wonderful boys.

Acknowledgments

I want to express my heartfelt gratitude to my three wonderful boys, who have been my rock every step of the way. Through this journey, I hope to show them that whatever you set your mind to, you can achieve—no matter how challenging it gets. Keep pushing forward, embrace the learning process, and never regret the obstacles along the way. Keep looking ahead, keep dreaming big, and never stop believing in yourself.

I will always love and support you all my boys. All of you will always be in my heart and be my strength.

I also want to give a big thank you to Gary, Noalene, and Ciara.

Thank you for all the help and support you have given me in this journey and the encouragement for me to continue. Not even a thank you is enough for everything you have done for me. I love you all!

I also want to give a big thank you to all: Gary, Noalene, Ciara.

Thank you for all the help and support you have given me in this journey and the encouragement to continue. Not even a thank you is enough for everything you have done for me. I love you all.

This busy Mom of three boys, loves playtime and adventures with them. She never lacks excitement in her life as long as they keeps her on her toes. Cassandra also has many passions and interests in her spare time, which involves a great love of being creative. This has enabled her to teach her kids that whatever you put your mind to—if you put in the effort, you can achieve it.

Chapter 1

Let me invite you to read about my story through my words and, the words of those who were around me from as early as I can remember:

The rain started to pour down on the land. It was one of the worst rain storms to hit the country in two hundred and fifty years. The torrential rain cascaded down in sheets, drenching everything in its path. The storm unleashed its fury, causing trees to sway and groan violently, sending shivers down my spine. The air was charged with electricity, creating an atmosphere of both awe and terror.

As the rivers rose above their banks many of the roads were washed away, going on to create newly formed lakes on the fields they covered. Lightning intensified fast and fierce—the storm was close—the deafening cracks of thunder following immediately after every sizzling flash. It was so bad that you could feel the vibrations reverberating throughout your chest. The vibrations subtly changed, becoming more intense. The ground beneath your feet seemed to quiver. It was as if the very fabric of reality was being torn asunder. A disquieting high-pitched siren was beginning to sound its lonely wail. Then all the cries and the sounds of screams began to echo throughout the area.

"Run, my love, run for your life! Don't look back. Whatever happens, please go and find a safe place and stay there hidden. I promise I will come and find you, when it's safe again here so we can be together again. Please don't trust anyone; trust yourself and follow your heart. Never reveal your true self. Trust should be earned and not given freely to just anyone. Just run. I promise I will come after you, and bring you back home again to us to our home, just please run. I love you so much, my sweet child never ever forget this. You are the only reason for me to continue fighting for our life. I will see you soon, my dear daughter. Now run, don't look back, just keep running."

Then she started to push me towards the clearing in the direction of the forest. As I began running towards the opening to get into the cover of the thick woods, the heavy rains began to increase. My thin pink nightgown soaked through, clung to me like a desperate spider web ensnaring its next victim. I began to sob and run, but the tight, wet cloth made running impossible. Every step became treacherous. The very surroundings seemed to be out to get me; tree roots and rocks appeared to be blocking my path to safety. My face was turning red, my eyes were puffy and blood red from all the tears rolling down my face, allowing me to taste the bitter salt they contained, that the torrential rain could not wash away. I could barely breathe, my breath coming in short rasping gasps. Exhaustion began to creep in from the running and tripping all over the roots and stones on the ground, and again my wet, constricting nightgown wasn't any help either. The soft moonlight that began to appear between banks of clouds as the storm began to dissipate made seeing stinging nettles and thistles all the harder, scratching my arms and legs, pulling at my hair as if someone behind me was gripping my body. The fear in me kept me running for my life, not knowing where I should go or what I should do. Hearing the screams of people from far away and the twigs breaking behind me made chills run down my spine. I started creating an image in my head of my worst fears coming true, making me cry even harder to the point of panic. The surroundings were so scary, the tall trees looming overhead and creating strange, ominous shadows that the wind shaped into nightmarish moving apparitions, which gave me the feeling of not knowing if anyone was around me. The sinister movement only fuelled the fear in me even more. In the distance, a road came into view and you could see the headlights of the passing motorists, causing a zigzag pattern in my head. Streetlights lined the middle of a curve, and a shadowed area became visible where one of the lights had stopped working. I just ran straight to the road, avoiding the shadowed area hoping I wouldn't be hit by any cars. The closer I got to the road, the more and more headlights were beginning to blind me, but no one saw me there as the commuters focused on the wet mist filled road. Well, anyway, who would see a small little girl next to a heavily trafficked road in the dead of night. Luckily, not too long after I got closer to the road, a car stopped, and a couple jumped out and started jogging towards me. I remember their voices; they felt warm and welcoming to me that I could be safe with them. After they put me safely into their car, I lost all consciousness, falling into the dark abyss. However, for some odd reason, I remember someone softly saying, "I can't believe it; the girl was right where she said she would be! Let's get our daughter home…"

Now I sit here reflecting on that one moment in time that this fucking recurring dream keeps haunting me. I can't even see the face that belongs to the voice anymore. It's just weird; it's like it's fading away, or I am somehow blocking the face out. This bloody dream is just driving me absolutely crazy. I just want to get a good night's sleep for once but this dream keeps recurring night after night. It seems like the dream has been repeated every night for the last fourteen years. It's so hard because the female voice feels comforting and loving all the time, but I can't remember who she is to me. Somehow, I must know who she is, where I came from or where I belong, but it is all but a forgotten memory to me. Everything in my life from before my adopted parents took me in, is a blur, and I don't remember a thing about my life before that. This dream, though it drives me insane, is the only thing I have to hold onto and is the key to unlocking all my answers. My mom says that the dream can't hurt me and that, in time the dream will go away. When I was a bit older, I was told how my adoptive parents had found me next to a highway. When they found me, I looked around four years old, at least what they thought. It was apparently a stormy night with heavy rain and strong winds, and I was just dressed in a thin pink nightgown that was a little too long for me. I was wet, cold, and I had blood all over me from all the scratches from the thick branches and brambles while I was running towards the road.

My adoptive parents gave me the name, 'Jade.' It is such a pretty name and matches my eyes—I love it. I am also amazed how two strangers could open up their hearts and home for a child, giving that child all the love and nurturing she needed to grow into a well-rounded individual. I love them with all my heart and see them as my parents no matter what. I'm really thankful and lucky that they found me. Who knows where I would have ended up if it wasn't for them. I guess now would be a good time to tell you a small bit about myself.

I'm 5'3", short—I know, but taller than a hobbit, and at least I have all the curves on my slim frame in the right places, so I have been told, thank God for that. My green eyes are a shade of Jade, found only in dragon pendants of old, which stands out from my dark brown glossy hair. I let my hair grow down to my lower back in soft locks, perfectly framing my oval face. If there was one thing I could change about myself, it would have to be my lips; they are too thin and to me, they don't seem very kissable. My parents insist that I am a normal girl, just a bit on the strong-willed side; however, they are parents and are supposed to be encouraging.

My Dad, Jake, is a tall man of 6'5" and has a really imposing muscular frame. He is a proud man with brown eyes, almost black and a short black military crew cut. Dad calls me his princess, but he would still challenge me to learn new things or encourage me to test my limits. Samantha is my mom, and she is the most gorgeous woman in the world with golden locks that flow down to the floor. She has a slim build with some muscle but not overly muscular, more in a soft feminine way. Her sparkling green eyes give a shine full of life to her face, and she always has a warm loving smile on her full lips. Samantha and Jake have been my parents for the last fourteen years and I love them to bits with all my heart. However, it is time for us to take off again, to start the next story in our lives. With all my education complete, we are off to New York, where my parents are going to help me start my business. So now we need to catch the plane. I keep telling Mom and Dad that it would be so much easier if we just could fly to where we are going, but to stay hidden, we must act like every other person in the world. It's worked for the last couple of years, even if we had to move a lot in my younger years. Mostly because of me but sometimes because of my parents, the apple doesn't fall far from the trees.

Well, let me take you all back to the beginning of my story.

Chapter 2

"Mommy… Daddy, where are you?"

"In the kitchen love, but Daddy's out at the moment. "

"Mommy, can I have blueberry pancakes for breakfast with Nutella?

"Of course baby, anything for you."

"Good because that's my favourite breakfast," Jade said with a mischievous smile.

At the moment at the grocery store:

"Wonder what I should surprise my princess with today…

"All this moving is not good for my little princess. She will never have a normal childhood or teen years, but at least we are safe for the moment. It's been a hard year for Jade, to take control over her power as it is. I just hope one day we can find some other witch to help her with her magic, well only time will tell. Samantha asked me to get veggies but my princess hates them. Hmm, maybe I can slip in some extra meat for her and some chocolate cupcakes as a treat if she eats her veggies. Why must all humans look at me this way? It's really irritating."

"OMG girl, did you see that hot guy over there!" A woman was pointing at Jake.

"Oh, shit he doesn't just look hot, he's like a fucking god," the other woman answered her friend.

"How's my hair and make-up?"

"It's amazing why? What are you going to do?"

"What do you think? I'm going over there to talk to him."

"Good luck girl!"

The woman walked up slowly towards Jake, in the sexiest walk that she could muster, but ended up looking like a baboon in four-inch heels trying to walk on a frozen pond, and slid her arm around his waist.

"Hey there, handsome. Are you a personal trainer?" the woman asked in her overly sweet, husky voice as she tightened her grip around his waste.

"Oh, um Hi. Well, no I'm not. Not to be mean or disrespectful, but I'm very married and do not appreciate that you are touching me. Could you please remove your arm from me?"

"I don't see you with anyone here and what she doesn't know won't hurt her. Right now, your body is amazing to look at and to be straight with you, I would just love to see more of it," the woman continued to try to seduce Jake.

"Lady keep your hands off me and just do me a favour and go back to your friend there. I don't do trash; I only want to get out of here and go home to my family."

I will never understand how the human brain works. How can she even try after I told her that I have a wife? Very well, let's get the rest of the stuff on the list that Samantha gave me. Why the hell does Samantha make the shopping list so long? Well, most of it is for our daughter, how she can eat that much so young is impressive. I don't know where she puts it all. Eventually the list was finished, just time to pay and get the hell out of here.

"Sir that would be 3570 Sek kr. Cash or card?"

"Cash, please."

"Thank you, and here is 30 Sek back, have a nice day sir."

Why didn't I take the car this morning? Oh yeah now I remember my phoenix wanted to go for a flight to stretch out my wings. Shit, I hope Jade slept longer today, we still haven't told her what her mother and I are yet. I think it's time to tell her about us because we know someday, she will pick up on our power and I really don't want her to think we have been hiding it from her. She should know more about this supernatural world we live in and how it is around humans. We also should be preparing her for the future because one day she will find her true love, which we just hope will be supernatural or it is going to be hard to explain everything to a human that may not believe in the supernatural.

Well, when I'm back home I'll mention this to Samantha. Time to see if it's all clear in the back so I can shift and get back home to my girls again.

"Hey man, do you see that dude there, he could be an easy target for us," the one guy said to his friend with an evil smirk.

"Well, you try him, he looks well-built and I'm not getting my ass kicked again because you choose people stronger than us, Patric."

"You're a fucking pussy, Simon. We can take him on together. Not like we haven't been training the last couple of months for this right?" Patric said back.

"Yeah, that's true but come on, he doesn't look like an easy target and I do want to live a little while longer to get my revenge."

Both men started to walk the same way as Jake, wanting to try and take him by surprise. *That's funny I smell rogues, they shouldn't be out at this time normally they would be out at night*, Jake thought to himself when he caught a whiff of a rotting meat smell.

"Hey buddy, yeah you, wait up let's go over by the trash bin, we need to ask you something! Jake looks back with a disarming grin and follows the two rogues. Patric and Simon crowd their target, one on each side of him. "Stay where you are and give us your stuff or you will be sorry," Patric yelled at Jake, as they crowded even closer towards him.

"Well, well what have we here, two lonely rogues out this early in the morning?" Jake answered back with a mocking smile.

"What do you mean by that and how the hell would you know if we are rogues?" Simon asked. This was the first time Simon had been called rogue so openly.

"Well, that's a weird question coming from you, rogue," Jake replied, raising an eyebrow. "The distinct smell emanating from you gives away your rogue nature, in case you weren't aware. However, it seems like you're new to this whole rogue business, am I right?"

"Give us the stuff or we will kill you old man. I am not going to tell you again," Patric screamed furiously at Jake, before Simon could answer Jake's question.

"Ha-ha I would like to see you try young man," Jake burst out laughing, like it was the funniest thing he ever heard this morning.

"Hey man, let's get the fuck out of here, this guy knows too much and he is making me nervous. I'm staying out of this," Simon told Patric nervously.

"You are a weak worm Simon, never come near me again you weakling or I will kill you!" Screamed Patric in pure hatred! Simon, feeling the weight of Patric's words, cowered in fear. The harshness in Patric's voice cut through his already fragile confidence. The anger emanating from Patric's every word was overwhelming, leaving Simon trembling in his presence.

Patric transformed into a light brown mangy wolf and started lunging towards Jake, with yellow eyes glaring in hatred and glistening teeth bared. Jake just stood there and looked bored. Jake took hold of the wolf's neck and twisted it fast and hard, breaking it with one quick snap! The fight was finished before it even started, Jake casually turned, looking over towards Simon with a look of 'you're next.'

"Please don't hurt me!" Simon cried out, scared and pissing his pants, as a steaming pungent puddle formed at his feet.

"Just go try to find a new pack that will take you in. Trust your instincts and never underestimate your opponent. Good luck kid!" Jake advised him.

Shifting into his phoenix form on the spot, Jake flew off to get home. He had wasted enough time already this morning with all this shit. Thank God no one else saw me fly away, but it was really a great flight and well-needed. I will need to tell Samantha about the rogues I encountered today; it's not every day you meet them in the morning. The closer I got home I could hear my next little problem. My princess was awake and chatting away with her mother, how adorable it sounded. Hopefully, she will be too busy to notice that I'm coming in for a landing. But of course, I wouldn't have that luck on my side. Both Samantha, and Jade came out to say hello to me. What surprised me was that Jade came running to my phoenix without any fear in the world for her safety. I just hope that she wouldn't run up to anyone like that, that would really be terrifying to see but we did raise her well, I hope at least.

"Darling what's happened, did I miss the memo or something?" I telepathically asked Samantha.

"Love I told her about us during breakfast because I thought it was the best for all of us. She needs to know that she can trust us and we can't keep that part of us hidden forever. We will never know If we need to fly away again," Samantha silently thought back.

"Daddy, you are so beautiful. Mommy told me about you and her being supernatural. I'm so jealous. I want to be a phoenix too. It's not fair, I'm not a phoenix, I also want to fly over the clouds." Jade with jealousy pouted her lower lip and put her small hands on her hips in a cute defiance.

I had to shift back fast so I could hug my princess for her compliment, it's so adorable with her little pout. Especially when she put her small hands on her hips in an attempt to be defiant and to be able to argue with us.

"Thank you, princess. But you and your mommy are the most beautiful ladies in this world to me. Did Mommy tell you about our surprise for you this morning?"

"What surprise are you talking about Daddy?" Jade asked with excitement in her tiny voice.

"Well princess you are going to start preschool tomorrow," answered Jake, back to his little girl with a big smile.

"Yay! You both promise? I can go, can I have friends? Can I go as a phoenix?" Excitement rolled from Jade in pure happiness.

"Yes darling of course, you can have friends. However, No, to the phoenix, remember what we talked about when Daddy was at store? So, let's go inside and talk when we eat breakfast," Samantha answered back with a small laugh in her voice over the excitement that her little girl had.

"Samantha, I really need to have a moment with you in private about something that happened this morning," Jake said.

"Oh, okay honey let's go into the kitchen while I unpack the groceries, and Jade can finish her breakfast in the dining room," Samantha replied with a worried tone in her voice.

In the kitchen Jake started to tell Samantha what happened earlier in the morning.

"Well, we need to be a little more careful during the day now because I had a rogue wolf encounter behind the grocery store before I was about to shift to come home. Funny story, by the way, one rogue to be clearer was the encounter, the other one chickened out and peed himself when I killed his companion," Jake explained to Samantha.

"He did what?" Samantha started to laugh hysterically that tears were beginning to roll down on her face.

"Well, he peed himself and was scared, the poor kid. I don't think he was older than maybe seventeen or so. I felt sorry for him and let him be, I told him to find a pack to take him in. Then he saw me shift and he started to run into the woods. I just wanted you to know that someone saw me today, but I don't think he would talk a lot about this, it's kind of embarrassing for him to tell everything to anyone," Jake added between laughter.

"Okay honey but we do need to be more careful who sees us. Think of Jade, if they find her, they will take her away from us. You did kill a rogue in human territory, you know. And the law is really strict with this. I do understand that you just defended yourself but you know the rules. I really don't want to take away the preschool for Jade because we need to move again all because of one stinky rogue. I want Jade to feel like a normal little girl with friends," Samantha answered in a worried tone.

"I understand darling; I will be more careful if there is a next time. Which I hope happened again for our princess's sake," Jake told her back.

Tomorrow morning finally arrived an eternity for young Jade.

"Hurry up Mommy and Daddy, we will be late. You both take forever," Jade exclaimed.

"Calm down little one; we will get there in time, I promise," Jake chuckled.

"Well love, at least she wants to go there; that's a good sign," Samantha said, laughing a little.

The family stood in front of a large, colourful building, decorated with <u>Sesame Street </u>characters. There was a fenced in yard with an entire playground set up with a giant sandbox filled with all different toys and tools.

The start of the day began well, as the first days go in preschool. But soon, you can say all kids aren't angels to you, some are really spoiled, mean bullies. It didn't take long before Jade had some girl to begin hard and mean to her, every day it escalated gradually to one awful day.

"Sara, please give back the book to me. I wasn't finished yet and I had it first," Jade said tearfully.

"Well, you are done because this book is mine now. And everything I want, I get it, so it belongs to me. There's nothing you can do about it." Sara stuck out her tongue with a mean smirk.

"I will tell the teacher then you'll need to give it back to me," said Jade.

"Well go ahead do that then she will not do anything to help you. You are ugly," said Sara, sticking out her tongue again.

"Miss Svensson. Miss, can you help me? Sara took the book I had and won't give it back. I just want to finish it so she can have it after me," Jade explained everything to the teacher.

"Oh, stop it Jade, I did see she had it first and you took it from her and you are trying to put it all on her. Stop lying and stand in the corner so you know what is right and wrong. Don't ever come to me with your lies," The teacher told Jade off.

Jade stormed off to the corner with her hands defiantly on her tiny hips. At this moment I wish I could cast a spell on this place and on all of the people in this room. I never want to come back here; I thought school should be fun and I would get friends but that stinky Sara girl is taking all my new friends from me and telling them I'm a liar! Plus, it smells like a dead wet dog in here; I bet it was Miss Svensson that farted. Suddenly, my head started to hurt a lot, but Miss Svensson wouldn't believe me if I went to go and tell her, she would just yell at me to get back in the corner. I just want to go home and be with my mommy, and make today as it was before coming to this place.

The pain in my head started to get stronger and stronger. Not being able to handle it, I started to cry. Without warning, in the back of my head I started to hear a faint voice that was getting clearer as every second went by.

"Hi Jade, please don't freak out! I'm Aria, and I'm your vampire soul, I'm not here to hurt you," my head voice said.

"Um, okay, hi Aria, no, I'm not afraid, just confused. Am I a vampire? Why does my head hurt? I want to go home! Why are you in my head? I thought I was only just a witch. How can this be," Jade thought, sneaking a peek out of the corner to make sure the whole class could not hear her chatting with her new friend.

"Well Jade, you are so much more than that, I will explain in a bit. First, shall we see if we can get the book back that you were reading, I really would like to know how it ends?"

"Aria, I'm not allowed to go away from the corner before I know right and wrong, you heard what the teacher said I think."

"Jade, you never lied. That teacher likes her more than anyone else. That Sara girl can do as she pleases without any punishment and that's not even fair for anyone in here. Let's ask the teacher if we can leave the corner?"

Jade started to raise her hand to get Miss Svensson's attention. Miss Svensson looked at Jade and snapped at her.

"What do you want, little liar?"

"Miss Svensson, may I please go and play?" Jade asked as politely as she could.

"Well *Jade*, that depends on you. Are you going to apologise to Sara, for trying to take her book from her and then trying to lie about it to get her in trouble?" Miss Svensson answered with a snarl.

"Yes Miss. I will apologise to Sara," Jade hung her head low and sheepishly answered.

Jade approached Sara; she was really nervous to apologise.

"Sara, I'm sorry for trying to take the book from you earlier. May I please borrow the book from you again?"

"No, this book is mine and you can't have it ever again."

With an evil sneer, Sara slapped herself on the face to make a red mark on her cheek just to sell it even more to Miss Svensson.

"Teacher, teacher Jade, hit me," Sara screamed with fake tears.

"Damn that little bitch is going to get hers back ten times worse when I get out of here," yelled Aria in Jade's head now completely pissed off. Miss Svensson ran over to Sara to check on her, she then grabbed my arm, dragging me out of the classroom and into the hallway. In a rage, Miss Svensson hit me, but not just one time. She hit me four times on my face.

"What the fuck did *you* do? That you actually have the nerve to hit Sara. I hope you are proud of yourself now. I hope you feel the pain Sara got from when you hit her, you disgusting little *witch*," Miss Svensson yelled between hitting me.

"What do you mean Miss Svensson? I never hit her, she did it to herself," Jade cried out between each slap.

"You need to know your place in this world, you little shit," Miss Svensson spat out at her, as flecks of spittle splattered into Jade's already wet tear-stained face.

"What do you mean a witch?" I started to get worried.

"Yeah, that's right little *Jade*, I know exactly what you are and how to put you in your place. You witches think highly of yourself, you are nothing in this world. You are just existing and shouldn't even do that, you are just low-level scum, the bottom feeders of our world."

"Jade, let me take over so I can drain this old bitch for putting her hands on you," a pissed off Aria roared in my already hurting head.

Seconds later Aria took over my body. You can at least say she was pissed off. My green eyes started to change colour to dark red, my hair turned crystal white; no brown could be seen. Aria completed the transformation without Jade's permission. Jade was confused and hurt but could do nothing to resist Aria's will.

"How dare you lay your dirty hands on my human. And tell her stuff like that! What kind of fucked up teacher are you?" Aria, hissed at Miss Svensson.

"I dare say I'm more superior than her. I stand over all these filthy witches," Miss Svensson growled back at one pissed-off Aria.

Then Miss Svensson slapped Jade, again not knowing that Aria was in control of Jade's body.

"Well, you stink like a wet dog that needs to be put in a dog house." Aria menacingly laughed back at Miss Svensson. "Put one more finger on my human again and I will suck you dry." Aria gave Miss Svensson her last warning.

"And what would you possibly be able to do against me? A fully grown wolf!" Then her wolf started to shine in her eyes as a warning. Then one more slap came even harder than any other one before that, sending Jade flying into the wall on the other side of the hall.

That was enough for Aria. "I warned you dirty mongrel. Jade is not just a witch; she is part vampire. I'm amazed that you missed that one. Maybe your age is affecting your sense of smell. You are not as smart as you think you are. Now for your punishment, I feel quite hungry and I do have a hunger for dirty mutt blood. I can give you ten seconds to run, your choice." Aria smiled gleefully at the teacher.

The fear in Miss Svensson was real, she really did miss the smell of a vampire on this girl. She started to back away, beginning to run for her life, arms flailing every which way and you could see she was having a hard time keeping her balance. Just as Aria hit the dreaded ten, Miss Svensson skidded into a classroom filled with children.

"Ten!" Aria yelled and started to fly after Miss Svensson.

We ended up in one of the other classrooms, where the kids and teachers began screaming and freaking out at the terror in front of them. Aria tripped Miss Svensson, who landed on her back, and sunk her teeth into her mid-thigh, starting to suck her dry from the femoral artery. I managed to get control at the very last second to stop it. Blood was trickling down from the corner of my mouth. The whole classroom was still screaming and staring at me all wide-eyed. On the floor, Miss Svensson was lying close to death in a quickly growing pool of steaming iron-rich blood, her breath coming in short, laboured gasps. One of the other teachers came to start to apply pressure to the wound to help her out. Miss Svensson had lost a lot of blood and was as pale as fresh snow. Light slowly faded from her once bright amber eyes as she lost consciousness.

And this is how my first and last day of preschool went. I will never forget how that classroom looked. You had all the ABCs on the walls with different animals and tools with the first letter. The blackboard in one of the corners, the teacher's desk next to a big window, play dough stinking up the room, and the reading corner exactly as it was before all hell broke loose. The last thing my classmates would remember of me would be a pale face and bright red blood, so much bright red blood.

Chapter 3

The headmaster's sudden entrance into the room left him visibly shocked. His face contorted with surprise and disgust as he took in the entire gruesome scene before him. I observed his eyes cloud over, and within seconds, he reached for his phone to call my parents. The events that followed Aria's takeover of my body happened so quickly that my recollection of them is hazy at best. However, I can sense that something has changed within me. Shortly after the phone call, my parents rushed into the school, their expressions filled with genuine concern.

"Headmaster, you called us. What seems to be the problem?" Jake asked.

"Sweetheart, what happened to your face? You are covered in bruises and what's this blood around your mouth?" Samantha asks with a lot of uncertainty in her voice.

"Well Jake, Samantha, your daughter almost killed her own teacher today by biting her, in the classroom with all other students and teachers present in it. Are you aware that she is a vampire-witch hybrid?" asked the headmaster with a raised eyebrow and an air of superiority.

"Yes of course we knew about that part but her vampire soul was not supposed to be awakening for a few years. If she has been awakened today then it has to do with something extremely traumatic that happened to our daughter at this school. Have you seen the state of her face?" Samantha questioned in return.

"Well of course, I have seen her face but it doesn't matter right now. Because she almost killed her teacher who also is a werewolf and belongs to a pack here," the headmaster explained, disregarding Jade's state of condition as if it didn't matter to him.

"I want this abomination out of my school. I will make sure to make your life a living hell for the rest of your life until my dying days. Because that teacher that she tried to kill is my mate. I can't kill you or your disgusting offspring in a human town. I will never forget what happened today; let us hope we never have to meet again," the headmaster yelled at my parents with venom.

Mommy turned from me, looked the headmaster directly in the eye and said, "Maybe you should learn to control your pack better; perhaps they need obedience training." Samantha turned back to examine Jade's horribly bruised face.

"Mommy, Daddy, can we please go? I'm scared. I'm so sorry this happened. I'm really so sorry that I hurt Miss Svensson," Jade told the headmaster with sadness in her voice.

"Yes, sweetheart, we are going home now," Samantha said to Jade.

We started to walk home but we had an uneasy, weird feeling that someone was following us all the way home. At home we decided to have a family meeting about what we should do. I was really scared and I told my parents that I didn't want to go back to school, thinking that I will allow myself to be taken over again.

"Aria was trying to defend me today and everything went bad," Jade tried to explain as good as she could.

"Oh sweetheart, it's Aria, your vampire's name… it's really beautiful, and I know sweetheart she only protected you from a mean person," Samantha tried to convince Jade.

"Darling, we need to pack our bags. I don't think we can stay here much longer because of the danger we are in right now. And I also think we have to be fast because we are under watch, one wrong move from our side will not end very well," Jake told Samantha, with trepidation clearly in his voice.

"Mommy, Daddy, I am really sorry. Aria just took over my body. I didn't know what to do and Miss Svensson kept slapping me. My head hurt so bad then bang! Aria was in control. I messed everything up today. It's because of me we have to move, isn't it?" Jade said while tears running down her face

"Oh, sweetheart it's not your fault; we both know that Miss Svensson treated you really badly today, and Aria only defended you. Just go upstairs and start packing your bags. Please do what you have been told sweetheart," Samantha instructed Jade, with a slight quiver in her voice.

Jake's thoughts were spinning out of control, bouncing around like a child's rubber ball.

I really think we need to leave tonight for all of our safety. It pained me to see her worry about all this stuff. I should have taken out that pack headmaster for what they did to Jade. Maybe I should go back, no that would make things worse. I know that we can protect our family completely fine, but all this worry on her face... it's really scary how a really confident person like my wife is, to see them being scared. But well... I'm also really worried about what's going to happen after today, if hell will break loose or not.

"Jake, do you hear me?"

"Oh, I'm sorry honey, I was stuck in my thoughts."

"That's okay love but go and pack our bags as well. I am sure we will have some visitors soon, and all the bags need to be packed by then okay? Can you do that for me? Meanwhile, I will have to look out for anything," Samantha informed Jake calmly but also with a bit of sternness in her voice.

Meanwhile at the Swan Lake Pack...

"So, headmaster, can you please tell me about what happened in the school today and what started everything?"

The headmaster started to tell a twisted side of the story to his Alpha about what he had encountered at the school during the day, just to make sure he and his mate looked innocent in their Alphas' and packs' eyes.

"Alpha, we need to do something about this disgusting, irritating hybrid. She almost killed my mate without any remorse or reason. I almost lost the love of my life and she is fighting for her life in the pack hospital," the headmaster complained.

"Headmaster of course I do understand what has happened, it is really irritating and hard to accept, but it's still just a child we are talking about. I do need to hear their side of the story and understand what has transpired as well. It is unforgivable what has happened but what triggered all this is my question. And that question… you refuse to answer me in full detail. I will not risk going to war against a hybrid that can have a vampire clan and a witch coven behind her. It is too big of a risk to do. I really hope you understand I need to think of the pack as well," the Alpha answered back.

"She almost killed her, Alpha," whined the headmaster.

"I do understand your feelings but we need to be careful. I have them guarded and surrounded just in case. But we need to be smart about this family. So, tell me about her parents."

"Well, not much I can talk about them more than what they told me about themselves. They are supernatural people but they weren't witches or vampires. I'm not sure what they are; they hide it really well and didn't answer me about it either; just told me that it wasn't important. They told me a little about their little girl that she is a witch. Seems like they didn't tell me everything in that way."

"I understand. Well, I'm going to their house soon to talk to them. A punishment needs to be served either way; one of my pack members got attacked."

Alpha began to formulate the beginnings of a plan:

"Let's get going so we do not delay this any longer. I'm also interested to meet this kid; I have never met a hybrid before."

The Alpha and some of his pack warriors started to move out from the pack territory to get to the family's home. The ride wasn't too long, maybe a thirty-minute car ride to the family's house.

Alpha knocked softly on the door and waited patiently.

"Who is it?" Samantha asked from behind the door.

"Alpha Kim of the Swan Lake Pack ma'am."

"Oh! What do you want?"

"Well ma'am, let's talk about what happened today. Can you please open the door so we can speak face-to-face like adults?"

"Um, are you alone? We don't want any trouble with your pack Alpha Kim."

Alpha Kim started to get a bit annoyed but his hackles started to rise. He began to mutter under his breath, *the nerve of this woman!* "I just want to talk!" he exasperatedly stated. Finally, the goddamn door opened up. Then he saw her, she was the most beautiful woman he had ever seen, too fucking bad she has a husband otherwise, he would have his way with her. She had long golden blond hair pulled up in a ponytail, big light blue sparkling eyes, and that body exuding a very sweet, almost intoxicating aroma around her. He felt his dick twitch involuntarily in his tight jeans as he eyed her ample size breasts. Holy hell, when she turned around, he saw her ass swaying as she walked, full and round almost heart shaped, making for a good grip if he was to take her from behind.

"Well Alpha, are you coming in, or are you going to stand there and drool over me all night? I can sense that my mate wouldn't appreciate the way you're looking at me. So, I advise you to roll that tongue of yours back in your face."

Alpha taken aback by the comment, responded, "Whaaaa? What do you mean by that? Actually, never mind that! Let's go in and talk. I'm also curious to see your daughter because I heard she attacked her teacher—a member of my pack."

"Well, she's gone to bed and feels really bad for what happened today but she will not be going back to that school ever again. With what happened she already apologised as many times as she could. Besides the fact that *your* mangy, uncontrolled pack member attacked my daughter unprovoked!"

"Well ma'am a punishment needs to be doled out because she did attack one of my pack members and there are laws about this. Maybe you know about them?"

"We know very well about the laws, especially if she was the one who started it. But our daughter told us it was your flea-ridden pack member that started hitting our daughter; Jade was only defending herself. So yes, I agree a punishment does need to be given out. How does doggy obedience training sound for Miss Svensson and the rest of your pack?" Jake sharply called out the Alpha, coming down from upstairs, pissed off that this prick of an Alpha wanted to punish his little angel.

"Excuse me, how can you be so rude as to interrupt my discussion with this lady?" Alpha Kim asked really irritated.

"I'm Jake, the father and that lady happens to be my mate and wife. I thought Alphas were to be well educated and smart when it came to the laws and to the etiquette for one to conduct themselves!"

"Jake, stop that right now please," Samantha requested to Jake.

"No Samantha, this prick of an Alpha is checking you out; he has a fucking boner in his jeans and is thinking so highly of a pack member that slapped a five-year-old little girl multiple times, yet the mongrel that he is, willingly wants to punish a girl of five-years-old, a little girl I might add who was slapped multiple times. He has no respect; he hasn't even asked about Jade's side of the story or he doesn't care about that. Get the hell out of our home, inbred flea-ridden mutt! I will give you five seconds before I turn you into a pile of dust."

"Alpha, I think it's best for you to go. Your narrow-minded view point and refusal to see the truth is what is the problem here. Plus, I also did warn you about checking me out, now goodbye."

"How dare you speak to me this way? Do you know anything about me at all? I can have your family killed right now," sputtered Alpha Kim.

"Well, there we have it, darling. He had us followed and surrounded by his mutts; you weren't wrong in your guessing Samantha. Do the scruffy little doggies here want to know what we are, love?" spoke Jake with a tight jaw filled with fury

"No darling, I believe he is attempting to solve the problem by himself. Perhaps we should lend him a hand? What do you say?" Samantha suggested.

"Well, Samantha, his allotted time has elapsed. Should I allow the mutt to begin running now?" Alpha Kim confusion evident on his bearded face

"What in the world!" he exclaimed, bewildered. "Are they toying with me?"

"Warriors, I command you to assault this residence and administer punishment to them as a collective!" Alpha Kim mentally communicated with his warriors stationed outside the house.

"Well darling, time to shift, he has just sent for backup. After you love!" Samantha told Jake.

"Holy fuck, they are phoenixs! I thought those were all gone from the world." In front of Alpha Kim stood two very angry and burning Phoenixs, the walls were starting to catch fire. Alpha Kim began to look for an escape route out of the house.

"Now Alpha, scream with your warriors because you will not be getting out of this house alive," Jake's voice came out a little darker.

All Alpha Kim could think was fuck this is not good everyone here is in danger, just because of him. How could he have been so stupid and not just listen to them before I took up punishment on a little girl. These parents really mean business about protecting their child and have no cares what would happen to them as long as their little girl is safe from anyone.

"Everyone back off and try to get out of here. They mean what they say, that they will kill us all. We didn't take them by surprise; they knew that we were coming before we even decided to act," Alpha Kim mind-links everyone in the house off his warriors.

The temperature inside the house escalated rapidly as the fire consumed everything in its path. Samantha and Jake's fiery determination mirrored the intensity of the flames, rendering their attempts to communicate with their spirit animals futile. Suddenly, the sound of tiny, hurried footsteps echoed down the staircase, sending a shiver down Alpha Kim's spine. Holy shit, It was clear that awakening their daughter would not sit well with them.

"Mommy, Daddy, what are you doing? You are hurting them really badly; let them go," a small cry came from Jade. She had been woken up by all the sounds in the house.

"Oh now look what you've done Alpha, you just woke up my baby. Get out of our home, and don't you ever dare come close to us ever again. The next time you will not be this lucky in keeping your life," Jake's spirit animal yelled back at Alpha Kim.

Alpha Kim's thoughts started rapidly ricochetting around in his head: "Did we just get saved by a child, the very same child that almost killed one of my pack members? This is all so confusing and so fucking embarrassing; there is no way in hell we can get out from here with my head held high."

While Jake had spoken up towards the Alpha in his fury for waking up his precious baby, Jade had come down from her room and stood on the last step on the stairs, listened unwillingly in to Alpha Kim rapids thought and before she even could react. One of the warriors seizing the opportunity, launched an attack. Then a sudden a piercing scream erupted from the little girl, causing everyone's ears to ring. To everyone's astonishment, her hair and eyes underwent a dramatic transformation. Her once brown hair turned an icy white, while her green eyes transformed into a chilling shade of blood red. She appeared utterly deranged, losing all control as she began conjuring a spell around herself.

The force of her power was demonstrated when one of the warriors was flung across the room, crashing into the wall with such intensity that cracks began to spiderweb across its surface. The warrior lay incapacitated, unable to rise to his feet. Meanwhile, Alpha noticed another warrior, who had reverted back to his human form, sprinting towards the girl.

With both parents now fully focused on their daughter, Alpha Kim's mind raced with a devious plan. He contemplated eliminating them and seizing the girl for himself. Perhaps he could train her to follow his every command, thereby enabling him to gain control over the entire werewolf realm.

While both parents were distracted, he decided to strike and kill both of them and would not think of a surprise attack from behind.

"Alpha, look out!" a warrior screamed.

As Aria started to evoke her chant, the warrior fell down on the ground lifeless. Black smoke started to spread within the house but it was not from the fire. It was fucking coming from the girl. Alpha Kim swore she could read his mind, as the smoke was going towards him. His breathing started to get harder and more laboured, for every breath he took felt like an elephant was sitting on his chest.

"Jade, darling stop… Please stop! Take down the spell now," Jake exclaimed to Jade.

"But Daddy, he was going to attack you and Mommy. I heard him… he wants to hurt you; can we please go? I don't want to stay here anymore. Why is Mum still in her phoenix form?"

"He planned to attack us, princess?" Fury in Jake's voice clear as day.

Jade only nodded her head in confirmation to her dad.

"Samantha, darling, put the fire on the house. Kill anyone that dares come close to us. Jade is scared; it's time for us to go."

I only saw my mum's phoenix nod her head and started to glow a bright white, accelerating intense heat around her to make the flames grow higher. We ran upstairs to get our bags. A few warriors were running after us in their wolf form, stupid mutts.

My dad shifted back into his phoenix and told me to jump up on his back. He picked up our three bags in one of his great talons and started to take a stand to fly off, but not without a great swipe of his blazing wing, taking a hard wing slap from my father's wing at the warriors, making them fall to the floor with their clothes on fire having instantly transformed into their human form in a smouldering death.

"I will find you and I will kill you all, mark my word!" yelled Alpha Kim up towards the sky as his eyes followed the phoenixes flying away.

Alpha Kim was in disbelief at how effortlessly their enemies had escaped. Despite having their best warriors by his side, the two parents seemed unfazed by the encounter. The skirmish had taken a toll, leaving Alpha Kim with a loss of ten warriors, three of whom had sustained severe burns.

Determined to seek justice, Alpha Kim resolved to gather the packs' allies and plot a strategy to bring down these insolent foes. The gravity of the situation demanded that this act of aggression not go unpunished. As per the laws that governed their realm, the fallen warriors must be avenged.

Chapter 4

Growing up was a constant whirlwind for Jade. With her family moving from one country to another since she was five, she often felt like the anchor in a storm. Each relocation brought a mix of excitement and anxiety, but deep down, she believed she was the reason for their restless lives. The weight of her parents' struggles and the chaos of adapting to new cultures pressed heavily on her young shoulders, making her childhood feel anything but normal. Jade wrestled with feelings of guilt, convinced that if she had been different, maybe they could have stayed put. The only relief was that she would not have another shift or would have any more changes within her before she turned eleven. Well, that was until we had settled down in Nepal in an area called Samagaun village, in a small cottage under the shadow of Manaslu, the eighth-highest peak in the world. It was a lovely little place with thick shrublands and turquoise lakes, gave off a feeling of isolated freedom with the huge mountains all around. Lives were different here; there were very few children my age, and everything was slower. Donkeys and mules did the majority of the hard labour and life was just unhurried. One day, as I was pacing back and forth inside the cottage, my mum started to speak to me.

"Jade, maybe you should go out for a run? That could do wonders for you, as you're wearing a path on the floor darling!"

"Yeah, maybe that's a good idea, thanks Mum, I will try to do that. The only thing is, I'm feeling a bit weird; my body feels extremely warm with a tingling sensation running all over my arms and I think that something is about to happen to me."

"Watch out, Mum!!!" Jade exclaimed in a terrified screech.

Just then, an icy blue fireball blast erupted from my fingertips straight towards my mum. Thankfully Mum was faster and got out of the way just in the nick of time.

"Honey, that was a close call. I can sense that something is changing within your inner fire once again. The fireball that came towards me had an unusual arctic blue hue, and strangely, it didn't emit any heat. This is not typical of your powers. Perhaps I should discuss this with your father while you go for a run in the forest. Jade, please hurry and venture deep into the forest, just to ensure that no humans witness any potential incidents."

"I'm so sorry Mum, I didn't mean for that to happen. Please forgive me, it's like I can't control my magic at the moment," Jade said with tears in her voice.

"It's okay honey, you did scream out before it even happened. I'm completely fine, no harm done. To be honest, I don't think your fire would burn your family. It seems that your powers are growing more within you. So, get out there, run off some steam and try not to burn down half of the forest. Everything is fine, don't you worry about this anymore. I love my baby girl."

"Mum, I will see you soon. And yes, I will try not to burn anything down to the ground. Tell Dad everything is fine and that I will come back soon, you know how he can be. Bye Mum!"

I walked out of the cottage and walked slowly towards the pathway that started at the tree line. At the start of the path I increased my pace from walking to slow running, feeling free from all the worries that were always around me and my family. My slow running started to increase to a faster speed where you could see the tree blurring next to you, jumping over fallen trees, rocks and roots. I eventually came into a nice little clearing with a pond and a rock covered in soft green moss lying next to the water. I choose to take a break, sitting down to take in a few deep breaths after my running, feeling the sweat trickling down on my forehand and back. My head was pulsating, feeling like it was going to explode, and the pain was just increasing tenfold... when I remembered it's the same pain I had when I was five and Aria came to life.

"This will hurt Jade, be prepared," a voice spoke up in Jade's inner thoughts.

"What, who's there, what will hurt?" Jade screamed out loud with confusion lashed in her voice.

"It's time to shift right now," the voice said again with more power.

Jade, fell down from the rock she was sitting on, in agonising pain, holding her head between her hands, while a snapping sound of breaking bones could be heard miles away. The pain was just increasing for every break and snap within her. Jade couldn't keep a hold of her head any longer. Her nails started to fall off, and claws were growing out followed by white fur slowly growing from her skin. Her legs breaking and dislocating into an unnatural position for a human girl, followed by more and thicker fur spreading all over her body. Ripping the seams on her clothes slowly as her body was growing with every breaking bone in her body. The final breaking point for Jade was when her jaw dislocated and started to elongate and some of her front teeth began falling out from her mouth to make room for her four new sharp canine teeth. Her nose turned into a black snout with whiskers on the side; the ears started to grow longer and wider, forming into a triangle shape. After the transformation, Jade's senses became remarkably heightened. Sounds that were once distant now reached her ears from miles away, while the scents of various animals permeated the air, from the tiniest mouse to the majestic Asian elephant. Overwhelmed by the experience, Jade collapsed onto the ground, utterly exhausted. Gasping for breath, she inhaled deeply, trying to fill her lungs to their maximum capacity.

"Hi Jade, my name is Sapphire and I'm your panther soul. I'm sorry that I forced myself to come out. The reason is that your magic is increasing too fast and making it unstable and hard for both you and Aria to control. I do apologise for scaring you in the beginning, but the fire was starting to consume you slowly."

"Wait what? How can I have two souls within me, is that even possible? I'm getting so confused now."

"Of course that is possible, and you are one of few shifters that has it; you should be proud. I can also explain the whole reason how babies are made as well if that would help you understand more on how it comes to why you are special. That would mean all the juicy details as well, just to make it more fun!" a small laugh came out from Sapphire.

"Omg no, please don't, it's bad enough that Mom will have that talk with me when I'm older," a very embarrassed Jade answered back.

"Jade, I think you should try to stand up and stretch out our muscles after the shift. Then you can take a look in the pond and see how we look. I know it's painful but it would help out with the soreness," suggested Sapphire in a calm voice.

Jade tried to stand up but was whimpering from all the stiff muscles and wanted just to lay back down again, but her curiosity was greater than the pain in her body. She took small, wobbly steps towards the water and looked down to see a panther face with snow white fur and Sapphire blue eyes staring back from the surface of the water. Jade stared down at the water, taking in every millimetre of her new form and noticed that her ears were shimmering with light shades of black and grey; she was also about nine feet long and thirty-three inches tall, well at least to her shoulders anyways.

"So Jade, what do you think about the new you? Aren't we beautiful?" snickered Sapphire

"Sapphire, this is you and me, and you are absolutely beautiful, I have never read about white panthers before, and your name is perfect with our eyes."

"Sapphire, you are absolutely beautiful and thank you for coming out so soon to help us both. We do need all the help we can get with Jade's magic. Do you have any suggestions to make her cool down with her inner fire? I have tried everything I know about to be able to handle as much as I can," Aria spoke up with a hint of worry in her voice.

Sapphire listened hard to what Aria said and started to think about some solutions to the growing magic within them, when she came up with an idea that probably could help them out to get the magic, under some control at least, so she got the hang of it. Then be able to control a third part of it at least.

"Jade, Aria, I think we should try to go for a run and do it as fast as we can manage if we all put in our speed in one go together," Sapphire said with a calm voice.

"I'm not so sure if we are able to run at the moment, we are still a bit wobbly on our legs," Jade spoke up with a hint of sadness in her voice.

"Come on Jade, we need to try it out, so let us see how fast we can be together and burn off some steam together," Sapphire chipped in.

"Oh Aria, don't hold back this time please. I do think this is the only way to take the magic under control and we are working together on the matter. So, what happened earlier will not happen again."

"Yeah, I wasn't thinking of holding back this time," Aria snickered little.

"Hold on for a moment Aria, you have been holding back your speed with me all this time? When we could have gone faster than we have done before?" Jade asked back.

Both Aria, and Sapphire started to laugh with each other at Jade's confusion. When Sapphire asked to have control over their mind and body for the run, she did notice a bit of hesitation from Jade at first. Jade decided to be more than happy to give Sapphire full control for this run so she could sit back and enjoy the ride that was coming. The run started slow, even for Sapphire but soon it became a faster pace. Not long they were running at full speed again making the trees blur of colours into nothing all around them. Sapphire let their tongue hang out from their mouth, flying and slapping them on their cheek. Jade closed her eyes in the mind enjoying every second of it; from within her mind it felt like they were flying through the woods. It didn't take long for all three to notice that the flame within Jade's body started to calm down from a burning hot flame to a low burning match. It was then Sapphire started to calm down the speed of their run to a slower, calmer pace again. She jogged around sniffing around when she came to an abrupt stop in mid-step laying her ears back, and a growl arose from deep in the throat. So, she linked to both Jade and Aria.

"Someone or something is keeping their eyes on us, and I can't locate where but I do smell them," Sapphire informed.

"That can't be possible, no human is this deep in the forest and I don't know of any packs or other shifters either," Jade replied.

"Well, apparently there is one pack around here, but they probably are keeping a low profile around us. I think we accidentally ran into someone's territory. Have you ever run this far in the forest before?" Sapphire said with a clear worry in her tone

Jade expressed her doubts about the presence of a pack in the woods, unable to find any evidence to support it. Worried, she turned to Aria and Sapphire, asking if they could determine whether it was a human or a shifter that was nearby. Aria and Sapphire, sensing the strong scent of a shifter, deduced that it was likely a leader or second in command. Understanding the danger they faced, they urged Jade to create a protective barrier around them, considering their lack of defensive training.

In the depths of the forest, a peaceful clowder of panthers lived harmoniously, preparing for their much-awaited ten-year celebration. They had been fortunate to avoid any attacks from hunters or rogues, allowing them to thrive in peace and tranquility. However, their idyllic existence was abruptly interrupted when a siren blared, accompanied by a telepathic message that reached every member of the clowder, young and old.

"Attention all clowder members," the urgent message echoed in their minds. "There has been an unknown breach in our territory. Exercise caution if you are venturing out and return to the safety of your homes until further notice."

"Guards follow me to our borders; we need to go check the perimeter and see if we can find the intruder and neutralise this possible threat."

The clowder dominant could only wish it's not a major threat for them; they all shifted into their panther forms and started to run towards the borders. In the middle of the dominant run, he saw something running extremely fast past him but couldn't really react as to what it was. It passed them all like a bullet that was just fired from an AK-47. The clowder dominant stopped in the middle of his run, only to get hit from behind by his guardsmen, who weren't paying any attention to what was happening. It was then that he decided to split everyone up so they could cover more of the groups' territory at the same time.

"Let's split up into four groups! One group of five goes up to the front border, the second group with five turns to go left, group three takes the right, and the last group is to head back to the main camp. Jonathan and I will stay here and look around to clear this area, then we will all meet up in the town centre."

"Yes," linked all the warriors back.

As I began to wander, carefully scanning the ground for any potential leads, I caught a glimpse of that familiar white blur darting by Jonathan and I once more. This time, however, Jonathan too had caught sight of it. I observed the perplexed expression on his panther's face and couldn't help but wonder about the nature of this shifter. Its incredible speed made it challenging to detect any distinct scent, leaving me increasingly bewildered with each passing moment.

"Uhm Michael did you see that? What can be that fast? It's outrunning us and we were running at full speed before," Jonathan linked his Dominant.

"Yeah, second time I have seen it now. I can't get any smell or a good view of it, and it is starting to piss me off. Let's hide in that big bush over there and see if it stops and we can get a better sense of it," I linked back.

"Michael don't go too deep in that bush, it has stinging nettles as well," linked Jonathan back fast.

Michael and Jonathon cautiously approached the bush, their steps silent and deliberate. They were mindful not to disturb anything or create any noise that might alert whatever lurked within. Suddenly, they observed a pause, as if the creature sensed their presence. Its ears flattened against its head, followed by a deep, ominous growl. As their eyes adjusted, they beheld a magnificent yet menacing sight—a towering white panther, poised to attack at the slightest sign of danger.

"Jonathan, do you see this or is it a dream? I have never seen a white panther before, have you? I have been told about them and they are extremely rare and some say that they hold unique powers but do not know for sure."

"Yes, Alpha Michael, I do see it but I can't get a clear idea of whether it's real or an illusion. I do think he/she has noticed us because it looks on high alert and very tense. I would say we should walk up slowly and one of us in human form so we can try to communicate with it."

"Yeah. That sounds like a great idea. I can shift back and you can stay in your form in case it attacks us," answered Alpha Michael.

A rustling sound alerted Jade, who was semi-hidden and her head darted directly to the sound, lowering her body to the ground, ready to jump for an escape as fast as it would be possible. Then the sound started to change to a bone breaking, the same sound that she had made when she transformed into Sapphire. A man came up in view in the bushes when another scent hit me. I started to giggle and also felt amused that he hadn't noticed what he was standing in. When she heard him yell out.

"Oh, for fuck's sake. Fuck, my dick is burning, not a fucking word Jonathan, you hear me not a fucking word."

Michael walked slowly out from the bush, holding both of his hands to cover his lower area, yelling and screaming, tears streaming down his round face. Michael's lower extremities felt like he was being stabbed by a million little shards of glass; even the slightest touch set off a million more shards. Michael had never felt such an intense burn, scratching and stabbing all at the same time. Both his legs up to his lower stomach were red and bubbly because he realised his mistake way too late and shifted in a bush with tall stinging nettles. In the background, Sapphire could hear a panther prowling around. The only thing she could probe from his mind was how much he was laughing because of his leader transforming in a bed of stinging nettles. Then he started to open his mouth to say something and got Sapphire's attention.

"I don't mean any harm, I only want to speak to you, if you are willing you can growl."

"What should we do, should we try to say sorry that we didn't mean to trespass into their territory?" Sapphire asked.

"Growl once at least, we can try to be civil and explain that we don't mean any harm either," Jade and Aria said in unison.

So, Sapphire growled once. Jade also let the safety barrier stay up around them.

"Okay. Would it be okay if my second-in-command joins us in his panther form? Growl once for yes and two for no."

Sapphire growled once again that she accepted it.

"Well, let me introduce myself, I'm Alpha Micheal. I'm sure you are aware that you're in our territory? Growl once for yes and twice for no."

Sapphire growled twice for no. She took in the man's appearance and estimated he was between thirty-five to forty years old. He had pitch black hair and dreamy hazelnut eyes, a deep rumbling voice not unlike a contented cat's purr that spoke with kindness and something more, maybe a curiosity. The confidence rolled in waves off him when he spoke.

"Would you mind to shift back, it would be much easier to talk; me and Jonathan can turn around so you have some privacy and can get dressed as well?"

Sapphire and Aria noticed Jade started to get nervous and hesitant with the shift, so they both started to give her comfort as well.

"It's okay Jade, we can shift back. Just keep the safety barrier up."

"I can't be naked in front of two men, what would Mum think? I would be naked, I can't do it."

"Oh, please girl, you are a witch; think of some clothes and spell them on to you," Aria snapped.

"I don't even know how to shift back to being a human."

So, Sapphire explained quickly to Jade that she should picture herself as a human. Starting from her toes, follow up all the way to her fingertips, and lastly think about her face, hair colour and all her other features.

Then Sapphire growled once again for yes and saw that both Micheal and Jonathan turned around as he promised.

Jade started to imagine herself and started to see pictures in her mind of how she looks. Not long after she could hear her bones popping into place for a human. It wasn't as painful as the shift was before when Sapphire took over in that forced shift. It didn't take long before Jade was laying on the ground naked, so she got up to stand and then started to spell on her clothes. The spell started to take form and the white fabric started on her shoulder, running down over her chest, not hugging her too tight, following her waist and falling down to her knees. After the white fabric was on her body big yellow/orange sunflowers popped all around on her newly spelled dress. Jade finished it up with some white ballerina flats on her feet. With a relief of being back in human form, Jade spoke up.

"Alpha Micheal and Subordinate Jonathan, it's okay for the both of you to turn around again."

"You are just a little girl," a very shocked Micheal said.

"Well yeah, I am, but I'm eleven so not that little."

"Ha ha, well little one, you don't seem like being a mean girl, just lost I would say. Where are your parents? And would it be okay if Jonathan shifts back as well?"

"Yes, Michael, it's okay. I'm so sorry for trespassing on to your territory I didn't mean to. I was enjoying my run, maybe a little too much."

Chapter 5

After Jade left for her run, I began to clean up the mess that just happened but unfortunately, I wasn't fast enough. My dear husband came home earlier than I had anticipated he would be back.

"Honey I'm home, where are you? The day has been painfully slow."

"I'm in the kitchen honey."

"Wooow… what happened here? What the hell, who pissed you off? I know I took the last steak for work this morning, but I didn't think you would burn down the kitchen for that."

"What? The last steak you didn't, and for the facts it's Jade's doing. She hasn't had any control over her powers today; she has been pacing around all morning. However, she did manage to warn me before a blast went off from her finger's tips."

"What do you mean? This is a bit worrying that her power is growing so fast."

"Oh. Love, the thing that worries me is that the flame was ice blue. Have you heard anything about that?"

"Ice blue, you say. Let me think I know I have read about it somewhere not too long ago."

Jake started to walk away from the kitchen towards his home office, where all his books were kept, still deep in his own thoughts.

I know I read something about fire in different colours. But Jade is only eleven so nothing major should be changing in her yet, I think. Well, she is not just a witch; she has her vampire soul also maybe that has something to do with this. Oh, my poor princess she must be so confused and feeling awful for what happened before with her mom. Come on, I think I know I have read about this not that long ago. It should be basic knowledge for everyone.

Hours started to roll by as Jake looked up from his books and notes, seeing that the sun had started to settle in the horizon.

"Honey… Jade hasn't come home yet? And I'm starting to get worried about her. Do you think she is lost? She has never been out this long before. This just is not like her," Samantha asked from down stairs.

"She hasn't? That's weird indeed. Why would she be out this long," Jake stated with worry starting to enter his voice.

"Damn it that's it. She is changing love, a huge change like a shift changes. Jake excitedly exclaimed. We need to find her fast; we need to shift and fly and look for her now."

"I would suggest staying on the ground. The Forest is really thick and wouldn't help us to see her from the air."

"Yeah, you're right as always, let's go and find her. I just hope she is safe and that nothing has happened to her. Hopefully she is not freaking out by herself."

Both Samantha and Jake sprinted out from their home in the direction to the forest; the only thing on their mind was finding Jade alive and well. Both of them were running around to cover as much area as they could but she was nowhere to be found. After a while they stopped to take a deep breath and Jake looked at his mate with concern and noticed Samantha's worried eyes had been tearing up, and tears were dripping down from the corner of her eyes. They were scoping around and looking for any sign of their daughter when a faint smell hit their noses that belonged to their daughter. When they noticed the small pond a little further away, they started to walk towards the pond quickly.

"Jake, look over there. I found her clothes and they are all shredded and torn apart. She has gone through the shifting all by herself. Oh, my baby," Samantha started to cry harder and grabbed Jake for comfort.

"Oh, thank God. She will be fine, love, look over there. Paw prints going away from the clothes. We just need to follow them. I hope she is fine that nothing has happened to her, and she is not too confused after everything."

"She is fine, you know how strong she is. She is stubborn, and Aria would never let anything happen to Jade, whatsoever," Jake said with a chuckle.

Samantha and Jake worriedly followed the paw prints away from the lake. They continued to walk after the paw prints and both of them started to wonder what she had been shifted into. The prints were not close together, so Jade had been on the run, and there were big gaps between the pads. There were no tell tale claw marks on the paw print, indicating an animal with retractable claws like a leopard.

"What she shifted into is god damn fast Samantha, we have never gone this deep in the forest before, and I'm afraid she may have accidentally crossed a territory without knowing about it before it's too late."

"Quiet Jake, I hear a man's voice and growling. Well, it doesn't seem like he is angry, at least we should go closer and listen in on what's happening."

"Yeah, it can be good, and we can see if they have our daughter."

Then a sharp snapping sound came up as if a femur had been splintered, and the growling stopped, and a little girl's voice came out.

"Listen Jake, that's our Jade's voice," Samantha spoke up.

We stared at each other in shock. There was Jade, standing fully clothed in a white sun flowery dress in front of two men and answering their questions, but she also had her safety barrier around her. So, she didn't feel completely safe around them. At least we trained her well. Not to trust every person she meets.

"Oh, thank the goddess you are safe! Why did you run this far in the Forest?" Samantha was running towards Jade.

After Samantha's outburst with all the worry laced in her voice, she was a bit calmer and turned her head towards the two men standing in front of her daughter, and rage started to build up within her. Then Jade spoke up and Samantha's attention went back towards her.

"Mum. I'm so sorry I didn't mean too; it was just that I was running around just like you told me to do. What are you doing here? Where's Dad, has something happened to him?" a shocked Jade replied back.

"I'm here princess, we were just worried sick about you. You have been gone for a while. Sorry, may I have permission to enter your territory sir?" Jake asked the two men standing in front of Jade.

"Well, it seems like this is your daughter and your wife just ran in here anyway. It's all okay, but I have some questions now. By the way, my name is Alpha Micheal, the leader of a small clowder of were panthers just through the forest and here is my second Sub Jonathan."

"It's okay miss, if you want to go to your daughter, I do understand that you both are worried. We only started to talk to her a few minutes ago," Alpha Michael said.

With that, Jake started to walk slowly towards Jade and Samantha with a perplexed look on his face, hoping Jade would understand. Jade looked at them and started to wonder why they looked like that. When

Jake stopped a few feet away from her then Aria started to explain to her why.

"Jade, you have the barrier up and they can't come to you if you don't open up a pathway for them."

With that, Jade swirled her hands a little and a pathway opened up for her parents so they could walk right into her. Jake engulfed her in a big, warm hug and just stood there then lifted his right arm for his mate so she could join in on the family hug as well.

"What just happened there?" asked a very confused Alpha Micheal.

"Um well you see, I'm a part witch, and when we had a feeling about being watched, I kind of put up a safety barrier around me just to make it a little safer for myself and I'm on someone's territory so it kind of makes a little sense," answered Jade with a nervous tone in her voice.

"Oh, shit that's impressive. I never had a chance to meet a hybrid before. I always thought they were just a thing of legend and yet… here you are. You seem to be a strong one also and are a well-mannered young lady. I do have to say I'm very impressed with your great parenting," Alpha Micheal praised Jade's parents.

Both Jake and Samantha looked at Micheal and noticed his face had changed into a smug look that started to tell them a different story. It was then both of Jade's parents started to get agitated and went into a more defensive stand.

"Well thank you for your kind words, Alpha Micheal. We should be taking our leave now and not disturb your clowder anymore. We are very thankful that you both showed our daughter respect and kindness, but we should get back home; it's a school day tomorrow, so Jade needs to get some rest before that," Samantha said.

When Jade heard that she was going to school tomorrow, she knew something was wrong; already at an early age she had learned different code words. Jade started to wonder what her mother had picked up on from Alpha Micheal. She looked at both her parents, and noticed that Jake was stiffer than normal and had a hard look on his face, but nothing told her anything what it could be. Other than feeling like the were wolf attack all those years ago. Smoke started to circle around her mother and then it hit her. Something was off and they needed to get out of there as soon as possible. Prying luminous eyes started to appear all around them in the shadows of the trees, and Jade started to feel uncomfortable in this situation and just wanted to go home.

Oh, shit here we go again, what have I dragged us into now. I only went for a run in the forest. I never meant it should go this way. How could I be so naive in this? I should have known better, Jade thought anxiously.

Then Alpha Micheal started to speak again after a while in silence. "Well, I'm insisting that all of you are staying for the night. I Would hate to make you all stay by force. It's amazing that your daughter is a panther/witch hybrid, and it can be really handy for us here in the pack.

So Jade, you stay here and your parents can go back home and come and visit sometimes!" Alpha Micheal commanded us with a wicked grin on his face.

"Who do you think you are to demand this of us and our girl?" Jake bellowed out.

"We would never leave her here, are you insane?" screamed Samantha.

"Oh, there you are wrong. I let her live so she owes me her life in return. She is mine to take, and she will do as I say."

"Jade, focus on Micheal's thoughts very closely," both Aria and Sapphire spoke simultaneously.

"What, why do we need to escape from here? This is insane. How can he even believe that I would stay here and leave my parents!"

"Just do it now. We have a feeling something is up."

That little girl is amazing, think of having a hybrid in the pack and what we can benefit from it. Well at least I will be having the full benefit from it. She will be my bed warmer during the night and a slave on the days. No one would ever believe a small child like her. Just thinking of her naked next to me makes my balls tighten up and my dick getting hard. The only thing I need to do is get her parents away from her, maybe get them captured. That would be easy and I can use them as an incentive to make her do my bidding. Well, if she doesn't listen to me, I have the dungeon to put her in for a little starvation that could get her to be the way I want her to be. Maybe I can force my mark on her little beautiful neck then she would never be able to leave me, Alpha Michael thought lustily, unaware his thoughts were being intercepted by the sneaky vampire Aria.

"I don't want any harm coming to my parents. I just want to go home." Tears started to form in Jade's eyes when she talked to her inner souls.

More and more people and panthers started to walk out from the shadows of the forest towards us. Jade started to feel how her panic was rising within her with every new pair of eyes she could see.

"Aria, can you mind linking my parents? Or at least try?"

"Of course, Jade. Now when Sapphire wakes up, we can mind link them anytime we want."

"Remember to tell them what we heard; we need to get out of here. They are too many for us to deal with and they are just listening to their Alpha. They don't know what is going on inside his mind," Sapphire reminded Aria.

Chapter 6

"Mum, Dad, do you hear me? Please respond by nodding your head or giving a signal. It's important," Aria broadcasted desperately, trying to create a mind-link with their inner souls.

Out of the corner of her eye, Jade saw that they responded and gave a comforting look. Jade's father lifted one of his eyebrows giving an indication he heard her.

"I heard Alpha Michael's thoughts and he is making me scared. I want to leave; there's no way I want to fight everyone here. I don't want to harm innocent people who don't know what is going on in his head."

"What do you mean baby? Tell us?" Mum's voice echoed in my head.

"I will just link over some part he said so you can hear it yourself. Is that okay?"

"Yes, princess, do that," Jake said in a calm voice.

That little girl is amazing, think of having a hybrid in the pack and how we can benefit from it. Well at least I will be having the full benefit from it. She will be my bed warmer during the night and a slave on the days. No one would ever believe a small child like her. Just thinking of her naked next to me is making my balls tighten up and my dick is getting hard. "This is what went on in his head not long ago," Jade embarrassedly telekinetically sent over to her mom and dad.

After that link you could see how the faces of Jade's parents shifted into pure rage, and they were on the edge of shifting into their Phoenix forms, doing some serious harm to Alpha Micheal. The normal colour of their skin started to change into a dark scarlet red like unoxygenated blood, and Samantha started to shake. When she turned this angry, it could be fateful for the receiver and she could be a very scary mother these times.

"You would do what with my daughter, you fucking ass-hole? I will tear you apart!" Jake yelled.

"What are you talking about Jake? You don't make any sense. Best for the two of you to leave," Michael answered back.

"Well let's go girls before anything else happens," Jake said.

"Jade will stay here," Alpha Micheal's alpha male voice boomed.

"And what if I don't want to," Jade answered with an attitude.

"You don't have a choice in this, you are mine!" Michael bellowed towards Jade.

"Attack her parents when they are not prepared," mind-linked Alpha Micheal to his guard contingent.

Several black panthers began walking around Jade and her parents looking for different ways to get them in a vulnerable state, to get a hold of them. Two of the guards saw one opening from behind and started to sprint towards their backs, when they suddenly ran into a wall and flew several feet back into a large old tree trunk. You could hear their spine breaking upon impact with the trees where the fell limply in a heap of half-transformed humans. The force was so powerful that the old tree quivered with the sudden impact of their panther's form, so they started to retransform itself into their human form, leaving them laying on the ground in pure agony, spitting up blood, tears falling down and screams that could be heard from far away. Several of the other guards left their position and ran to their comrades on the ground, looking them over, when the two injured members took their last breath, falling into never-ending sleep.

"Here *kitty kitty*, aren't you forgetting something? My daughter is part something of which you would never understand. If you think she wouldn't protect us or us her, you are sadly mistaken," Samantha laughed sinisterly.

"Jade, do you think you can put a spell on Alpha Micheal that could reveal who he really is? It's not fair to the pack members to get killed in the name of a hidden paedophile," Jake said with a vengeful look.

Sapphire agreed with their father and wanted Jade to cast that spell as well; she had enough of this prick of an Alpha. A leader that uses his power to get small kids is just a sicko. It was time for the pack to know the truth and let them make the decision of punishment for their own leader. Alpha Michael started to feel very uneasy and the shocked face showed them a lot that he didn't mean to show anyone. He started to speak up and explain everything to his clowder.

"I only wanted her to stay here with her own kind. With her help we would be unstoppable; just look at how easily she has taken two of our friends out. She is a murderer; we can't let her leave, thinking it is alright to kill any humans she comes across. We can't have that on our conscience."

The clowder members stared at their two fallen friends and felt anger at the girl and her parents but in the end, their Alpha was a fair leader who had never done anything to anyone in the clowder that they were aware of. He had always protected them, so the clowder chose to attack the intruder that not only killed two of their members but also offended their Alpha. Growling started to increase all around them, most of them had their ears back, showing them their teeth; the fur on their backs and necks stood up, and everyone started to crouch down in an attacking position, ready to leap at them at any moment they got the chance on Jade and her parents.

Jade looked anxiously around everyone. This pack had so much unwarranted hate towards them. She could feel the hate emanating from the majority of the clowder members. She knew if all of them would jump to attack them they could end up in the same fate as the first two did. She only wanted to protect herself and her parents, but now people were prepared to sacrifice themselves for a sick, selfish leader. It was then Jade decided to put the truth spell on the Alpha Michael before anyone else got hurt in this madness.

"Mom, Dad, I will start the truth spell towards Alpha Micheal; this madness needs to stop. Could I ask that one or both of you shift and make a firewall as a protective barrier to surround us? I need to take down the safety barrier to cast the spell," Jade linked.

"That's a good idea baby. They need to know the truth before they kill themselves or get badly injured. We both will shift; Dad will fly up and be over you, and I will make the firewall," Samantha mind-linked back.

As Samantha and Jake underwent their dramatic transformation, flame-red burning wings emerged from their backs, followed by elongating legs and erupting feathers of various colors. Talons with a sharp metallic sheen soon appeared, glinting in the sunlight, while their upper bodies turned vibrant with shades of red, yellow, and orange, proudly puffing up their chests. Their noses, chins, and mouths then elongated into hooked hawklike beaks capable of tearing apart medium-sized animals, with small puffs of angry black smoke emanating from their nostrils. Finally, their eyes transformed into fiery amber, aggressively locking onto Alpha's gaze with an intensity that caused Alpha Michael to drop his eyes with fear and trepidation.

Meanwhile I started to speak the spell against Alpha Micheal; each uttered word of the incantation caused the very fabric of the protection spell to disintegrate into a vapid mist.

"Leigh le fìrinn taobh deas an duine seo a
nochdadh leig leis a smuaintean a thighinn a-mach
agus a' bhreug fhuasgladh."

(Let truth show the right side of this person. Let
his thoughts come out and unmask the falsehood
over and over again.)

"What the hell are you doing, you little brat!" Alpha Micheal screamed while stalking towards me.

He was almost upon me when the spell kicked in on him and everything stopped for a moment.

"Don't you dare touch our daughter! You sick bastard, you are a fucking paedophile. You are just sick. She is only eleven years old, you sick fuck!" yelled Jake's phoenix.

"I have never done anything towards anyone. She can't be let free, she is a danger for every living being. She is a freaking abomination, you are the sick fucks bringing that into our world. How dare you!" Alpha Micheal screamed back.

After Alpha Micheal's last word left his mouth, the wind started to pick up all around in the trees, swirling towards Alpha Micheal's body making him shiver. The wind started to swirl up towards his mouth to force the truth out from his own lips. Every time he tried to close his mouth, the wind got stronger and made it harder to keep it closed. It didn't take long before every single thought he ever had erupted out, forced from within him by the strength of Jade's spell. All the pack members stared at him in disbelief at what they just heard coming out from their leader. Even so most of them shifted back from their panther form, not trusting their own inner animal to not tear him to shreds, which the majority wanted to do. Well at least not before they got their own answer from him, completely forgetting the respect they once had for him. At this moment, in their mind was the safety of their own children. Had he defiled any, had he planned to? Before they even started to bombard Alpha Micheal with their questions they turned around to Jade and asked.

"Is this actually true?" the clowder demanded in unison.

"This is all lies. Come on everyone! She is a witch; she can manipulate the words, forcing me to say stuff that's not true. I would never do anything like that. For God's sake, she is just eleven years old, and she is not even a member."

At that statement one of the clowder members screeched, "What the fuck does not a member mean, so your sick perversions are alright to you if she was a clowder member? So how many of our children have you molested, fucking pedo?"

Michael continued to defend his character, "How can all of you even think of believing her over me?" Micheal was furious that his inner thoughts had been exposed like this for all his clowder to dissect. Michael fearing for not only his leadership but also for his life. That fucking little girl was ruining everything.

"To answer your question, yes, it is true and no, I can't manipulate someone's thoughts; I'm so sorry. I only did this so all of you know what you are fighting for," Jade mumbled sadness in her voice.

All the members of the clowder turned their heads towards Alpha Micheal and then started to walk slowly to him. When one of the guards who was closest to him punched him so hard he fell to the ground right on his butt.

"My daughter is ten years old you sick piece of shit," the guard venomously spat out.

"What the hell are you thinking you are doing? You can't just attack me like this, I'm your leader," whined Alpha Micheal.

"Leader? You are a weak worm and think way too highly of yourself, that little girl over there has shown us your true nature, a disgusting, sick piece of shit. Not one of us has ever seen before, but I fear that you actually have molested a young child," the warrior spat back.

Jake looked at everything that was unfolding in front of them. The energy from all the members of the clowder was changing into utter hostility towards their ex-Alpha as well when he decided to tell Jade. "Princess I think it's time for us to leave. I don't think you should see all this, and it's a busy day tomorrow for you as well."

Jade and Samantha looked at each other and nodded their heads. Then all three turned around and started their long walk back to the cottage that they called home.

"Alpha Micheal, have you ever once in your life as our leader touched or had inappropriate thoughts for one of our kids in this clowder? I do advise you to speak the truth, thinking of the spell this girl put on you. Lie to us and the punishment will be severe," Jonathan spoke up with a clear anger in his voice.

Jonathan stood and looked down on his so-called Alpha and friend, hoping for everything to be a bad joke, but unfortunately, he wasn't that lucky. He was forced to keep his anger in hold to not just rip his Alpha and friend to pieces. Jonathan had to mind-link every pack member there not to touch him before they got to know everything there was to know. Then, they all could make up their mind about what kind of punishment they should be giving him for the crimes that he had committed. To his luck the pack members took a small step back but were ready to kill the ex Alpha as soon he told a single lie to them.

"I would never touch or have any thoughts about any girls or boys. What are you all taking me for? I'm like an uncle to every kid in this clowder. We are a big family together and you would never do stuff like that to your family," Alpha Micheal yelled back.

All the pack members listened carefully to what Alpha Micheal just said and were just waiting for the wind, to know if it even was the truth he had spoken to them. It didn't take long before the wind started to whistle up around Alpha Micheal again, forcing his mouth open and pulling out the truth from the depth of his soul. Everyone stood there in pure shock, not knowing what they should do. One thing they knew was that he could never be their leader or around their families anymore. It didn't take long before every clowder member of age shifted into their panther forms clothes were ripped into confetti and were flying around in the air.

When Micheal saw what just happened in front of him, he shifted as well and, turned around and sprinted away for his life. He ran as fast he could, but hot on his tail all the warriors and his own best friend tearing after him. Several times, he got yanked by his tail when he felt a hard pain spreading from his mid tail making him stop in his run, crying out in pain, which made it easier for Jonathan to grab hold of his friend's back legs, biting down and breaking them in four different places. The pain was so bad for ex-Alpha Micheal that he shifted back to his human form, letting out screams of agony, looking at his friend's panther in pure fear. Jonathan shifted back to his human form to scream back.

"How the fuck could you do this. I believed you; I stood behind you. I was prepared to give my life to save you. You are just a disgusting human being and shouldn't be in this life. You are dead to me; try to stand up and fight me."

"Jonathan, you are our new Alpha. The clowder has made their decision about that piece of shit. He needs to suffer the consequences for raping our kids, and we all agree with death for him."

"Is everyone in agreement on this, speak up now, or stay quiet," Jonathan boomed out silently inside every clowder member's head.

Jonathan got a mass link back to him with a big *yes* even from the kids. He knew it was bad but not this bad. He never thought his own friend could do this behind his back and be able to hide this. He was just hoping everyone would believe him after this, that he had no clue that this was going on. Because he would never allow it for any reason.

"Well, the clowder has spoken up Micheal. It's time for you to ante up for your crimes and accept your punishment like a *man*."

"And what would that be? I'm still the Alpha here," spat Michael back.

"Nothing you have to be worried about, considering you are no longer our Alpha. This is your own doing; enjoy the last bit of life you have. You know the clowder law on these matters. You made them yourself or were you thinking our laws do not count for you."

Jonathan's mind started to wander as the stress of the day increased:

It's unbelievable that a pervert has been my friend for so many years. What that poor little girl did for our family here is amazing and she just accidentally ran into our territory with not a single bad bone in her body. She saved our kids from any more harm from that bastard. He refuses to admit that he has done anything wrong at all and only blames a little girl for his misfortune. I do understand how all the members of the pack are so angry, even I'm pissed off over this, so when everyone wanted him dead for his actions, I couldn't agree more.

Jonathan shifted into his panther form and was softly growling, bearing his enormous teeth, saliva dripping down to the ground from his two four-inch front upper canines. Everyone started to stalk slowly towards Michael, furious growls from the depth of their bellies growing with each padded step. Micheal started to get nervous, muscles taut, whiskers twitching and began to bunch his own body readying for the eminent fight, fearing for his own life. At the same time cursing in his mind about what Jade had done to him to make him suffer like this.

Alpha Jonathan's panther backed away, letting the pack have their fun ripping the bastard's carcass apart. Some of the guards stopped fast, staring at their new Alpha with questioning looks. The only thing Jonathan could say in our clowder link was, "Go and have fun. I will stand back from this, not because he was my friend but because I have no children. This is your kill to make him suffer and atone for what he has done to every one of your children in thought or deed. Do this for our clowder and for all our future children that he would have had access to. We have a lot to thank Miss Jade for, but for a chance meeting she unknowingly saved our clowder from our own sick leader," Jonathan stated silently to his clowder.

With a sharp nod, the guards pressed on, drawing nearer and nearer to Michael. Their paws swiped at him, leaving small scratches in their wake. They toyed with him, passing him between each other like a ball of yarn. It was difficult not to find amusement in the sight of these majestic panthers playing with their prey before delivering the final blow. It didn't take long for Michael to meet his demise, lying lifeless on the ground. His last vision was that of a mother, accompanied by her three daughters, approaching with an axe in hand. With a mighty swing, she severed his head from his shoulders. The mother, aided by her friends, then erected a pole in the ground. As the gruesome finale, she impaled his head on top and spat upon it, unleashing a piercing yell.

"You are not a man; you are a flea on the dirt. Rot in hell, you sick son of a bitch."

Then she skipped away, happy and content with cheers from the rest of the pack. The only thing Jonathan could do was laugh, not at the grizzly scene before him but at how one tiny girl could have such an enormous impact. There was one small problem though, no one in this clowder would ever trust an Alpha again around their kids, even if he never did anything. The trust was broken and morale was as low as we could go.

There is one way for me to earn their trust again I need to find Jade and her family. The only thing is I don't have any clue where they are and they left a long time ago. Well, I need to speak with the rest of the members and tell them my plans for them as well. Hopefully, they will agree with the plan. I can only hope Jade will help us this time. I wouldn't blame her if she refuses, thinking how she was treated before all this. When we all got back to the outpost, I started to speak up.

"Attention, everyone! I have made a decision. I will make another attempt to locate that young girl and request her to cast the same spell on me. My intention is to ensure that none of you develop any trust issues with me. From this moment forward, I am prepared to live a life devoid of lies. My sole objective is to prioritize the well-being of our clowder, for we are family."

"Alpha Jonathan, I don't think you should have the spell on you for all your life, you have always been there for everyone to make sure we all were protected," a small girl said, coming up running towards him.

"We appreciate your idea and the commitment you show to ensuring our safety and trust. If you're open to it, I have another suggestion," a woman's voice chimed in.

"I'm all ears," Jonathan responded with a slight smile, addressing his clowder.

"What if we all had that spell on us? We might have noticed the signs that were right in front of us, but no one paid attention to. With the spell on all of us, sick fucks like Michael would never be able to molest again," the woman proposed.

"Does everyone feel the same way about this? Those who don't agree with this can leave this clowder with my blessing no questions asked. You have twenty-four hours to make your decision if you want to stay or leave. Any who choose to leave us have no obligation to tell anyone you are going."

"Excuse me, Alpha, I saw them walking towards the village to the south. You should start in that direction," A member suggested.

Jonathan nodded his head, thanking the guard and started to walk away into the forest, following the direction that the warrior told him about. It didn't help that they were starting to lose light. The only thing Jonathan was hoping for was that they left some smell for him to be able to track them from. They weren't dumb either. She had two parents that were immensely powerful, they would have covered their steps very carefully, well at least he would have done that. Jonathan was walking for a few hours thinking how he could talk to them. When he stopped looking forward a little, he saw a small cottage at the end of the forest, so he walked slowly up, preparing a speech in his head and wishing himself good luck. Hoping he would be alive after this small visit he was about to do. Jonathan stopped himself from knocking and began doubting himself over what he was doing. It was late and he was an intruder as well this time, but his duty towards his clowder was more important for him than his own life. He just wanted to make it right and be there for them all. So, he raised his hand towards the door and with a huge intake of air, he knocked on the door…

Chapter 7

"Knock, knock!"

Jonathan could hear footsteps coming closer to the door and a woman's voice erupting through the other side of the door.

"Who is it?"

"Uhm it's Jonathan. We met earlier today and I'm so sorry to bother you at this late time."

The door flung open with a furious Samantha, standing there still fuming after the event, wisps of smoke rising from her hair and ears. The smell of burnt feathers lay heavy in the air.

"Who do you think you are coming here after that shit your Alpha tried to pull? Leave and don't show your face in front of my family ever again."

"I do apologise for what happened there. I didn't know anything about that shit. I came here because I didn't have a choice. I'm the new Alpha of the clowder after the other members executed the former Alpha Michael. I wouldn't come here if it wasn't necessary. Trust me, you people scare the shit out of me!"

"What could be so necessary for you coming here? Just spill it out, Jonathan! Jake, come down here right now!" Samantha yelled into the cottage, her eyes never leaving Jonathan for a second. The tension was so high you could cut it with a knife.

Jonathan's thoughts raced at a mile a minute, sweat beading on his forehead despite the cool mountain air.

Oh, fucking hell, she will burn me to a crisp, I shouldn't be here to bother them. I really do understand why she is pissed off; my own so-called friend was going to take their daughter by force. Of course they would never help me out. It's hard as it is not to show any fear but God damn, that woman is scary as hell.

"Honey, stop screaming after me. Who are you talking to?" Jake asked while he was striding towards the front door.

"Oh, my dear you will love this, it's that second in command, his name is Jonathan," Samantha announced to Jake with distaste in her voice.

Jake looked at Jonathan with a hard, penetrating stare not showing any signs, but he noticed Jonathan's eyes dropped faster than anything. Whether out of fear or embarrassment was not known, but Jake could see the fear clearly smouldering in his eyes.

"Why are you even here? Was it not bad enough in your clowder earlier?" Jake asked with a raised eyebrow.

"Oh, honey he's saying it was necessary for him to come here, but I can't fathom why," Samantha said.

Suddenly Jonathan fell down on his knees, clasping his hands together like a praying monk and started to spill out why he was there.

"Please I don't mean any harm towards your family. I have looked for you for hours just so I can beg for forgiveness and help. I had nothing to do with what Michael did before. I had no clue that he was a child predator, and if I did… I would have ended him a long time ago. Can you please accept my apologies!"

"Honey, what did you do to him?" Jake started to laugh.

"I haven't done anything yet. Well, more than calling for you and being pissed," Samantha answered.

"Would it be possible for me to speak with Jade and apologise as well for what happened earlier? I also would like to ask her to put the same truth spell on me and the entire clowder. Unfortunately, my clowder has serious trust issues after the reveal from Michael, and everyone has agreed with this, I came here as a representative for all of us."

"Oh, this is our problem, how?" Samantha asked.

"Samantha, I know you are still very angry but we can't put everything on one person. Jonathan came here knowing he could get killed, he is on his knees begging us. I think this is up to Jade, we will be there behind her to have her back and protect her," Jake said with some sternness.

"I do know, Jake you do not have to tell me. Jonathan, stand up you look pathetic on the ground. Jade," Jake's deep booming voice reverberates through the cottage.

"Let's see what she thinks about all this," Samantha said clearly, irritated still.

"Jade, can you come down please? Someone is here and wants to speak to you," Jake raises his voice towards the stairs.

"Okay Dad, I'm coming, just give me a few seconds," Jade yelled back.

Jade sat in her room, the sound of voices and her mother's anger filling the air. She couldn't shake off the sadness she felt about what happened with the pack they had left behind. It was difficult to comprehend how the entire pack, or whatever they call themselves, turned against him, making his situation undoubtedly challenging. Reflecting on the truth spell she had cast on him, she couldn't help but feel a twinge of regret. However, deep down, she knew that it was necessary for the truth to be revealed for the safety of everyone, especially the children. It was a tough decision, but a part of her knew it was the right thing to do.

As she sat there, lost in her thoughts, her parents abruptly instructed her to pack her bags once again. And now, in her room, she found herself surrounded by two bags filled with her belongings. Curiosity gnawed at her, wondering what was happening downstairs. The anger in her mother's voice persisted, but now there was another man's voice mixed in with her father's. It didn't take long before her father called out for her, signalling that it was time to join them downstairs.

"Okay Dad, I'm coming down in a few seconds," Jade answered back.

Meanwhile, in my room before heading downstairs, I discovered just how fascinating my magic power really was. I began experimenting with spells, realizing that I could create my own and manipulate them as I pleased. And in no time, I found myself teleporting outside, appearing right behind Jonathan.

"Hi Jonathan," Jade said, popping up behind him.

"Gaaaah!!!! Fuck kid, you almost made me shit myself. Oh no." A really red-faced Jonathan stood there, completely embarrassed.

Jonathan stood frozen, unsure of how to react. Jade's sudden arrival had clearly startled him, and now she regretted her impulsive action. As a breeze carried a scent towards her, Jade's remorse deepened, wishing she had chosen the stairs instead of relying on her magic.

"I apologize, Jonathan, for frightening you," Jade said, her voice tinged with a hint of amusement. "Let's head indoors so you can use the restroom."

"Jade, what's wrong?" Jake asked.

Then the smell got to his nose as well and he couldn't keep his laughter in.

"Hahahaha."

He stood there for a few seconds, trying to regain his composure and to let the poor man go inside.

"Omg, Jonathan are you okay? While you are there, I will go and get some clothes for you," Jake had remorse in his voice.

"Okay thank you. I wasn't prepared for that one. This is embarrassing and I'm sorry for causing even more trouble for the three of you," Jonathan said, completely embarrassed, eyes downcast, not able to look up to their faces.

After letting Jonathan inside the house and showing him to the toilet. Jake walked to one of his bags in the master bedroom, picked out some sweatpants, a t-shirt and a pair of socks. He placed the clothes outside the bathroom door and walked into the living room where Samantha and Jade were waiting. It didn't take too long for Jonathan to clean up but he did still feel very embarrassed over what had just happened outside. He walked slowly out of the bathroom and walked carefully towards the living room, where he saw all three sitting and waiting for him, Jade was first to open her mouth.

"Jonathan I'm so sorry for scaring you earlier; I didn't mean to do that."

"That's okay little one. I should have been more alert as well as the new Alpha of the pack," Jonathan replied with a small, embarrassed smile.

"So, Jonathan, what did you want to ask our daughter?" Mum asked with a serious tone.

"My question to Jade is that I'm wondering if she would be willing to cast that truth spell on myself and the rest of the group. The clowder asked this as well. No one is trusting anyone after what happened with Micheal. In order to get past Michael's horrific acts, something drastic needs to occur, otherwise we will not be a clowder anymore," Jonathan explained to the family.

"Is it that bad over there? I'm so sorry I created so much problem within your clowder. The thing with the spell is it never goes away, it stays on as long as I have not reversed it from you all. Unfortunately, no other witch would be able to break it either. So, my question back to you is, are you willing to live a life never to be able to tell a lie again? And is your clowder willing to live like that as well?" Jade asked seriously as she explained how the spell works.

Jonathan looked at Jade for a short moment and then his eyes fogged over, as he created a telepathic mind link to his clowder family. Jonathan explained to them how the spell would work. Jonathan asked every clowder member if everyone was okay with this or if they wanted to back out, but he made it clear he was going to follow through with his plan. Jonathan reiterated that any or all members could freely back out before Jade cast the spell. It didn't take long before all the clowder members agreed and asked if Jade would come back to the pack or if they should start to walk towards her home.

During the time, Jonathan was his telepathic link, Samantha started to ask Jade. "Honey, are you sure you want to do this? It's going to be a lot of people to put a spell on, the physical drain will be extraordinary? Not to mention the complete depletion of your mental energy will leave you exhausted and vulnerable."

"Well Mum, Jonathan did come here to ask for help, even if he knew it could kill him. Also, if his clowder understands the rules of the spell, I'm all for helping if it gives them peace of mind as well, so they can rebuild their lives again. I brought this on Jonathan's clowder earlier inadvertently and I feel like I need to help them out."

"My apologies. I just wanted to give them the same information you just passed down to me. Their only question back where, do you want to come back to the pack or should they start to walk towards your house?" Jonathan asked.

"Uhm, I don't feel safe to leave my home after everything that happened. If it wouldn't be too much trouble to ask, I would prefer they come to me this time," Jade said nervously her lower lip trembling with trepidation.

Jade, rest assured that they will come here to meet you halfway. We all understand the importance of accommodating one another in this situation. Can you please let us know when would be a suitable time for you? Your kindness and willingness to assist us are greatly appreciated, and this is the least we can do for you and your family. Samantha and Jake, you are doing a wonderful job raising such a polite and kind-hearted girl. I can only hope to repay her kindness someday. Jonathan expressed his gratitude with a humble bow. Jade looked at her parents, feeling very insecure about what was to happen. She had never done this huge of a spell before. Both Samantha and Jake looked back at her with big smiles on their lips, trying to send their strength to their daughter.

"I would like in a few hours as soon as they can be here. I will only go up to my room again to get some rest before I have to get the spell working," Jade said back in a small, nervous voice.

"Okay are you sure Jade? I don't want to ask too much of you. You had a very eventful day today, but if this is what you want, we will get it sorted," Jonathan said with a smile.

"It's okay Jonathan, Mum, Dad, can you call for me when they are here," Jade said before walking away to the tranquillity of her bedroom.

While Jade had gone to the bedroom for some well-needed rest, Jonathan's mind linked his pack members to tell them where they should walk to.

"They should be here in two to three hours. Do you think that gives Jade enough sleep?" Jonathan asked with a worried voice.

"That should be okay. We aren't so sure how her magic works or how much sleep she would need, but she has made up her mind to help you and your clowder, and we stand by her choice," Jake said.

Three hours had passed when Jonathan's people began to arrive at the forest clearing, making their way towards the house in small family groups. Jake diligently watched the groups from the kitchen window, keeping a close eye on their progress. When Jake figured the clowder had mostly arrived, he swiftly turned around to wake up Jonathan, who had fallen asleep on the couch.

"Hey Jonathan, your clowder is approaching. I better go upstairs and wake Jade up too," Jake informed him.

Jake walked up the stairs towards Jade's room, knocked on her door, opened it slowly and saw his daughter levitating over her bed and with a calm voice, he started to speak, "Princess, it's time to wake up. The clowder is coming closer to the house, your mom and I will be waiting outside for you."

Jade opened her eyes a little bit and noticed she wasn't on her bed but sank down slowly and softly. She flung her legs over to the side of the bed, stretching out her back like a cat, and her arms followed. After that she stood up and dressed with a large hoodie over her head and walked to the bedroom door. She opened the door and started to walk with heavy steps in the hallway to the stairs. Jade felt bone weary and just a little stressed over what she was about to do to other people. Her weighty steps took her down to the door leading out from the cottage, where she was met with a lot of people on their knees, bowing deep into the ground, submitting themselves to her like she was some omniscient deity with their very lives in her hand. Jade had never felt power like this; it was one thing to cast spells or transforming into an animal. *This*, this was on a whole other level; power like this was absolutely terrifying yet somehow intoxicating. Jade was very unsure she should do the spell, but then she became wrapped up in the fervour of their voices echoing out all around her.

"Thank you, Jade, for all your help; we are indebted to you until our last breath. You are our saviour."

"Please, you don't have to do this to me. I'm the one who created this mess from the beginning, and I'm deeply sorry for that," Jade stammered out.

"Sweet girl, you saved our children from a monster that we looked up to. We will always have your back whenever you call for us," a woman's voice clearly broke out.

"Does everyone here know how this spell will work on you all? I'm willing to do this for everyone but if anyone has second thoughts about this they should walk away now. The spell is permanent, no other witch will be able to take this away except me. None of you will be able to lie, not even to save your lives."

Everyone that was still on their knees didn't move a muscle and stood firm in their decision about the spell, it also shocked Jade to the core how the clowder stood by it. So willing to not be able to tell a lie in their life again.

"Okay I will start now then, please stay still because it's a lot of people to spell in one go," Jade spoke the spell over and over again getting louder and louder with each incantation.

"leig le fìrinn taobh deas an duine seo a nochdadh

leig leis a smuaintean a thighinn a-mach agus a'

bhreug fhuasgladh."

(Let truth show the right side of this person; let his

thoughts come out and unmask the falsehood.)

None of the members in the clowder dared to move before she finished her spell. When Jade spoke the last word in her chanted incantation, the wind started to pick up, swirling around each and everyone. It didn't take long for the wind to settle down again when the clowder members looked at Jade and saw her swoon, losing her balance and falling down to the ground as her knees crumpled under her slight weight from the exhaustive nature of casting a spell on such a large group. The whole group stood up in unison, clearly worried faces all over them, when at the last second, Jake got his hand under Jade's head, preventing it from hitting the ground. Jade opened her eyes slowly and said in a weak voice to the clowder.

"I, *I, I* hope this will make you feel peace within every one of you, and please remember to think before you do anything! To put yourself or others in danger."

"Princess, are you okay?"

"Yes Dad. I'm just very tired and need to get to bed to rest again. The spell took a huge amount of inner strength."

Jonathan ran up to Jake and Jade started to check her body over without touching her. He knew she never hit the ground but the worry within him grew tenfold in a few seconds.

"Jonathan, she will be okay. I think she used too much of her magic and strength. It was a huge spell to cover all of your pack members. She only needs to sleep it off. Tomorrow she will be back to normal," Samantha explained.

"I'm so sorry that I asked so much of her. I should have known it would take out a lot of her. Me and my clowder should leave; I will come back tomorrow just to check up on the family if that's okay? Just take her to bed so she can rest well. Good night and thank you for all the help you have given us," Jonathan said with anxiety in his voice and clearly written on his face.

"That's alright, we will see you tomorrow then, Jonathan. Have a safe walk back to your pack land," Samantha replied with a warm smile.

Jake had already started to walk into the cottage with Jade in his arms, she had fallen asleep right after she spoke to the pack members in her weak voice. He heard his mate talking to Jonathan and he was glad someone was so worried about their little girl, but also sad because they would leave this place tonight. So, Jonathan would be coming to an empty cottage tomorrow. Their daughter's safety was at top of their list. This clowder knows about them and about Jade being a hybrid and thinks what they would do if they knew she was a tribrid. Samantha walked into the house with a frown on her face and looked at her daughter still in her mate's arms.

"Honey, do you think we should be leaving today when she is this weak?"

"We will wait a little, at least so she can have some rest and she can tell us what she wants to do. Staying here is not an option for us anymore; they know too much already," Jake answered.

"I can only hope that Jonathan and his pack will forgive us for just leaving. They have been very respectful under the circumstances towards us."

"They all will, and they will understand why this is happening as well. A hybrid is rare, Jade is even more unique."

Samantha nodded her head to her mate and husband, and let him walk up to Jade's room to put her back in the bed. Meanwhile they sorted out the house before leaving. Jade woke up in her bed and drowsily looked around and had a faint memory of what happened, when she slipped out of bed, put on her fuzzy slippers to look for her parents. It didn't take long for her to locate them, and saw they were just finishing up packing the last stuff.

"Oh. Princess you are up how do you feel?"

"I'm okay Dad. Let me help out with our bags. I have one idea of a spell that could shrink it so it could be easier to move it."

"Honey, are you sure you have the strength to do that? You just got up after your nap. I don't want you to push yourself too hard."

"Mom I'm okay. It's just a small spell, and it would be easier for you and dad as well. We are still leaving right?"

"Yes, princess, if you feel up to it, let's get it done. We need to leave very soon. Dawn is approaching fast."

Jade started to chant the spell… *"Ar mo ghlao déan iad seo beag,"* and in front of the three large moving boxes started to shrink into small dice, and the bags that had all their clothes shrank down to small wallets.

"There Mum, I left your handbag so you can put everything in there and I will carry it when we take off."

As Samantha and Jake observed their daughter, a sense of disbelief washed over them. They were at a loss for words, unable to comprehend everything they had just witnessed. Their little girl seemed to be growing up in the blink of an eye. Samantha chuckled softly as she carefully placed the small packages into her handbag. With the packing completed, she handed the bag to Jade, signaling that it was time to leave the cottage.

Stepping outside, Jake transformed into his majestic Phoenix form. Samantha assisted their daughter in climbing onto his back, preparing her for her own transformation later on. Nestled between her father's protective wings, Jade found comfort as they soared high above the fluffy clouds.

Jade faded into the rhythmic beats of her father's wings, thinking about where the family was running to this time and when it would end. Jade's magic was growing fast, yet she still had no idea where her spells came from…

Chapter 8

During their flight, Aria and Sapphire started to talk calmly with Jade about some ideas they had and maybe could help her as well.

"Jade, I have been thinking a little… how about finding a coven of witches, it would help us with your magic. A coven could help you understand all your magic and teach you how to use it in a safe way as well," Aria started to say.

Aria's perspective on the matter is valid—your magical abilities are becoming stronger with each passing day. It would be wise to seek out a teacher who can guide and support you, not only for your own benefit but also for the well-being of all of us. Both Sapphire and I are capable of harnessing your magic in our transformed state; you are much stronger than each of us. You alone hold the key to your magic, now we just have to safely unlock it.

I agree with both of you. It's important that we involve our parents in this discussion. They can assist us in finding a suitable coven, if necessary. However, I can't shake this peculiar feeling that's been growing inside me. I can't quite determine if it's a positive or negative sensation. Do either of you share this uncertainty?

"Yes, we've felt it too. But until it happens, all we can do is stay alert and keep our eyes and ears open," Aria said calmly.

"One thing I do wish for is that we could stay in one place and maybe one day have some friends to run around with. Some days can be really lonely. I do understand we have to move sometimes, but most times, we only move because I have done something to give us away," Jade said with a heavy sigh.

"Jade, soon we will have a more stable place to live. I can feel it in my spine; just give it time," Sapphire said.

"And Jade… we are moving because it's the safest way to keep you safe for your parents. They love you more than anything. Don't take it too hard. You are the most important person in their life," Aria kept talking.

"For the second part, I hope we stay out in a very remote area so I can be out and running, and even Aria can come out and play as well," laughs Sapphire.

Several hours later, my parents began to descend, gliding closer to the ground to ensure a safe landing. Jade looked around and saw that they landed in a desert that had some caves and miles after miles of flat, barren lands with scattered rocks, shimmering heat rising off the desolate landscape.

"Mom, Dad, where are we?"

"We just landed in a place called Sturt Stony Desert in Australia, Princess. I know it can be a lot to take in but there's no population out here; we will be safe here," Jake answered Jade's question.

"So, which cave should we take for the night? Because I'm tired and need my mommy to sleep," Samantha laughed.

Jade looked around and found a cave that was a little cosy but nothing could be compared with a warm bed and a cosy home. So, she pointed towards the area, and her parents looked where her finger went, and they started to smile. They started to walk there and looked around, the cave was empty and looked clean. Well, if you didn't count for some spiderwebs and a few snakes in there anyway. Jake ventured deeper inside while Samantha got to work clearing out the webs and ensuring the snakes were gone so no one would get bitten.

Meanwhile, Jade stepped outside and was just looking around, taking in the heat and listening to the silence all around her. She was still feeling a little weak after the spell yesterday, but she wasn't going to tell her parents. They had been worried all night and day. It didn't take too long for Jade's parents to clear out the cave, and when they were done, they called for Jade to come inside.

"Princess, I think it would be best to sleep in your shift form tonight. It would probably be softer and warmer as well."

"Okay Dad. I will let Sapphire take over; it is getting colder outside as well."

Jade allowed Sapphire to take control, and this time, the shift wasn't as painful. It was still uncomfortable, but it passed much more quickly than before. Both Jake and Samantha looked at Jade with a proud look and smiled towards their daughter. The two of them shifted as well, lay down on the ground close together and fell asleep almost instantly. Sapphire looked at their parents and smiled to herself, shaking her head. She then stood up and started to walk outside to feel the cold air around her fur. Jade looked around through Sapphire's eyes, enjoying the calmness around them. After a while of standing outside Sapphire laid down on her stomach sniffing and having one ear open to be able to keep alert if anything would be approaching them.

"Sapphire, I just thought of one thing: our shift this time was easier than the first one we made," Jade said.

"I know Jade, and it will get easier every time we shift. I know the first shift was bad and hard for you to endure."

"Jade, Sapphire is right, it's only going to be easier every time you change, and then it will not hurt at all," Aria chipped in.

Jade's happiness filled her with a sense of contentment, causing her to grow increasingly fatigued. Eventually, she succumbed to drowsiness and began to drift off within Sapphire's mind. The atmosphere became serene and tranquil, enveloping them in a quiet stillness. This tranquility allowed Aria and Sapphire to relax, no longer feeling the need to be constantly vigilant for any potential disturbances. Soon enough, all three of them succumbed to sleep, seamlessly transitioning into the realm of dreams.

The dream

"Bang, bang!" the sky lit up, followed by a terrifying loud crack and a series of thunderous claps just seconds after the lightning flashed. A wall of ice-cold rain poured down from the sky, making it hard to see no more than a few feet ahead; everything was dark around. The ground was so saturated that the fields formed overflowing puddles that flowed down the streets, creating small rivers that surged between the houses. A few minutes later, a high-pitched alarm started to whine out over all the houses and mansions.

Terrified people were running around with tears and rain rolling down their faces. Some ran through the rain, clutching small children in their arms, desperate to escape whatever was hunting them. When two hands suddenly gripped Jade's shoulders and started to tell her what to do. Jade looked up at the face but couldn't see it clearly through the tears and pelting rain. Everything was a big blur. Then a man's voice came out from behind Jade, telling her to hurry up and that they were coming for them. Jade looked around and saw some bodies laying on the ground, blood slowly leaving their body getting washed away by the torrential rain.

Tears streamed down Jade's small face as sadness consumed her. An inexplicable urge compelled her to run, as if a voice had whispered in her ear. With each step, the voice grew louder, overpowering her thoughts. As Jade's tiny legs carried her forward, the voice transformed into a tangible sound, filling the air around her. The world seemed to come alive, illuminated by a newfound light that banished the darkness. Suddenly, Sapphire awoke from her deep slumber, startled by the sudden change in atmosphere.

Sapphire felt Jade's stress and it began to affect her as well. When Sapphire opened her eyes, the sky had started to act up a little a myriad of colours danced across the sky, like a melting rainbow shifting in different colours that got brighter and brighter. The light became so bright Sapphire had to squint. Then an even more dazzling flash of light appeared in front of Sapphire's paws and started slowly fading to reveal a woman in a flowing white dress. The sheer fabric enveloped her, revealing a glimmering display of delicate gems and pearls.

Sapphire was greeted by a warm smile and eyes that reflected warmth and welcome. Adorning her head was a silver leaf crown, an ancient creation adorned with two crescent moons and teardrops of topaz. Her long hair gracefully floated around her face, gently caressed by the light wind. As she leaned towards Sapphire, her hair cascaded to the side, intertwining with her garments. Then, she opened her mouth, and an angelic tone resonated.

"Hello there, my dear Sapphire. I hope I didn't scare you too much."

Sapphire looked at the woman and nodded her head in acknowledgment but never turned her eyes away from the person.

"Oh, Sapphire, you can talk like normal to me. That is what makes you so unique. I hope interrupting your dream didn't scare you too much either."

Sapphire looked confused, turned her head sideways and started to think that it was worth a try to see if what she said was the truth.

"No miss, was that you that was talking in our dream? I'm sorry for my rudeness, but who are you?"

"Oh, I'm sorry. I forgot to introduce myself," the woman said with a gentle smile. "My name is Selene. I'm the moon goddess and the first werewolf."

"The moon goddess? I'm a bit confused right now, I'm not a werewolf."

"Not yet, dear. Your wolf will wake up when you turn sixteen. Haven't you been informed about this and your heritage?" Selene asked back.

"Miss Selene, Jade is adopted and she doesn't remember anything from before she was four. What I know is that we are a tribrid."

"It's okay Sapphire; I know about that part as well, but let's go back to why I came down here. It's a warning of what is going to happen on your sixteenth birthday. Please let me apologise for this beforehand."

"What kind of warning are you talking about? Why must everything be so hard all the time for Jade? She hasn't had it easy in her young life; she has been on the run her entire life, with people and supernatural beings constantly trying to kill her! Jade has no hope for a normal childhood, let alone teen years; she has no friends or even peers of any kind to relate to. Her family is constantly moving, and she has no sense of what home actually is. It just isn't fair!"

"Sapphire, please calm down. I know Jade hasn't had it easy, I know of her pain in her dream as well. Just let me tell you about the warning. I don't have a lot of time left here, soon I need to go back to my home."

Sapphire nodded her head to stay quiet so she could let the moon goddess speak up about the warning.

"I do understand that all three of you have questions; I promise I will try to answer them within time, even through your dreams. The warning I'm giving you is that the year you turn sixteen is going to be filled with worries and heartaches, even giving you a feeling of insecurity in your heart. You will be meeting your mate that day as well, but I made a mistake of pairing the two of you together, and I'm so sorry for this. So, to my last warning, you need to find a white witch or a white witch coven as soon as you can. Your power will only grow stronger for every year that passes, so try looking into your past and finding the clues. I love all three of you so much, and I will be seeing you soon again."

"Wait, what? I'm not following at all. How can I find my way back if we can't remember anything from before? What kind of clues?"

"I'm so sorry my dear, my time is ending. Please follow your dreams, find the clues and remember my warnings. I will meet you soon again."

As Selene spoke her final words, her body started to gradually lose its colour, starting from her delicate feet travelling upwards. The last thing Sapphire saw was her beautiful face and the last words leaving her lips as a reminder—"Don't forget you are never alone…"

In Sapphire's mind, Jade was deep in her thoughts, asking herself what she should remember from her past. Everything from that time is so faded in her mind she can't even see any faces of the people in her dreams. Jade started to think of different ways to remember when she started to think that her mom and dad maybe had some information as well, it was a long thought but wouldn't hurt them or herself by asking. Then Jade began to think about the moon goddess apologising about her mate. How bad could he be for her to come down to us?

Jade started to think about if her own parents knew about the moon goddess so that she could appear in front of someone and talk to them. The thought also took her into how other kids have it compared to herself, they always look happy and content with their lives running around playing with each other. In the end of Jade's thoughts, she made up her mind about one thing: it's time to talk to her parents about all of this. They may think she went crazy but better to talk to them about it than not to. Jade's self-reflection was interrupted by both Aria and Sapphire when they raised their voices in their head.

"Jade, please listen to us now. We have amazing parents who love us over the moon and they will do everything for us to make us happy. Even if we will remember where we came from or our origins, the love we have from our parents it's not what everyone has. It may not look like it from the outside, but unconditional love makes us happy. Don't think so much about what others have. We will find out our past at the right time and not before that, doesn't matter how much we push on it. First thing when our parents wake up, we are going to talk to them about what happened tonight and see what we will do from there."

"I don't know what I would do without both of you. I know our first step should be talking to our parents but I also think listening to the moon goddess' suggestion about a white witch is a main priority for us and our parents. I think they will wake up soon because the sun is rising from the east at any moment."

"Jade, we wouldn't be who we are without each other. Like the moon goddess said, we are never alone. We have love and support. Nothing can beat that, no matter what."

One hour later, the sun had risen up on the lower end and the heat from it started to warm the ground and stones up slowly. When Sapphire started to hear movements in the cave, letting Jade take back control and shift back to her human form. Jade had remembered to cast a spell on herself, changing into jean shorts and a tank top. As she adjusted to the outfit, she started to hear her mother's Phoenix move around and scraping the cave floor before it shifted back to the human form.

"Good morning. I'm outside, it's a beautiful morning," Jade said into the cave.

"Okay baby. We are coming right out as soon as I wake up your father."

Samantha walked up to her mate's phoenix and started to speak slowly, trying to wake him up. He started to stir a little and made the shift back to his human form in a half-awake state. Jake opened his eyes slowly, looking at his mate with a loving smile. Then he looked around and couldn't see Jade anywhere.

"Honey, where's my princess?"

"She is outside waiting for us. So, get your butt up and get your naked body dressed," Samantha laughed a little.

Jake stood up looking for his bag, and remembered one little thing. The bags are still small, like wallets. Then he started to bellow out laughter when he looked at his mate, and she was still naked herself.

"I think our clever daughter needs to make our bags with clothes bigger so we both can get dressed."

Samantha blushed when she realised that she herself was naked and started to laugh as well. Jade heard her parents' laughter rumbling through the cave, and then it hit her: their luggage was still in wallet size. So, Jade snapped her fingers twice, and in the cave, her mother's handbag started to rip apart and exploded sending the boxes and bags flying open. In the middle of all this, Jade heard her mother scream in shock and then their laughter got even louder. After a little while, Jade's parents walked out from the cave still laughing and looking at their daughter.

"Next time give us a warning; you almost gave your mother a heart attack," Jake laughed out.

Jade looked at them smiling and only nodded her head, then she turned around and looked out over the barren land letting a deep inhale of breath coming out louder than she had thought about.

"Princess, is something bothering you?"

"Dad, I don't know if the two of you would even believe me. I'm not sure if I even believe it, and I am used to the strangeness of my life."

"Baby… it has to be something really important to make you act like this. Please tell us we will listen to you whatever it is," Samantha said with worry in her voice.

Jade looked at them fast then she opened her mouth with hesitation, letting the words spurt out from her in one breath.

"Mom… Dad, I don't really know how to explain this but the moon goddess came to visit me and apologised for my mate and said I must find a white witch or a coven of white witches and try to find my way back. Then she told me that, apparently, I'm getting my wolf when I turn sixteen. Then my magic will just increase for every year that passes. So, I would like to find some white witches," Jade blurted out in a single breath.

"Okay princess, please try to breathe. What I just got in my head was that the moon goddess came down to you and gave you warnings," Jake repeated.

"Yes Dad. You believe me?"

"Of course, we both do, so our next step is helping you to find at least one white witch who is willing to help you, my little princess. You need to understand if she came down to you, it's a huge honour, and we need to listen to her as well. About your past, it will reveal itself when it's time to remember that we will always help you along the way."

"So, what are we going to do?"

"First thing first. We need to find a white witch, and we will start with that after breakfast. Then I will fly around and look from the sky and surrounding area as well. Meanwhile, your father and you will go to the city and look there. Witches love being around humans because they do fit in with them better than other shifters," Samantha explained her the plan.

"That is a great plan, my love. Promise me that you will be careful while doing that and we will as well. But you are right about witches like being around humans, so that would be our best bet to find them."

"Oh honey, you know I'm always careful; I have a feeling that the two of you will find someone before me. At least I can cover up more area here for safety and see if I can find a new home instead of this cave. Even if it's comfortable, a house with a bed is always better."

Chapter 9

Samantha walked back into the cave digging through the boxes for something to have for breakfast. She found a jar with Nutella and some bread as well; she carried it outside, where Jade and Jake had sat down and waited for her. They ate in peace and when they finished, Jade stood up and took it back inside again. She looked at her parents and saw they were getting ready to shift.

"Dad you can stay in human form; I have a spell that can help us." Jake looked at his daughter and nodded his head meanwhile, Samantha shifted into her phoenix form and took off into the air, leaving a swirling cloud of dust in her wake.

Jade waved her hand after her mother phoenix and then turned around to her father smiling and said, "Hold my hands and hold tight and don't let go of them."

"Siùbhlaidh sinn aig astar deallanach. Thoir sinn do'n bhaile mhòr as fhaisge."

(Let's travel at lightning speed. Take us to the nearest city.)

The air around them started to get warmer with every word that left Jade's mouth, and all the small stones scattered on the ground began to tremble, swirling with the wind. Friction crackled in the air, and tiny blue flecks of energy sparked to life, forming a shimmering ring around them.

It created a sudden spark and flames began to erupt around Jake and Jade—dancing wildly but never touching them. Jake looked amazed at the flames but never let go of his daughters' hands, the flames carried a sense of welcoming warmth and swirled around them as a warm hug. It didn't take long before they got engulfed in a vortex of flames and sucked away and appeared in a deserted back alley in the big city of Sydney.

"That was amazing, princess! Where did you learn that spell?"

"Well, it's the same spell I used when I scared the crap out of the new Alpha Jonathan in Nepal, remember? It was the fastest and maybe safest way for us to be travelling."

"Well, should we go and look for some witches? Do you have a spell for tracking them as well princess?"

"No Dad, I don't have it. And honestly, I don't think it's a great idea for me to try making up a spell in a middle of human city at the moment," laughed Jade.

"You are right there; better to stay in the safe zone with your magic. Remember to cover up your smell princess."

"I already have done that and only let my witch smell be exposed, just in case we will come across other witches."

Jade and Jake walked street after street looking around in stores and restaurants, but didn't have any luck. They even looked into different tourist places, but even that was a bust for both of them. Jake looked around and started to feel hungry and began searching for a place to sit down, grab a bite to eat, and have something to drink. And then he noticed a small little café in the corner of a house going down to an older part of the city. Jake pointed towards the café's direction to Jade, and she nodded her head and started to walk towards the café.

The closer they got, the more they noticed the darkened shades covering the windows, making it hard to see through them. The windowsills were lined with pots after pots with plants and herbs. Over the door hung an old wooden shop sign swinging after the wind. The door was of old hard oak with black bolts and black wrought iron trim through the wood with amazing carved designs of different animals and plants.

Jade looked amazed at the door letting her fingers follow the carvings like she couldn't help herself. So, she pushed opened the heavy door and a small bell chimed softly—once as it swung open and again when it closed behind them. They got hit by the smell of lavender and chamomile but also the smell of smoke, creating a calmness from within them.

Both looked around and noticed a darker décor, with deep purple walls and candle holders mounted throughout. On the ceiling hung a large chandelier with lit burning candles. Rivulets of deep red solidifying wax slowly trickled down the blood-red candle. The floor had a long, deep blue carpet with the moon's phases embroidered within, heavy russet brown drapes hanging over the window and some very old-looking tapestries hanging between the different table stalls depicting various street life scenes.

They walked a few steps, absorbing the mysterious yet inviting atmosphere. Just then, a woman approached them with a welcoming smile.

"Hello, and welcome to Morgana's Café. Would you like a table?"

"Yes, please would it be possible to get one of the tables that is more private?"

"Yes, of course, sir, no problem. Please follow me and I will take you there."

The tall and slender waitress with her silver hair started to walk, recounting the history of the café

"The cafés building was built around 1788 and the main building is still in its original state. The building has maintained ownership by the same family name throughout its existence. The main building has survived countless fights and went from being an alehouse to a restaurant to a late-night pub and finally to a café. The café building itself has also gone through being a seamstress building and to be a clothing store. You can see some of the café's history in pictures all around on the walls and also some paintings that have been made over the years."

Jade noticed the bar standing in the center of the area, and it was herb after herb hanging by the stems from the ceiling, teapot standing in warming chambers. She couldn't take her eyes off all the small details around her, and she couldn't help but notice the curious glances from the other patrons. She even took note of all the guests looking at them with raised eyebrows, and even the staff stopped working. Yet, their waitress remained unfazed, leading them deeper into the café. She guided them to a table with the same russet brown drapes hanging all around it that was covering the window. On the table were already two menus laying next to a napkin and sparkling silverware tucked in neatly between the folds. A bottle of water, beads of condensation adorning its surface, was standing in the middle of the table with two red wine glasses next to it. Jake walked to one of the chairs, pulled it out for Jade, and let her sit down; then he pushed it in. He walked around and sat himself down on the opposite side of his daughter.

"I will come back a little later and take your order."

Jade looked up at her and nodded her head, and smiled back.

Both of them looked at the menu and saw several items they liked.

"Excuse me, are you ready to order?"

"Yes, may I please have a large cola and a double ham sandwich with extra meat on it? Please," Jade asked.

"Of course, sweet child. Sir, what would you like?"

"I would like to have a double espresso and a ham sandwich as well," answered Jake.

The waitress wrote down their order on a notepad, offering them both a warm smile before making her way into the kitchen so she could speak with her boss about Jade and Jake, who were sitting at the table.

"Morgana, there is something worrying about the new guest that walked in. The young girl is sending out waves of magic from her, but the man seems to be just an ordinary human."

"Do you think she is an old dark witch? Who is using a youth retention spell."

"I'm not sure if I am going to be honest. You have more experience in this than me. Should I ask Lillian for help in this?"

"No. Let her be, she has a few customers already. I will deal with it. I will call for you when their order is ready."

The waitress nodded her head, gave Morgana the order slip, and walked out from the kitchen. Morgana looked at the order slip and smiled.

Morgana placed the meat into the sizzling frying pan, the rich aroma filling the air as she skilfully mixed it with rosemary and garlic. The fragrant herbs masked the distinct scent of one specific mix of herbs she uses to get intruders very drowsy so they fall into a deep sleep. Only she could wake them up with a homemade liquid that she stores in plain sight in the bar.

While the meat was resting on a wooden chopping board Morgana went to the bread and put it in the oven to heat it up for thirty seconds. She started to chop up veggies and organised them before she assembled the full sandwiches. When everything was done, she called for the waitress so she could collect the food from her.

"Thank you, Morgana."

"Nothing to thank me for. You didn't forget their drinks, right?"

"No, they are ready to go with the food."

"Okay hurry away. Don't let the sandwiches get too cold."

The waitress took the food and started her walk down to Jade and Jake, and when the food arrived Jade looked at her and said with a warm smile, "Thank you so much, this looks delicious."

The waitress nodded her head and smiled back and then left them to enjoy their food.

Jade looked down at her food, inhaling the rich aroma of spices and the savory scent of meat. But when her nose got a whiff of something different—that didn't sit well with her. She couldn't quite place the mixture, but the more she breathed it in, it made her feel a bit sleepy. She looked up at her dad and saw he was about to grab his sandwich and take it to his mouth when Jade reached across the table, grabbing his wrist to stop him. And began to speak to him in their mind link.

"Dad, don't eat the sandwich."

"Why not princess?"

"I'm not sure, but I smell a small peculiar scent from just the sandwiches. I'm not certain what it can be. I have never come across it before. It could be harmful for us."

"Very well, is my coffee good to drink?"

"Ha ha, yes Dad, the drinks are okay, no weird smell coming from them."

"So, princess, do you think it safe for you to try out one of your spells here?"

"Yeah, I would be able to, but I have a feeling that we won't be needing the spell."

"Why do you believe that princess?"

"Because Aria and Sapphire are telling me to stay alert and be prepared, but also yelling at me not to eat the food, but they are still calm. Oh, Dad, do you mind letting your scent come out as well? Just to make us known."

The waitress walked to the table and noticed that they hadn't touched their sandwiches at all, and a new scent hit her from the man in front of the witch girl. Which worried her even more now, but she had to act like she didn't know about their true nature.

"How was everything?"

"Well, the coffee was great, but I think your boss should go through the fridge and pantry. The sandwiches have an odd smell coming from them, unfortunately."

"I do apologise about that; let me take them from you and see if the cook can make something else for you both."

Jake handed the waitress both plates and gave her a polite smile. She took the plates, walked back to the kitchen, and started to explain to Morgana what just happened out in the café. Morgana looked at her, confused and also concerned.

"Can you explain the smell the man gave out for me?"

"Of course, Morgana. He has a smell from a cedar tree and smoke mixed in with it. The feeling from him is calming but also very captivating."

"Oh my. That's not good, not good at all, and the girl is giving out magic. I think we need to close the café early today. Alert Lillian for me."

"Morgana, what is he?"

"With that description you just gave me I would guess he would be a phoenix, and they are fiercely protective over their mate and their family. I have met a phoenix before but that was a long time ago. Please hurry up and tell Lillian to close the café early. This can be dangerous for humans and us."

The waitress ran out of the kitchen to find Lillian. She was at one table talking to some customers. When she turned her head and saw the waitress was stressed and waiting patiently, Lillian excused herself to the customers and walked away.

"What is it?"

"Morgana told me we need to close down the café early."

"Early, why?"

"Well, we apparently have a phoenix in the café and a young witch. They noticed the sleeping drug she used and didn't eat any of the food."

"Oh, fuck that's not good. I will go around and tell the customers something has happened in the kitchen, and they will have to leave; no one will have to pay today. Can you go to the door and give out coupons for their next visit?"

"I can do that. Thank you, Lillian."

Jake's sharp eyes scanned the café, immediately sensing that something was off. He noticed a young woman was walking around to customer tables in the café, and not long after she spoke to them, they stood up and walked out of the cafe.

"Princess, something is up."

"I know Dad. I have noticed it, and I also heard that they are closing the café early. I think it's because of us."

"Why would you think that?"

"Because no one is coming over to our table and telling us to leave. Plus, I have started to feel magic around the area, and it's powerful as well. So, if I'm guessing right now, we walked right into a witch coven without knowing about it."

"Oh, shit and me letting go of my scent probably made it worse."

"Well, it got a reaction, didn't it?"

Chapter 10

Jake smiled at his clever daughter and shook his head a little, starting to prepare for the worst. Then yet again, he looked at his daughter, and she sat calmly in her chair, sipping on her cola. When all the customers had left, Morgana walked out of the kitchen and began to walk straight towards Jake and Jade, letting her powers be known to them. Behind her walked Lillian, her power plainly on display for those who knew what to look or feel for. Jake felt the power from both of them, an uneasy feeling developing in his gut, still Jade didn't move a muscle. She only turned her head and smiled widely in the direction of the two women walking towards them.

She took in how the first woman looked with her round face, her head covered in raven black hair pulled back in a tight bun with two chopsticks poking out. Her makeup was bold, with a sharp cat-eye and vibrant eyeshadow that made her striking violet eyes stand out even more. Deep red lipstick on her lips, she looked to be around five foot four inches with large curves around her hips. Then Jade focused on the woman behind her with blood red long hair pulled up in a high ponytail. Glacial Blue eyes that could make you freeze by looking into them for too long, light makeup, and she was about the same height as the first one with a similar shape on the face. The only differences between them were that she was very lean and had a different, more

116

elegant grace. Neither of them were smiling, having only a stern look on their faces, made worse by the tight bun and ponytail. As they approached the table, the woman with black hair was the first to speak.

"What is your purpose here?"

"I'm sorry if we created any problems for you all. We came here to look for a teacher or mentor. That could help my daughter here with her magic."

"Tell me how she can be your daughter. Where are her real parents?"

"Well, me and my mate adopted her when she was four years old after we found her near a highway. We don't know anything about her real parents. Jade here can't remember anything about her life before we took her in."

Morgana could sense the truth when she looked into Jake's eyes and made a decision to hear them out.

"Okay, what kind of witch are you looking for, if I may ask?" The dark-haired woman turned her head to Jade.

"Miss, I'm following the moon goddess' advice and looking for a white witch or a coven."

"Well, let me introduce myself. My name is Morgana, and the girl next to me is Lillian; she is my niece. It's your luck that you walked into a white witch coven, and I happen to be the high priestess."

"Miss Morgana, would you and Miss Lillian pull down your power a little? I think it's making my dad uncomfortable."

"Of course, we can and stop with the miss. Just say our names that's fine."

"Jade, can you tell me a little about what the moon goddess spoke to you about? It's very important for us to know if we are going to help you," Lillian spoke up.

Jade started to explain what the moon goddess and she talked about. Both Morgana and Lillian's faces were on her the whole time, and she wasn't sure if they even blinked. She noticed that Morgana nodded her head a few times, you could see that she was thinking.

When Jade was done explaining everything to them, Morgana asked, "Could you let out your powers so we can feel the strength in it?"

"Yeah. But I haven't told you everything about me yet."

"Okay, what we know is that you are going to be a hybrid on your sixteenth birthday. What more can it be?" Lillian asked.

Jade looked nervously towards her dad, and he nodded his head, letting her know she should tell them.

"The thing is, I'm already a tribrid."

"Jade sweety, that is impossible. Let's see what kind of power and strength you have," Lillian giggled a little.

Sapphire was growling in Jade's head and started to yell.

"Let me out and I will show them."

"Sapphire, calm down. I have the situation under control and we will keep you hidden a little longer. I think this is going to be fun later on," Aria started to laugh.

After that, Aria started to take some control within Jade's body, making her green jade colour darken into blood red, changing the hair into a silvery white shade like a frosted winter window. The change took Morgana and Lillian by complete surprise. Morgana looked at Lillian, shaking her head towards her niece, and then the power floating out of Jade was making them take a step back, holding their chest. They looked at each other, and their faces only showed shock and confusion, eyes wide with not only fear but also curiosity. Aria started to take in the power again, but she also knew she didn't let go of the part Sapphire was holding onto. She knew blasting off all that power could be too much for them to handle.

"Jade, did you let Aria show herself?" Jake asked carefully in their mind link.

"Not really; she and Sapphire were angry they didn't believe me, so Aria took some control and let loose some of our power," Jade linked back.

It took a moment for Morgana and Lillian to collect themselves again and take in that Jade's herbal witch smell had been mixed in with blood and mouldy wood scent.

"So, Jade you have a vampire within you, so I take it that what you said about being a tribird is true. So, what is your third centre soul?" Morgana asked after catching her breath.

"Aunt she is very powerful for being so young. If the moon goddess come to her, we need to help her, and if she as well getting a wolf, that magic power is going to be even greater."

"Lillian, I'm going to train her. Jade, would you like to have me as your teacher? I believe you, and I think you came to us at the right time."

"For real, you will teach me? I'm so happy."

Jade's elation was palpable as she found a willing witch to help her. Unable to contain her excitement, she began jumping up and down, completely oblivious to Aria's presence. In her jubilant state, she momentarily lost control over her magic, causing ice-blue flames to erupt all around her and engulf her body. The flames quickly spread, igniting the floor and carpets in their wake. Concern etched across Morgana's face as she swiftly erected a barrier around Jade, attempting to contain the spreading flames. However, to her surprise, the flames began to devour the barrier, leaving her to ponder the immense power possessed by this young girl. Jake, noticing the dangerous situation, immediately reached out through a telepathic link with his daughter.

"Jade, princess, you need to calm down before you putting the café on fire. Losing control over your magic is extremely dangerous."

After the telepathic lecture, Jade stopped and looked horrified over what she had done. Aria had retracted back into her mind, giving back full control to Jade. When Jade had calmed down fully, she noticed the damage she had made on the floor and how the rest of everyone in the café had sweat beads on their foreheads. Her whole face started to show embarrassment, and she was ashamed of what she just did. Tears started to fall down on her cheeks. Lillian noticed it and rushed over to hug Jade, telling her, "Jade it's okay, everything is alright. This is not the first time this has happened. My aunt has a spell to fix it, trust me."

"I'm so sorry, I didn't mean to damage your café, Morgana."

"Sweet child. Open your eyes again; everything is fixed. There are no more damages. Things like that happen to us all, so don't worry about it okay?"

Jade looked around and everything was back to how it was before her little excitement. So, she bowed her head towards Morgana and apologised again. Then Jake noticed a pondering expression on Morgana's face and asked her.

"Morgana, what are you thinking about?"

"That we need a safer place to train Jade in. In the middle of the city of three million people wouldn't be ideal. Because her flame ate up my safety barrier as well, we will need someplace desolate.

"Dad, why don't we teleport back to where we are staying, that's out in the middle of the desert? I couldn't possibly do much damage out there, right?" Jade asked.

"That could be the best place for us to do it. Just let me get some books and so on because you need to read up on magic history as well. It can be good for you to know where your powers are coming from."

Jade nodded and waited patiently as Morgana walked off to retrieve what she needed. Luckily it didn't take long before Morgana remembered one thing,

"Jake, Jade, what made you not eat the sandwiches?"

"Jade smelled something and she told me not to eat it."

"What did you smell, Jade?"

"I smelled herbs, but it also made me a little sleepy by inhaling the smell, so I figured out it was something bad."

"You are a smart girl and have a good sense of smell as well as a survival instinct. I put in a sleeping herb when I was cooking the meat. You are an impressive young lady. No one has ever noticed it before. Back to what you were saying earlier, where is your family staying."

"We landed out in the Sturt stone desert yesterday, so we are in a cave," Jake said, a little ashamed.

Morgana appeared to look up into nothing, staring off into space but then she turned her head to Jake and spoke.

"That's nothing to be ashamed of, and it would be a perfect place to be in, safe for everyone. Lillian, you are coming with us as well. We will need your earth power."

"Okay Auntie. What are you planning? One more question: how should we all get there?"

"I can help us there; I have a spell we can go with," Jade said proudly.

"Jade, I have one question, if you never had training, how come you know spells?"

"Well, I don't really know," Jade shrugged. "I'm playing around with words most times and sometimes the spell comes by itself to me."

"Okay, that is very dangerous to do Jade. I'm amazed no one has been hurt, or you have not exploded yourself. Don't worry about it let's see how your spells are working for you."

"Can everyone stand in a ring and hold each other's hands and don't let go of the hand, please."

After a brief moment, Morgana took Lillian's hand. Lillian took Jake's, and then both Jake and Morgana took hold of Jade. When Morgana took hold of Jade's hand, she felt sparks of magic between them, and in ancient books that was a sign that they belonged together as the true teacher and student. It was very rare for this to happen, and Morgana had felt this three times in her long life. One had already passed away in the war, and the second was a woman she lost contact with. The third one was her own niece, and now Jade. She felt honoured and was going to do whatever she could to help Jade out in her life to the day she wasn't needed anymore. Jade started to say the spell and Morgana's head turned right away because of the languish she was speaking in.

"siùbhlaidh sinn aig astar deallanach. thoir air ais
sinn don fhàsach às an tàinig sinn.
(Let's travel at lightning speed. Take us back to
the desert we came from.)"

The air around them started to get warmer with every word that left Jade's mouth, and sparks started to be created again. Wind started to circle them and small dust got swept up all around them, letting flames be created. It started to make a mark on the carpet again in a giant way but never spread from that area. Flames started to grow higher around them all and sucking them up in the vortex again. Seconds later, they ended up outside the cave, and the flames calmed down into nothing. Morgana looked around and saw they stood in a giant circle together when she let go of Jade and Lillian's hand to examine it.

"Jade, how powerful are you?" Lillian said in pure shock.

"I don't know, that's why I asked for help. I know I lose control sometimes."

"Jade, where have you learned that language from?" Morgana asked.

"Well, my spell always comes to me in that language; I don't understand them myself. So, if anyone knows what it is, please tell me."

"My dear, what is a very old language, coming from Scotland and Ireland, very few speak it, let alone in spells. So, if I'm right, your ancestry is from there, and your magic is magnificent and very special. I do have a question for you, Jade."

"What can that be, Morgana?"

"Did you feel sparks from me when I took hold of my hand?"

"When you ask me yes, I did but it wasn't uncomfortable at all. But why did that happen?"

"It means… I'm meant to teach you I will be at your side to the day you die or don't need me anymore."

Jade looked stunned over what Morgana just explained to her. She wasn't sure how to handle that information. It has only been her and her parents against everything. So, now, there stands a woman and her niece who are willing to stick by her side as well. Then she got a clue to where she could be coming from just because of the language her spells are from; it was a lot for her to take in for the day. But deep down, Jade had a sinking feeling that this was only the beginning of what the day had in store for her.

"So Jade, are you okay to start with a test to see how powerful you are?" Lillian asked.

Chapter 11

Jade looked at Lillian and nodded her head.

"Jake, you are going to stay out of this. Nothing we are doing is going to hurt Jade in any way. Even if it looks like it."

"Okay, I'm just going away. Would you mind linking my mate and telling her we are back and we found you two?"

As soon as Jake walked away, Morgana nodded her head to Lillian, and she gave a sly smile back. Twisting her fingers and letting her wrist roll around a little. Her blue eyes began to shine little, and a wicked smile spread on her lips. As the stones around Jade's feet began to tumble and roll away, cracks emerged from the ground, spreading rapidly in all directions. Jade stood frozen in the center, her body trembling with fear, desperately yearning to escape. She realized that her father would be unable to come to her aid this time. Suddenly, she lost her footing and tumbled down into the gaping chasm beneath her. Petrified and unable to resist, Jade could only listen helplessly as Morgana's voice echoed through the rumbling earth.

"You should fight back, save yourself. Jade, you need to believe in yourself and your power. Take help from your centre souls and seek after the inner power."

The cracks suddenly started to close in together again, with Jade locked between them, when Sapphire had enough and took over full control from Jade. A high, murderous growl left Jade's lips followed by a shift into the white panther. Clawing herself out for the gap that was holding her, then tapping into the magic within her and Aria. She, for the first time, let out all of Jade's magic power blast all over the area. The fiery sparks erupted all around the white panther, the sky lighting up like a supernova, making Morgana stumble back and Lillian lose her control for a few seconds. Both women looked at Sapphire growling, who had her ears folded back and blood-red eyes, giving a death glare, bunching her muscles taut to make herself ready to go on full counterattack.

Lillian's horror intensified as she gazed at the imposing figure of the large white panther. Jade's earlier claim about her immense power now seemed undeniably true. Overwhelmed by the mounting pressure, Lillian struggled to maintain her composure. It was evident that the panther was far from pleased in that moment. Lillian's attention shifted slowly towards Morgana, only to discover that even her aunt was struggling to remain upright, taking a few steps back in the process. Realizing the urgency of the situation, Lillian attempted to ease the spell's intensity, but to her dismay, she realized that she had lost control over it. Taking a few steps back, Lillian urgently called out to Morgana, voicing her growing concern.

"Aunt, I no longer have control over the spell. It feels as though it has slipped from my grasp," Lillian exclaimed, her voice filled with desperation.

Morgana, taken aback by this revelation, responded with equal urgency, "That cannot be possible. The earth element resonates the strongest within you. Are you absolutely certain?"

Earth of stones started to rise up around Lillian, trapping her in a cocoon, shaking her around making it hard to stand up. The intensity of the quaking burgeoned when Lillian fell down on her knees. Water came in hard with the wind circling in between the walls of stone, lastly ice blue flames started to rise up from the outside of the nest, creating a bell jar over it, making it hard for Lillian to breathe. At last, Jade let go of her own hold of her power, making Morgana fall to the ground unable to use her own magic to save her niece from her trap. Jake walked out of the cave and got to see the scene in front of him, feeling the magic push from his daughter's panther, making him fall to the ground as well. When he started to yell towards his daughter for the first time in his life.

"Jade, you are killing her. Stop, this is madness; this is not you."

Sapphire's head turned towards Jake, not fully recognising him by face, but the voice made Jade snap back into the real world, forcing Sapphire to shift back. Jade moved with vampire speed, dismantling the spell binding Lillian while simultaneously gathering her scattered magic. Tears streaming down her face, Jade slowly created clothes on her slender body.

"Lillian, I'm so sorry. I didn't mean for it to go so far; I lost control. Please forgive me. I have never had to defend myself before."

"Lillian, can you hear us? For the moon goddess's sake, answer us," Morgana yelled from where she was laying.

Jake rushed over to Morgana to help her up and letting her pull her arm over his shoulders so he could help her over to her niece. Worry was plastered all over his face for what he had witnessed Jade do to the young woman on the ground. Jade was sitting next to her head and started to reach for her head when Lillian started to move slowly and speak up.

"Holy fucking shit!"

"Lillian, thank the goddess. I didn't kill you," cried Jade.

"Jade, I'm fine. I just passed out because I didn't get any air; your spell cut that out. It's amazing how you can control all elements. You are one hell of a powerful girl, you know that?"

"Thanks, the heavens, you are okay, Lillian and you too, Jade."

"Morgana, I didn't mean to hurt her. I lost control and I have never had to defend myself before."

"Sweet girl. You are okay. We shouldn't have tested you so hard without knowing your true inner power. I should have learnt that lesson years and years ago," Morgana explained.

"Sapphire wants to come out again. Is that okay for everyone?" Jade asked.

Everyone nodded their head and let Jade shift back to her panther form. Sapphire carefully crawled towards Lillian, examining her with concern before standing up and circling around her. Emitting a gentle purr, she then settled down beside Lillian's motionless form, providing both warmth and comfort. After a moment, Sapphire began to speak.

"Lillian, Morgana, I'm so sorry for letting my anger take over; it will never happen again. Dad, thank you for bringing Jade back to control. I couldn't recognise you in my anger."

"Sapphire, everything is okay. Now that we know the power the three of you are holding, we can work with that, but I think we need help from others."

"Morgana, what do you mean by help from others?" Jake asked.

"Sapphire, can you shift back to Jade? She needs to be a part of this discussion as well?"

Sapphire stood up and walked away a little so she could shift back into Jade. When the shift was done Jade walked back fully clothed.

"So, Morgana, what did you want to speak to us about?"

"I have been thinking over how to help you Jade, in the best way possible. Even outside the magic part, and you are going to need teachers in every shift you have. I have seen the deep connection you have between Sapphire and your vampire side, and all of you working well together sharing control as well."

"What do you mean, Morgana?" Jake interrupted.

"What I'm trying to say to Jade is that you need teachers who are Panther, vampire and wolf. To learn to defend yourself in every situation. I can only teach her how to control her magic part in defence and attack. My gut feeling is telling me she needs to master all parts of herself."

"Neither my mate nor I associate with other shifters. We have been trying to stay clear from them as much as possible. The few we associated with ended up being assholes before we had Jade. After she came into our lives, well… let's just say one pack of wolves is not around anymore, and the ex-leader of a clowder of panthers, Jade accidentally, met the same fate as the wolf pack; however, not by our hands."

"No, but I know a few people I trust. That kind of trust, I would do anything for them, and they for me."

"Aunt, wait a little, you are not thinking of assembling them all in one spot?"

"That is exactly what I'm thinking. We need them, and they are the best of their species."

"Who are these people you are talking about?"

"Well, Sylvestro is the vampire, Sylvia is the panther, Sarah and Ash are werewolves. I do think about taking in a dragon as well. And his name." Morgana was cut off in the middle of her sentence by Lillian.

"No, Aunt. Not him; it didn't end well the last time we met."

"That is because you broke his heart. Back to the dragon's name. His name is Stefan, a royal prince."

"Why do we need a dragon?" Jade asked.

"He is the only one that can stand your fire. Your fire is incredible and very powerful."

"I have heard of these people. I think it was around eight or nine years ago. They are known as the war team and work together with two witches. Are those two you?" Jake asked, looking at both Morgana and Lillian.

They both only nodded their heads in unison and smiled shyly. Jake had his mouth open and looked at them not knowing what to say or do about this. The only thing he could think of was to tell his mate what just happened and see if she would agree with his plan for Morgana's. In his mind, it was already set, what was best for Jade he would go with, and what Morgana just said and spoke about was the best for her with the best trainers there were out in the world. Samantha got the telepathic link and answered him back.

"Love, whatever is best for our daughter. We will get any help we can. I also have something very important to talk to you about; it's urgent. I'm on my way back."

"Lillian, how do you feel?" Morgana asked.

"I feel fine; why do you ask?"

"I need you in Italy, now. Start searching for Sylvestro. In my last image, I had a glimpse of him being there. After you find his ass, you have to go to Brazil for Sylvia. Do you still remember where Sarah and Ash are?"

"Okay, yeah, I do remember the way to them. I will also make a stop in the highlands in Scotland as well. You talked about getting Stefan as well. That will be a fun meet-up, don't you think?"

"That will be interesting indeed. Just tell him I need him, and it's urgent. I do feel a little sad that I will miss the look on his face when he sees you show up to talk to him again after five years," Morgana started to shake.

"How fast do you need them all?"

"As fast as possible. I know Sylvestro can be hard to find, but try to get them within twenty-four hours. I know that is a short time span, but I have full trust in you."

"Okay, I will take my leave right away; no time to waste for me. I will return soon."

Morgana waved her hand to her niece when she opened up a portal to Rome, where Morgana last saw the image of Sylvestro. A swirling purplish archway appeared, and faintly in the background, a strange city street materialised. Lillian, without the slightest hesitation, stepped through the archway. When her portal closed, Jade came running and asked, "Where did Lillian go off to?"

"She is going to find your other teachers. She is starting by looking for the vampire in Rome. I gave her twenty-four hours, but she will probably need more."

"Is it hard to find vampires? I have never come across them besides myself."

"No sweet Jade. But Sylvestro is over four thousand years old and has a habit of acting like a petulant toddler three-year-old child when he gets summoned."

That made Jade crumpled over in laughter, so tears were falling down from her eyes, as she pictured a toddler vampire in nappies throwing a temper tantrum. Even Morgana started to laugh as well, loving this carefree child in front of her. When Morgana brought herself back under control, she asked Jade.

"So, Jade, are you up for some more training against just me this time?"

"Yeah, it could be fun. Hopefully, I will not lose control again."

"Don't worry about that; I'm not going to test the strength of your power more today. I must tell you though, that you are one of the most powerful ones I have trained, and it's very impressive. I can't wait to see you grow up and master everything within you."

Morgana's compliments flushed Jade's cheeks crimson. Dropping her gaze to the rocky ground and shuffling her feet nervously as Jake walked over to them.

"So, is there any more training today? I missed most of the first one."

Jade and Morgana, passed a wicked smile towards him, and Morgana sent away a red fireball against Jade and at the same time, yelled, "Protect yourself."

The fireball sizzled past Jake's head, making him duck, and then two more came from behind him, barely missing his his ears. With that he yelled out, "Hey, I'm not your target box. Watch where you are aiming those fire blasts."

Both Morgana and Jade started to laugh out loud, their smiles stretched across their faces. They threw spell after spell around them, and Jake ducked whenever he noticed them flying too close to his head. He caught Morgana deliberately aiming some his way, testing Jade's reaction. Suddenly, the ground under him started to shake and rumble. The small sandstones underneath him began to move towards Jade, slowly, he was also moving in Jade's direction, not under his own power but by force. Morgana noticed it as well. In shock she yelled out, "Jade, what are you doing?"

That only made Jade stretch out her arm against them, pulling it towards her body and making the small stone move faster. When they finally were within two metres of Jade, her eyes glowed up in a soft purple glow, and words started to leave her mouth.

"dìon an fheadhainn as fheàrr leam. airson a h-uile buille a gheibh thu a' dèanamh an sgiath nas làidire agus barrachd cron!"

(Protect the ones I love. For every hit you get make the shield stronger and more harmful!)

"Jade, what are you doing?"

"Don't you smell it?"

Morgana looked at her young student and shook her head while she started to walk towards the barrier. Just then, Jade yelled out.

"Don't touch the wall, Morgana. I don't know how much power I put into it!"

Morgana turned her head to Jade in shock and started to feel within her magic how powerful this barrier was. Then Jake could hear faint howls in the distance, making him turn his head to Morgana mouthing.

"Did you hear that?"

Morgana looked at him and shook her head again, not understanding what was going on. She started to feel more uneasy by the second.

"Jade, would you mind me putting in a spell on yours?"

"Of course not. What is it you will put into it?"

"Invisible spell. I don't understand what's happening to you or your father at this moment, but something isn't right. Better to hide in plain sight."

Jade nodded her head in response and noticed her father's eyes were kept towards the south. Following his line of sight, she detected a disturbance. She had heard the howls long before he had, and that was why she pulled them into her. She started to feel small light vibrations on the ground floor and told Morgana.

"Hurry up. Something is closing in fast."

Chapter 12

Not long after Morgana got her spell up into Jade's, a foul smell of rotting meat caught Jade's nose, making her want to throw up. She was holding her stomach, tears flowing down her face while the acid taste built up in her mouth.

Jake's phoenix shifted abruptly as he caught sight of Jade's visceral reaction to the putrid smell. In an instant, the noxious odor overwhelmed him, causing him to grasp the gravity of Jade's earlier ordeal. From within the safety barrier, Morgana watched them with growing concern. She couldn't fathom why the Phoenix appeared so enraged. Recalling that Jade had fallen ill due to something and witnessing Jake's transformation, Morgana's attention returned to Jade. To her astonishment, she noticed Jade's hair gradually turning a silvery white shade. A single thought raced through her mind.

"Oh, great, her vampire side is back; this must be serious."

A few minutes later, she began to hear howls, and her guard went up tenfold. A smell of rotten meat and ammonia tracked its way into her nose. Then ten wolves came skulking around the corner of the rocks, sniffing around, softly growling deep in their chest. The head wolf nodded its head to his group and shifted back to his human form.

"Search the place, don't leave anything untouched."

The other wolves spread out at their leader's command; they walked all over the area, eventually into the cave, where one started to howl. Making the leader walk in there, letting out a menacing laughter. The crack of bones echoed out from the cave, and two men walked out dressed in Jake's clothes.

"Hey man. Do you smell all that magic? It's strong here."

"Yeah, I think we found the place where we are going to stay for a while, at least until they come back."

"What are we looking for?"

"We are looking for a child. That is all you need to know. That is what we are getting paid for. So, no more stupid questions."

"So that's why you have been dragging us around half the world for a fucking child. Are you stupid? I'm not dealing with this. I'm out of here."

"If you go away, it's just showing how weak you are."

The other man just looked at his so-called friend, slowly turning his back walking away. Looking straight into where Jake, Morgana and Jade were, mumbling something for himself.

"I know of this man; he is an honest, hard-working man. I wonder why he was with this group," Morgana said in a low voice.

"Morgana, why are they smelling so disgusting?"

"Have you never met a rogue before?"

"What is a rogue?"

"Oh dear. It's people that have been mean or done unforgivable actions in their former home. But some haven't done anything and choose not to live with a pack. We also have those that were born into this life."

"How do you know that man?"

"He had done some work for me; he is one of those who had to leave for a reason that he never told me about, and I did not think it was any of my business anyway. I do know he doesn't have a bad bone in his body."

Jake's phoenix nodded its head and kept a link open to his mate not only so she knew what was going on but also to tell her to hurry up home. When suddenly, one of the rogues walked right into the barrier hitting it with his left side. The pain was instantaneous, and he started to yelp, rolling on the ground in agony. The left side of the wolf's face began to sizzle into a smoking liquid dripping down to the ground, making the foul smell of rotten flesh permeate the air even more. Where the oozing substance touched the rocks, craters formed, as if the wolf's very essence had turned to acid.

The other wolves, confused and sensing a strange scent, sniffed the air intently. However, all they could detect was the odor of burnt flesh and fur. Overwhelmed by the pain, the wolf transformed back into a woman. Her dark brown hair was tangled and unkempt, resembling someone who hadn't showered in months. Her face bore significant injuries; with her cheekbone exposed down to her lower mandible, her face was etched with a permanent evil grin, and her own tears mixed with blood as they dripped onto her bare breast and leg. The excruciating pain caused her screams to reverberate throughout the open space, echoing around the cave in a cacophony of agony.

"Gest me some ucking wader," her injuries caused her to mispronounce her request.

The other wolves stood in place, confused by her request yet still feeling aroused by the naked body in front of them. Even her screams in pain and agony helped increase their climatic fervour. There wasn't anything better than a woman's scream in pain. She looked at them, realising what was going on through the haze of pain and started to shield her naked body from them as best as she could. However, there was a significant issue that she encountered during this process—the melting liquid from her breast began to spread to the other side, causing her further distress. As time went on, the pain intensified, making it increasingly difficult for her to endure. Suddenly, to her horror, her left breast slowly detached from her chest, falling to the ground with a splat reminiscent of dough hitting the floor.

The sizzling from the dropped fat clump could be heard by everyone as it made a puddle-filled crater on the cave's rocky floor. A smell faintly reminiscent of bacon being fried in oil spread through the cave. Eventually, she had a full open wound that was still dissolving; her ribcage was very noticeable, with snow-white bones being exposed where the acidic ichor ate the flesh away, pink lungs weakly pulsing with each ragged breath behind them. In the centre, you could see her heart beating frantically, trying to keep the body alive as Jade's barrier continued its morbid journey. She fell to the ground when her left leg couldn't hold up her body's weight any longer. All her muscles had been destroyed, and her femoral artery gave a mighty spurt but was soon closed as the ichor fused the ends in a sickly form of cauterisation.

The only thing left under her was the leg of the skeleton. Under her was a pool of her own flesh and blood and some fat cells bubbling, making her scream more. The liquid started to slowly make its way up her bum and into her private area. She started to scream loudly until the liquid reached her larynx then the screams quieted down abruptly. All that remained was a steaming, festering pool of melted flesh, with the faintest remnants of a body still twitching. Everything got too quiet in the cave after all her screaming. The ominous quiet was worse, closing around the other wolves stalking around slowly, looking for what could have done this horrendous thing to their member. The *leader of the group* snapped at them.

"Don't go near where that thing is laying; something made this spectacle out of her."

So, the wolves walked away laying down outside the cave and resting. Meanwhile, Samantha had picked up her speed towards her family when she linked her mate.

"I will be there in one minute; stay strong."

The smell had gone up in the air, and she could smell the rotten flash and a faint, strange bacon-like smell, so she was preparing herself for the worst. Jake managed to take back control from his phoenix and shift back to human so he could tell Morgana and Jade that Samantha was close to them. A smile of pure relief formed on Jade's face.

"I just hope they will leave soon; what kid are they looking for?"

"I wonder that as well. Jade, you and your dad stay in here, I will teleport out of here and get some answers."

"Morgana, I can open up the barrier behind us for you, so it looks like you are walking up to the site," Jade said.

Morgana nodded her head and walked behind them and waited for Jade to do her thing. A small crack opened up for her so she could pass out when she heard Jade's voice.

"Whatever you do, don't touch the barrier."

"Like I want to end up like melted ice cream. I do have some more years left in me still," Morgana smiled back.

Morgan went outside, and the crack she passed through closed up in front of her eyes, she started to make her walk so it would look like she came up from the canyon. She made herself look like she was around eighty years old, full of wrinkles and hunched back harmless; she also had a walking stick to help her around. She purposely did not take notice of the wolves laying outside the cave, and their heads raised up as soon their noses got a whiff of her human smell. Deep growling echoed around the area. Then from the shadows, a man stepped forward to investigate.

"Oh, my dear, I'm sorry sir if I took up your cave and your dog's home," Morgana stammered out.

Jade had a hard time to keep herself from laughing; her stomach started to hurt from keeping it to herself. She could also see her dad had a hard time keeping from laughing. Morgana's eyes sparkled a little between her blinks, trying to read the person in front of her.

"Ma'am, do you live here?"

"Yes, child I do. I will remove my things and give back your cave. I must say you have beautiful dogs."

"They aren't dogs; they are wolves. I do believe you are lying to me. It's kids' stuff here."

"What are you implying, child? Can't an old lady keep old stuff from the past? And your wolves look like obedient puppies, but I do think they need a couple of baths."

That comment made the remaining seven wolves growl, baring their yellowed teeth towards Morgana. It didn't faze her; she only rolled her eyes and smirked within herself.

"Old hag. Do you have a death wish? In that case… I will grant it to you."

The sun got brighter, the heat intense, and a menacing hissing squawk sound with a faint crackle sounds blaster out from the sky. A furious red-orange bird on fire dived down for landing between Morgana and the rogues, flames burning everything around it where the bird landed. Making angry noises, letting the flames flare up higher, when a second firebird came out from the canyon, letting its presence be known. Morgana let out a smirk towards the rogues and let down her disguise to speak up.

"Let me introduce some friends of mine."

"You are a fucking witch, leave this place."

"Not before you answer some questions of mine first. What child are you looking for, and for what?"

This made the two phoenixes' flames grow even hotter, and their glare burned holes into the rogues. Making some of the wolves back away a few steps; they weren't prepared to fight against firebirds.

"None of your business witch."

"Well, you made it my business, so open your disgusting mouth and spill it, or I will let loose my friends on your asses."

"I would like to see you try."

That started to make Jade pissed off, and she began to lose some of the control over her magic, well it didn't help that both Aria and Sapphire were exploding inside her head either. The earth started cracking up, stones falling down in the cave and rolling out from it. One of the bigger boulders rolled over onto one of the wolves, crushing its back leg and hip before it stopped, still over the wolf. Howls interrupted the area and the man lost his focus on Morgana and her two friends. It was then Morgana took her chance and sprinted up to him; knowing both Jake and his mate would protect her, she grabbed hold of his arm and teleported back into Jade's safety barrier. Jake noticed Morgana's move and spit out a wall of fire to keep her safe on her move. Samantha looked at the woman and recognised her, and linked Jake.

"Darling, that's Morgana, the head witch of all white witches. She is an old acquaintance from years back. You have met her, but she changes her appearance every so often."

Jake's Phoenix looked at his mate and wife, twisting its head to the side when he noticed in the corner of one of his eyes making it turn again, and a high-pitched squawk left his beak. Some of the wolves had hunched back, putting themselves in an attacking position towards them. When he rose up at his full length, raising his broad wings to the sky, letting the flames bloom up over his head, then stretching the head out, clawing into the dirt on the ground with his claws. It didn't take long before all seven wolves came running towards Jake and Samantha, trying to get close to them.

Everything Jade and Morgana could hear at that moment was screaming howls and sizzles following it. Heat came blasting from the outside of the barrier in waves hotter than the desert itself. Eventually, it calmed down from the outside, so Jade looked up. Beyond the barrier, charred corpses smoldered, the acrid scent of scorched fur and flesh filling the air. Amidst the destruction, her parents standing, talking to each other calmly in a warm, soft hug. So, she took down the barrier around her and Morgana. Unfortunately, Morgana didn't notice it. She was deep in the man's head, reading every single memory she could get her hands on. When she was done with the mind-reading spell, she looked at Jade and spoke softly.

"Jade, would Sapphire like to have some play time before we continue the magic lessons?"

With that sentence, Sapphire's head perked up and was begging Jade for some playtime. Jade could only chuckle and let her have her way with this new toy of hers. She shifted, and the man's eye grew wide and began screaming out.

"You are the child I have been looking for. You are going to die for everything you are going to do towards me; my followers will avenge me."

Samantha looked at the man and recognised him from earlier on the day when she was flying around when she started to laugh like a mad woman. Which made all heads snap towards her with raised eyebrows.

"Why the fuck are you laughing, you outrageous disgusting woman?" the man yelled out from the ground.

"You mean the small pack of sticky piles of asses a few miles from here? In that case that would never happen. If you don't survive my daughter and know how to raise the dead, she will forever be safe. Go on Sapphire, have some fun ripping him apart. I have heard brains are a delicacy in some countries."

"Samantha is that you? Are you Sapphire's mother?"

"Hi Morgana, long time no see, I thought it was you. Sorry for being late, but I did stumble on some nasty pieces of shit on my way around here that needed to be taken care of."

"Sapphire, do have fun; remember what your mother said; even dumbasses can taste good in some areas. I will go and talk to your parents for a while," Morgana said and walked away with her parents.

Sapphire looked at the man, giving away a cat smirk, putting her two front paws on his chest. Pulling out the claws and then pushing them into his front ribcage, hearing his scream was music to her ears when she lowered her head down to his ear.

"Scream some more."

Then licked the side of her face, meanwhile pushing down her one paw, letting the five claws slicing his chest open down to his stomach. The blood poured out from his wounds, tears falling down on his dirty face. The man was begging for his own life, but everything fell on deaf ears. Sapphire had started to hum to different songs that his screams could match with. Meanwhile she was slicing and dicing him slowly when Jake came out from the cave and spoke up.

"Sapphire, stop playing with your food. You still have the training to do."

Then she snapped out of her head, letting go of the man for a few seconds when he tried to crawl away with his injuries. When he noticed her crawling slowly next to his head, and spoke.

"Bye, bye little toy."

Then stood up, taking her canines over his bare neck, clamped down, twisting it to the side, and ripped the head off its shoulders, and his limp body fell to the ground, hot blood gushing out as his heart not realising it was dead still beat. Letting the body spasm on the rocks while she walked away while shifting into her human form again.

Chapter 13

Meanwhile everything that was going on in the Sturt Stone Desert, Lillian walked the long streets of Rome looking for Sylvestro getting more and more irritated over it. She found solace in the fact that she could at least enjoy the breathtaking beauty of the city. The predominant colors of the buildings, ranging from shades of yellow, orange, and brown, were complemented by small windows and dark grey shutters that added charm to the architecture. The presence of green plants hanging from rooftop pavilions provided a refreshing contrast to the warm hues. Despite her fascination with the city, she couldn't shake off her concerns about Jade's increasing power. She could only hope that her aunt's decision to bring these people together would be beneficial for Jade in the long run. As she strolled past the Magnificent Trevi fountains, virgin waters babbling, memories of her time with Stefan came rushing back, flooding her mind.

Lillian's mind drifted to her strolling alongside Stefan towards the magnificent Trevi Fountain, its intricately carved marble structure captivating the attention of everyone in the square. Lost in conversation about their cherished memories. But their bliss was suddenly shattered when a woman rushed toward Stefan, throwing her arms around him in a tight embrace.

"Oh, there you are! I've been searching for you everywhere. Your parents were quite upset when you left without a word last week," she exclaimed.

"Leave me alone Gloria. We are nothing, and I don't want to see you around me again."

"Stefan, who is she? And why is she hugging you?"

"You stupid bitch! You should address him as Royal Highness, and I'm his fiancé. So why are you walking around with my fiancé here?"

"Gloria, I have already told you and my parents NO! This will never be happening."

"Stefan, is this what you wanted to talk to me about? Why didn't you just tell me straight up? Do you know how humiliating this is for me?"

"Yes Lillian, but it's not what you think. I never agreed to this. I only love you that's why I took you here to give you this."

Stefan took up a small crimson velvet box out from his jacket, and opened it in front of the crowd that had developed from the commotion, tears streaming from his eyes. Without warning, Gloria snatched the box from his hands and started to scream with joy.

"Thank you love. You have no idea how much this means to me and our families."

"Give it back Gloria; it has never been meant for you. You and I will never be together; get that into your thick skull."

"I'm leaving; I can't stand this anymore," Lillian cried out and started to run away through the narrow, crowded streets.

"Lillian, wait please. I can explain everything."

Lillian continued to run between crowds of people, feeling her heart break hundreds of times over and over again. She could hear Stefan running after her, screaming for her to come back

As she arrived at a secluded back alley, she noticed it was empty except for a fat black rat twitching its whiskers nervously. Without hesitation, she teleported herself away from that place and never once glanced back at the man she had once believed to be her true love.

As the memory faded, Lillian blinked away tears hastily, remembering it like it was from yesterday. She knew Stefan had been looking for her everywhere but she always slipped away at the last minute from his hands. She walked away from the place into a back alley again and made up her mind to try a location spell to find Sylvestro faster.

"Show me the last image where Sylvestro was last seen?"

Scenes flew around in her mind about Sylvestro's last location. The last image she was able to scry was that he had left the country, and with that, Lillian signed deeply, knowing that her work would be ten times harder to locate him. So, Lillian started to think of her next step and made the choice to travel by plane to Brazil and get to Sylvia's place. She and Sylvestro have always been close; maybe she knew something that could help her out later on.

Lillian took a taxi to Rome Fiumicino airport and was there in good time to purchase a one-way ticket to Niquelândia Airport. She only had to wait for about one hour before a voice broke out in the central speaker system, calling for the customers to make their way to the gate.

"Flight 2678 to Brazil Niquelândia Airport, please make your way to gate 7 for boarding. Flight 2678 will soon be departing."

On board the plane, Lillian found her seat and put her bum down for some relaxation when a couple came down the narrow aisle, squeezing closely past her. She could hear that the woman was clearly upset and irritated at her husband.

"I told you we wouldn't find the little girl here. No one has seen that girl for years; no traces of her anywhere."

"Darling, please remember we are on a plane filled with humans. I know what you're saying but we gave our word to look everywhere and anywhere."

"I just want to go home to be with the rest of the family, to start creating our own family. It's not our fault she sent her away; who knows she can even be dead. In fact I wish she was; then we could get on with our own lives, not having to look for some snot-nosed brat!"

"I know darling, and we will have our own children soon enough. If this stop is a dead end, we will go back and tell what we know that we haven't found a single trace since eight years ago. That is what we at least can do for them."

All their bickering made Lillian listen in more to their conversation, and she was lucky that they had a seat directly behind her. She started to tap into her magic carefully to not elicit unwanted attention, she noticed that they were werewolves and of higher ranks once as well. She got very interested in that girl they were looking for. Lillian made up her mind to try to get more information using mind reading. The problem was that the spell was more effective with physical touch. But this time, she would have to chance it without touching. Lillian started to mumble the spell under her breath, slowly trying not to make it too noticeable over the spell she was engaged in. It didn't take too long for Lillian to begin hearing the couple's thoughts:

"I can't imagine how they are feeling. I know that he was pissed off that the Queen sent their only daughter away. Especially after what had happened to their son two years earlier. Who would have known that the alliance would become a reality before the war broke out, a war because the Queen rejected the mindless lord.

"Everyone closer to the royals knew that they were to keep their daughter a secret. A very small handful of people even got to meet her in the flesh. It was after a while the demon lord got news about the child.

Last time we were at home was almost seven years ago. We had won the war and captured the Demon King's brother—our prized prisoner. everyone enjoyed torturing him day in and day out. No one ever expected the Queen to be down in the dungeon, and in a moment of blind rage, she lost all her control over her magic. Everyone in the kingdom fell to their knees, including the King himself. The power radiating from her struck the demon, igniting him from the inside out.

"The demon's eyes became flood lights, filling the entire dungeon with their eerie green hue, as the Queen's fury intensified. His ears, nose and mouth were an Industrial Revolution smoke stack billowing toxic black fumes. Yet the queen did not relent, her rage inconsolable. All, everyone, in that room could hear was his screams for revenge that no one would ever forget about him. The hatred in his voice was real—palpable—but it was nothing compared to the Queen's seething wrath. It didn't take long before the creature was a steaming pile of ashes. At that moment we all knew who was the boss in the kingdom.

"She wasn't a weak or simple person that she had led people to believe. My respect for her grew more, and so did my wife's. She adores the Queen, and they have a sister bond between them and we never had to be scared to voice our opinions to her about anything. The King was a bit angry but mostly ashamed that he had submitted to his own wife, so when the Queen asked my wife and I for help finding her daughter, we never hesitated. She explained she couldn't find any leads through her magic and was left lost. The last she could find was in Sweden, but that went cold fast. I do have to give the little child some credit for hiding. My wife is the best tracker, even better than me, and when she

says she can't find a single kernel of information, we are dead in the water.

"The thing is, when we were in Sweden, we did hear rumours about a vampire child with two Phoenixes as parents. We went to the house that we found abandoned. Well, it was more than half of a house standing there, burnt down, but the place reeked of magic and fire, so we were still looking for that smell only so we could find the source, and hopefully it could be the princess. Both me and my wife knew there were more people looking for the princess. We had been crossing paths with a few over time. Most of them had been rogues and the last one we met up with, told us something disturbing about a witch claiming herself to be the Queen of all shifters.

"Hopefully my contact in Brazil has some information that we can use, otherwise we will go home. We both are missing our families and need to go back. It's going to be hard to tell both the King and Queen about our search that we have nothing to show them. If we by any chance find the girl, the whole kingdom will be in pure happiness and joy will be spread again all through the kingdom, with big celebrations yet again."

Lillian listens to the one person's thoughts and starts to become alarmed over what it was about. She knew Morgana was a dear friend to the Queen but she always stayed hidden for security reasons. It was also a long time ago Morgana had contact with the Queen, maybe she should make a stop and see what is going on. If Jade were the princess, she would be in great danger. Lillian made up her mind. As soon as the toilet opened, after the seat belt light went out, she was going to the toilet and teleport herself out of the plane. She had no more time to spend; she needed to get to the bottom of this and find all their friends and fast. Lillian started to tap into her magic to see if there was any other witch on the plane, but luck was on her side this time.

The rest of the passengers were only humans, lucky because one dumb fuck could spill everything and anything to someone that shouldn't have at all; that could be dangerous. *Loose lips sink ships,* as the saying went. Not long after Lillian dispelled her magic, the seatbelt sign flicked off. She unbuckled herself, stood, and made her way toward the front of the cabin to use the restroom. But in her haste, she made one crucial mistake—she hadn't fully concealed her scent. After she made the spell, and looked if there were any other supernatural beings around them. When she passed the two wolves to get her carry-on bag, she looked at them fast and then quickly continued forward when the woman reacted to the whole thing and smelt something was off with her.

The two other passengers Lillian passed.

The woman looked at Lillian and noticed that she was looking at them, so she took a deeper breath and could smell magic on her, but with very little power.

"Dear, did you notice that woman that just passed us? She looked at us very intensely and she also had a small bit of magic smell on her."

"Yes dear, but mostly she has a human smell, so relax. She could have been in contact with a wizard or witch earlier; you know how their magic can stick on sometimes to humans. I have been thinking about us going home; if my contact doesn't have any information, we will go home and explain to the Queen."

"You mean it honey? I miss our families so much. The last time we met them was when your sister just had a baby."

"That baby isn't small anymore, and I think it's time for us starting our own family as well."

"That's true, do you think the Queen will be angry at us? We don't have any proof about her daughter or the lost son, for that matter."

"Dear, she needs to accept that we can't find anything, but this will be my last try. We do have our lives as well that we have put on hold for our Queen and friend. I do think she would understand."

"I can't get my mind off that girl that walked into the toilet; something is up, my gut feeling is telling me that. Something is very wrong."

"We can't do anything on a plane either way, there are too many people on here. Maybe what we can do is confront her after we have landed."

Time ticked away, and Lillian still hadn't emerged from the restroom. Inside, she focused on her spell preparing to teleport as close as possible to Sylvia's location. The woman started to get more nervous because she noticed Lillian hadn't left yet and was still in there when she got a plan in her head.

"Darling, I think we should let one of the flight attendants know that they should check on the girl. She hasn't come out and others need the use of it."

So, the man stretched up his arm to call for one of them. It didn't take long before one came over to them so they could explain what the problem was. After they told the attendant about their concerns, she walked up and knocked on the door but received no answer back from them. The attendant walked back to the couple and said no one was in the bathroom, so that it was free for them to go; after giving the answer to the couple she walked away and continued her work attending to other needy passengers. So, the woman chose to go up to the toilet and knocked herself on the door. She didn't get an answer, she took her hand to the doorknob, and the door opened up. The smell of magic hit her like a ton of bricks, and her nose wrinkled up. She walked into the toilet to pretend to use it. The move was only so she could get the smell of the women using the magic and see if it was a dark witch or a white witch. Unfortunately, all she could sense was raw magic, with no clear allegiance. After she had done her business, she walked out back to her seat and started to talk to her husband.

"Dear, that woman was a witch the whole restroom reeks of magic."

"Oh boy, that's not good. Do you know what kind of a witch it could be?"

"No, there was way too much magic smell, so I can only wish for it to be a white one this time. Wonder what it was she had on her mind."

"Well, as soon as we have landed, we are going on a hunt for that witch. My contact has to wait; this is more important."

They looked at each other and nodded their heads together and sat down for the time being.

Chapter 14

At the same time as everything that was happening in Rome and on the airplane, a man was walking into the rainforest following a small walking trail. With each step, the sounds of the jungle grew louder—nature's symphony in full force. High up in the trees, vines hung, twisting in the breeze that never reached the ground, with some growing clinging next to the thick tree's trunks in all different directions, and wild orchids bloomed everywhere, spreading their enticing scent. From every corner, you could hear the screaming from the red howler monkeys, hissing noise from the ground of a huge coiled-up anaconda perfectly camouflaged in the steaming wetness, its forked tongue tasting the pungent air. The deeper he got in the forest, the thicker it got, making the trail tighter and harder to walk on, roots sticking up all around, making him trip as he tried to thrust forward. Brightly coloured poison dart frogs jumped from leaf to leaf, avoiding him as if his touch would poison them.

From time to time, he had to duck his head and body from flying toucan bird to the smallest paradise tanager, but only because he got too close to their nest and eggs. He walked for hours before he started to notice the place he had been looking for. Even before he took a step forward, three jaguars jumped out, growling with pure anger, swiping their front paws directed to the man's middle section and lower parts.

He was starting to get irritated and showed them his own fangs and began hissing back. His sharp nails extended instinctively, ready to defend himself. The three jaguars backed off and ran into the woods again, letting him walk closer to the place in front of him.

He walked closer to the two huge trees that had roots growing over his head thick and strong close together, and between the trees was a weaved door in vines from the forest. Small holes were made, allowing the air to let inside. If you looked closely, you could make out a balcony hanging out from one of the tree trunks. Flowers grow all around, covering up the house that was hiding within it. To be able to find this, you had to know what you were looking for, and then the man took a deep breath, letting it out slowly. It was almost twelve years ago he talked to her, and it didn't end well for them both, he was here to beg for her forgiveness. He had a speech ready to tell her and wanted to make his present known, and he knocked on the door. Noise started to erupt from the inside, and the door opened up, and a voice broke through.

"What are you doing here, Sylvestro?"

"Sylvia, it's been a long time. Would you let me in?"

"Over my dead body, you have nothing to talk to me about; now go away. I have already told you to stay out of my face and never come looking for me."

"Sylvia, I just want to talk to you. Please let me in; we need to fix this."

"We have nothing to talk about; you made that perfectly clear last time we spoke. Get out of my place, and don't ever come back here."

"Please let an old man speak with you."

"Old man? Go and fuck yourself."

After that, Sylvia slammed the door in Sylvestro's face and walked away. She couldn't believe that he had the nerve to come to her home to try to speak with her after so many years. Sylvia's panther soul started to speak to her in a weak voice.

"Sylvia, I know he hurt you, and he hurt me as well, but we can't continue like this much longer. You, of all people, know how much we need him back in our life just to survive again. We're too young to fade away, and with each passing year, we grow weaker. I know you've noticed it too. Remember yesterday?"

"Sly, I know that as well. But I'm scared that he will hurt us more this time, and that would take our life. That we are becoming weaker and dying slowly isn't too bad. And about yesterday, I wasn't careful. I will do better next time."

"Sylvia, wake up; it took me almost twenty-four hours to heal the claw and bite marks after the fight with the jaguars. To be honest, I still want to live for a bit more. Let's at least hear him out this time."

Sylvia never got to answer Sly within their link before Sylvestro slammed her door open, furious that she refused to listen to him. She turned around, clearly angry at what he had just done. He's not respecting her wants or needs by thrusting himself into her sacred space.

"Sylvia, I have had enough of this fucking game you are playing. This time you are going to fucking listen to me."

"Get the hell out of my home. You are a fucking leech and have no fucking respect. I accepted your fucking rejection and let you fucking leave. So, now you are here after almost killing me with that shit stunt you pulled on the battlefield."

"I did that to save your fucking ass. People were after me, and you, being my soulmate, would have put you in more danger. I have already told you this, and still you are so stupidly stubborn, refusing to listen or talk to me. Have you a brain inside that fucking beautiful head of yours."

"So what? We could have fixed that together, but you were not even man enough; you are a fucking coward. Just leave and never come back to me again."

"Sylvia, please…"

"Get the hell out of my home. I don't want to see you ever again. I'd rather die than be in your company."

"Baby, I do love you; I have always loved you."

"Go and fuck yourself; you don't know what love is. Go and find a human to play with; just leave me alone."

As the last sentence was still leaving Sylvia's lips, Sylvestro drew from his vampire speed and grabbed her, moving them to the back wall in a tight hug, refusing to let go of his strength more than a match for her weakened state. He didn't care about curse words leaving her mouth; he put his face in the crook of her neck, letting tears fall slowly from his eyes and whispering low.

"A day doesn't go by for me without thinking about you. My whole body is aching and falling apart each and every day that I'm not next to you. You are the one and only love of my life."

After a few seconds, Sylvestro lifted his head and looked at Sylvia, at his heart pounding as he noticed her face had gone deathly pale. He started to scream and yell for her to wake up, shaking her body. When nothing worked for him, he started CPR with three blows of air in the mouth and ten hand compressions on her chest. He repeated the movements frantically for several minutes, sweat beading on his forehead, arms beginning to ache, when at last, she started to cough. He lifted her head up slowly and laid it on his legs, letting his tears fall without a care in the world. He knew he looked pathetic however, he felt his whole body was shutting down with his true love's limp body. Sylvia opened her eyes and turned her head away from Sylvestro, throwing up blood directly on the floor in her living room. The colour of her skin was still pale like untouched morning snow, and her pulse got weaker and thready. This was the first time she had ever collapsed like this, and dread settled deep in his chest.

"Sylvia, what is going on with you? Talk to me."

"Sylvestro, it's nothing to worry about. It will pass soon."

"No, you are going to tell me, this is not normal for you. You don't have any injury that would do this."

"You are wrong there. I do have one, and it's the one you made a long time ago. You are the one that is killing me from the inside."

"What are you talking about? I have never hurt you!"

"So now you are a liar as well as a coward. Your rejection of me ripped my heart out; you have been killing me because you are too stupid to understand anything. Can you just leave so I can die in peace?"

Hot, salty tears were streaming down Sylvia's face in hurt and agony. She still loved him but she wasn't going to let him hurt her ever again. She had promised herself this on the day he rejected her as the only way to keep her safe. Unfortunately, the result is that it is killing her instead, slowly and painfully draining her will to exist. Sylvestro looked at her with sorrow showing all over him. He lifted her head up to put it down slowly on the floor again so he could stand up, then he walked into the kitchen, made some herbal tea and came back walking to the sofa with two cups.

He noticed Sylvia hadn't moved from the spot, so he walked back to her and crouched down to scoop her up in bridal style. Sylvia was too weak to fight back and let him just pick her up. While in his arms, she crawled closer to his chest, and she felt his lips on her head, leaving a soft, tender kiss. After Sylvestro got back to the sofa he sat down with Sylvia on his lap and stretched out one of his arms for one of the cups to give to her. Letting one of his hands run over her back slowly while kissing her temple in light, soft caresses, whispering calmly and slowly.

"Why didn't you ever tell me about this? Do you really hate me this much?"

"I don't hate you. I have always loved you, but you never wanted to be with me. Can't you understand you hurt me so badly? A vampire can reject their mate, but a panther dies slowly if they reject or get rejected. I knew this would be my future after you told me those words. That's why I never told you this, as it would never change anything. Sylvestro, I may be dying, but my love for you never has."

"That is not true, my dear. I have always loved you, but I never showed it. When the bond between us was created, I only got scared and worried. All I wanted was to protect you. I may not have handled it right and done some wrong things, but I never intended to hurt you this way. Is there any way that I can save you and us? I would honestly die myself if it meant you lived instead."

"You already know the answer if you really think about it."

Sylvestro stopped rubbing her back and looked right into the wall in front of him, letting his thoughts run through his mind. During this time, Sylvestro was overwhelmed by his own thoughts; Sylvia had taken her free hand and laid it on his chest to feel his calm breathing and barely beating heart. She also took in the smell of coconut ice cream that was coming from him, making Sylvia start to doze off, feeling calm and relaxed, letting this happy time be the last she remembered before she would leave the earth. When Sylestro yanked up, noticing her heartbeat had slowed down rapidly beneath him and started to yell.

"Sylvia, I don't care if you're going to hate me for this. I will not have you die not here, not ever!"

She didn't have time to react before she felt two sharp fangs puncturing her below her earlobe. A soft, weak moan left her lips, making Sylvestro groan and feeling himself getting lost in Sylvia's intoxicating blood. Sylvia dropped her cup of tea onto the floor, taking both her hands up to his face, then down and around his torso. Letting soft moans leave her, though she started to feel stronger, and her pale skin started to get more colour like a blossoming sunrise, her cheeks becoming rose blush.

When Sylvestro finally let his fangs slide out from her and he licked his mark on her pale skin. In an instant, she jolted upright from his lap, a smirk curling her lips. With a slow, deliberate sway of her hips, she walked further away from him towards her bedroom, beckoning with a single long, slender, elegant finger. For a few seconds, Sylvestro looked confused, but when he heard a room door open up, he jumped up on his feet, sprinting to where the sound came from. There stood Sylvia, unbuttoning her shirt. She then took up her pointing finger and started to bend her finger again, luring him closer to her. Sylvestro got the point and stalked closer to her, when finally in front of her, he took his arms around her back, pulling her closer to him, leaving a deep, tender kiss on top of her head. He let go of his arms around her and took a step back, looked into her eyes and noticed that her panther was in half control only because one eye was green and the other one was black. He took it in and asked, "Are you okay, my love?"

"Never better!"

Then her fingers trailed up on his chest, and Sylvia's head tilted up and she raised herself up on the toes to kiss him on his jawline, which still had this morning's stubble. When she kissed his jawline, she let one of her fingernails turn into a claw, sliding it over his Armani shirt buttons and ripping them loose. She glanced up slowly as his shirt parted to see his eye looking down at her, shifting between grey and blood red. Everything stood out from his pale skin; he didn't make one move to stop her. Sylvia continued her kisses down to his throat, nibbling a small bit on his collarbone. Hearing his hiss and groan made Sylvia even happier, and took it as a sign for her to continue. She kissed her way down towards his torso, deep, soft kisses stopping at the line of the upper ripped shirt.

Sylvia took both her hands on either side and separated the fabric in one pull, letting the few buttons that were left fly in all directions in the room, ricocheting off the wall. As his shirt tore off, Sylvestro's nipple stood up in front of her, and she couldn't resist licking the right one, swirling her tongue in tight little circles and letting her left-hand slide over his other. Making him hiss out loud, his body quivering a little in pure pleasure. She allowed his body to calm down slightly. Sylvia could feel his hand in her thick hair, gripping it tightly but not painfully. She could still move around but also knew his strong grip could restrict her movement at his pleasure.

She started to let her right hand glide down over the eight-pack on his muscular stomach. Until she came down to the buckle of his belt, unbuckled it and took a step back to yank the belt from its place in one swift move. Letting the pants fall down to the floor of the room, she looked down and saw his hardened member being free from the restriction of the pants. Sylvia let her index finger float light further down, letting it follow the contours of his swollen member, feeling it pulsate for every place her fingers touched. He followed every move she made with her lustful eyes as she began to crouch down to her knees, desiring to have a taste of his enthralling flesh.

She lifted her head up to meet Sylvestro's hungry eyes on her. With pleading eyes from Sylvia, he nodded his head and let go of her hair, letting her do as she pleased with him for the moment. Sylvia turned back her head and began blowing warm air from her hot, slick mouth over his thick, hard member before letting her tongue make small, slow circles around the top. Letting the first salty pre-cum taste drip on the tip of her tongue, she moaned at the taste, desiring to take more of it, letting it slide deeper down into her throat.

The moaning from her throat vibrated all around his hard member, making Sylvestro's knees become weak. He started to rock his hips with her movements, taking every part of her mouth and throat. Grasping her head forcefully, pushing Sylvia's head down further on his quivering shaft. Sly started to take over Sylvia's body little by little just so the clothes on their body could rip apart. As soon her clothes were ripped to confetti, Sly sank back into their mind, letting Sylvia have full control again. Sylvia started to let one of her hands go down towards her dripping-soaked lower part that was aching of need. Sylvestro noticed her move and stopped with his assault on her mouth.

"Don't you dare touch what is mine to play with!"

Just his word made Sylvia stop mid-way, pulling away from his hardness, looking confused. Before she could utter one word, Sylvestro grabbed hold of her hair, pulling her up off her knees. To then started pushing her towards the bed, making Sylvia fall down on her back. He separated her legs wide open so he could look at her beautiful body. His eye landed on her moist, pink, pulsating treasure of joy. Sylvestro started to kiss her feet, going towards her knees and followed them down to her soaking wet core. Letting his tongue slide between her folds and his thumb on her nub, making tiny, quick circular movements, and the other arm around her waist to hold her down. Sylvia was turning her head from side to side, screaming in pure pleasure. Stars danced behind her closed eyes as waves of passion overcame her.

"Come for me, baby. Let me taste all of you."

After the last word left Silvestro's lips, Sylvia's pussy exploded in a gushing quaking orgasm as she screamed out his name at the same time.

"Are you ready for me, baby?"

"Mm, come closer… I need you."

With that, Sylvestro got into position between Sylvia's legs, letting his hardened member slide between her folds, spreading her juices around himself. When he felt that both of them were ready, Sylvestro began to push himself inside into her core. Breaking her hymen, he stopped and didn't move for a while letting Sylvia get adjusted to his size. He looked at her and saw tears had fallen down, that made him worried. He laid closer to her so he could kiss her on the mouth. Sylvia started to move her lower part slowly to make sure he knew so he could start moving again. Sylvestro started slowly pulling out; meanwhile he had his elbows close to her body. He could feel her taking her legs around his hips and pushing him closer to her.

"Baby, I'm trying to go slow. Calm down."

"Fuck me, fast and hard."

Sylvia whispered softly back into his ear; then she bit down on his ear lobe hard. Making him yank up in surprise, slowly taking up the pace and making him groan loudly. Sylvia's moaning increased with every thrust he made, and she started to grind her hips along with him. The room started to fill up with the musky smell of arousal and sweat when Sylestro pulled out and grabbed Sylvia up, to place her on top of him where he was laying down on the bed. Placing her over his hard shaft, letting her slide over him as deep as he could get inside of her. The moans coming out of her were of heaven for every stroke that took place within her. Fully inside of her, she started to grind on top of Sylvestro, making harder and faster pulls between them, letting Sylvestro's head hit the headboard of the bed a few times when he moaned out.

"Come for me, baby."

It didn't take much before Sylvia bucked her hips and squirted all over Sylvestro's stomach and chest. Letting Sylvestro take back some control over the speed between them, when she bent down over him, letting her breast grind against him. Her erect nipple tingling against the hair on his chest while she was kissing his throat and neck, whispering between the kisses.

"Now it's your turn, my love."

Then her canine teeth thrust forward and penetrated his skin between the neck and collarbone. Making him push up hard and spreading his own seed inside her, covering her already moist walls. The both of them were panting and breathing fast, trying to calm down their bodies, when suddenly Sylvia sat up in the bed listening to something she just heard. A low growl left her lips, making Sylvestro on high alert. Then the bedroom door cracked open, and a female voice shrieked out.

Chapter 15

"Oh, my fucking god. I'm so sorry Sylvia," Lillian said, covering her own eyes.

"Fucking hell Lillian what are you doing here at this time. Are you trying to get yourself killed?"

"Would it be possible for the two of you to get some clothes on and meet me in the living room, please? I can't stand here trying to talk to both of you like this."

Lillian hadn't expected to find Sylvia and Sylvestro tangled together in bed like this. The last time she met them was at the war a long time ago. Although she was happy to find both of them together, one less problem for her to deal with. Not long after she left the room, Sylvestro stormed out in a pair of tight joggers, raising his voice towards Lillian.

"Are you that dumb to just show up uninvited?"

"I'm sorry, Sylvestro. I was in Rome looking for you, but well you weren't there. Morgana sent me."

"Love, calm down. She didn't know you were here, and besides, didn't you just *show* up uninvited as well earlier today, we both know how that played out," Sylvia intimated. "Lillian, what does Morgana want?"

"She is in need of help with training a girl that we came across in Australia looking for white witches."

"Tell me why we should help with training a witch. It doesn't sound like we would be much of a help for her, we do not know the first thing about training witches. I don't think Morgana has lost her head so what is really going on? There seems to be something you are not telling us."

"Well, Jade isn't just a witch; she is also a white panther, a vampire and she will also be gaining a wolf at sixteen. She was able to reverse one of my own spells against me while in her panther form and knocked me out within seconds. She is only eleven years old and is able to control her fire, which is ice blue. She also is able to create some powerful magic now with no training. The moon goddess paid her a visit in her dreams, foretelling her a warning and some information about her wolf part. Oh, I forgot, she controls all four elements too." The words tumbling over each other. Lillian was speaking so quickly.

"There is more on your mind, Lillian because you look bothered and quite nervous," Sylvestro asked.

"On the plane trip here, I tapped into a wolf's mind after overhearing the beginning of their conversation. He was thinking about a lost princess, and they were on their way to Brazil for a meeting with a contact. Do the two of you know anything about her? They also mentioned a prince as well."

"Wait, hold up. I know of two wolves coming to meet me someday this week but they wanted guides on their journey. From what I know about the princess is common knowledge. The Queen sent her away before anything could happen to her during the war. Now, about the prince, he was lost two years before the war, sadly. It almost broke the King and Queen's heart. No one has found the child after that day. It's like she never existed since being sent away. Many have looked for her, but they have always gone back with no information, not even a single trace of her being still alive or dead. Unfortunately, I don't have any more information on that matter. I'm sorry Lillian, it's already the knowledge you have," Sylvia explained.

"So, when did Morgana need us, and where are we going?"

"As soon as possible. Before I forget it, I'm so happy for the two of you about the time you got together again. Well, I should take my leave again. I still need to get Ash, Sarah and unlucky me, Stefan."

"She is assembling a war team again. Something is up, Sylvia; we need to leave right away. Your guest is going to have bad luck today. Morgana needs us, and she never called on us all like this, I think she will tell us all when we are there."

"Well, she is in the Sturt Stone desert in Australia. Safe travel. I will see you later."

"Lillian, would you be so kind as to open a portal for us and to help you on the way? Stefan is in Scotland, well to be more correct, in the highlands. Hope that will help you out a little on your quest."

"Of course. I was hoping to take Stefan last; I wasn't looking forward to meeting him again, but thank you, Sylvia. Lillian opened a portal to the Australian desert, convected heat distorting the view on the desert side. Say hello to everyone."

Lillian cheerfully said before Sylvestro and Sylvia stepped into it and waved fast as Lillian closed it down. With a quick wave, she sealed it shut, exhaling deeply as she composed herself. The moment of solitude was brief—she had her own journey to begin. Turning her focus inward, she started the spell for her teleportation towards the mountains of highlands in Scotland. She started the spell for herself when a knock came on the door. The only thought in her mind was, I wonder who that can be, and she stopped her spell and walked to the door to open it up. After she opened the door, a fist connected with her face, and she fell backward, hearing a woman's voice.

"Told you I smelt strong magic here, and look at this, it's the witch from the plane."

"Who are you?" asked the man.

Lillian took one of her hands up to her face where she had just got hit. Glaring at the two newcomers under her breath, she uttered some words.

"So, this is how two new mutts say hi to someone that opens the door. So shameful of the two of you, maybe you should run away with your tales between your legs, or better yet, chase speeding cars."

"How dare you. You are just a small, little weak witch. Wait until Sylvia gets back here she will take care of you," growled the woman.

"Darling, calm down. What if this witch is a friend of hers? She will be furious to know what we just did. Remember, she never let anyone just be in her house. In my knowledge, only the closest of her friends are allowed."

"I'm so sorry, miss. My name is Zane, and this beautiful woman next to me is Darla. Would you like to tell us yours?"

"I'm the niece of the high priestess Morgana. Lillian, and I'm one of her closest friends she left not to long ago. I was on my way to leave as well, not that it is any business of yours."

"Did you just say Morgana?" the woman gasped.

Lillian only nodded her head and saw all the colour in them disappear from their faces. She also notices that the woman stepped back and showed fear for the first time; the man who was trying to hold on to her meanwhile started to talk again, and you could hear the fear in every spoken word.

"We are so sorry. We didn't know."

"Well, how could you know when the first thing she is doing is to punch me in the face, and now I need to travel with a black eye? That is going to be fun to explain to everyone."

"Miss Lillian, I'm terribly sorry. I was wrong, but ever since the plane, I have been on edge."

"That is no excuse to go around hitting people when they open a door. I was going to tell you when I opened the door that Sylvia was out for the time being."

"Do you know when she will be back?"

"She has gone to Morgana, and I don't know when she will be back from that mission. I do think the two of you should go back home and start your own family. Just to make this clear, Mr. Zane, close off your mind next time on a plane. You both should be lucky it was only me on the plane that was a witch."

"Did you invade my mind?"

"Yes, I did, and I can also tell you Sylvia doesn't have any more information than what you already know. I had to ask her about it. Be careful next time. I do have a question: where do the two belong?"

"Oh, you didn't invade that much. We are the gamma couple from the royal pack. Your warning is taken in and I'm sorry I should have been more careful in the open."

"I need to move; say hi to the Queen from us. I still have some people to find before I can go back home."

"Miss Lillian, if I may ask, where are you going?"

"I'm going to Scotland. Do you need a lift, or are you trying to ask for a favour, Darla?"

"A favour, if it's not too much to ask of you, because of my wrongdoing."

"Everyone makes mistakes; it's how we learn from them that makes a difference. I'm guessing you want to ask me for a portal back home?"

"Yes please, if that's not too much to ask for."

"It's okay Darla, it's not. I do know both of you have been away for a long time. Is it okay if I open the portal in the castle?"

"That would be amazing, Lillian. If you ever need help you know where to find us," Zane said with relief.

Both Zane and Darla smiled at Lillian and promised to give the Queen the message. Lillian opened up a portal for them. As they stepped through, both turned back, bowing their heads in respect before she sealed it shut. Then she turned around to get her butt moving. She had already spent too much time here when she should have been looking for her ex. She still felt hurt over what happened five years ago at the fountain and didn't want to meet him ever again, but she knew that her aunt was right as always. After casting her spell, Lillian found herself transported to the highlands of Scotland, specifically on a snowy mountaintop. As she surveyed her surroundings, her gaze shifted towards the sky, where she spotted a magnificent dragon soaring above. Instantly, a mixture of excitement and nervousness overwhelmed her, causing butterflies to flutter in her stomach. The sight of a dragon always had this effect on her, making her cheeks flush with a rosy blush. He was a dragon, and she was even more annoyed by her predictable reaction; she couldn't help but feel frustrated.

Meanwhile, Stefan, who was flying among the clouds as his own dragon, noticed a sudden flash of brightness emanating from the mountains. Intrigued, he altered his course and descended towards the source. The dragon's unwavering gaze remained fixed on the figure on the ground, who was staring back fearlessly into its eyes. As they drew closer, Stefan's disbelief grew, and upon landing, he transformed back into his human form. Without hesitation, he sprinted towards Lillian, longing to embrace her in his arms once more. Lillian didn't have time to react before she was embraced in a warm hug and a chin on top of her head, and then she heard Stefan's voice crack.

"Where have you been all these years? I have been looking everywhere for you."

"Hi Stefan, long time no see. I have been around; you probably haven't looked hard enough then."

"Don't be like that, love. Why did you come all the way here?"

"You should save those words for your wife and not me. Morgana needs you, so she sent me to find you."

"Lillian, I don't have a wife. Is that why you left me five years ago because of that woman?"

"Will you go to Morgana, Stefan? We don't need to make this harder for either of us."

"I will go, but I need to talk to you. It has already been hard for me. My heart only beats for you; it always has. When you ran away, my heart was torn asunder. No one can take your place. That woman was someone my family wanted me to be with. I never agreed, and I will never do that."

"We can talk about that later. I need to leave again."

"NO! You will not leave me again I will not allow that again; I just got you back in my arms. I will be damn sure not to let you go ever again."

"I need to go to Germany. It's important."

"Germany? What aren't you telling me, Lillian? Speak to me. I may be able to help you."

"I need to go to Ash and Sarah. Morgana needs them also."

"Wait a moment, have you talked to Sylvestro and Sylvia as well? There is something more to this story."

Stefan moved Lillian from his grip so he could look into her eyes and see what was going on in her head. Lillian had a hard time not to look into his eyes either and started to tell him about Jade and that Morgana needed everyone's help. When she told him about how Jade turned Lillian's magic back towards her, he felt his anger rise towards the girl, but he started to understand why Morgana asked for help. Then he noticed the black eye she got earlier, and he started to scream out in pure anger.

"Who the fuck hit you?"

"Oh, I hoped it wouldn't show yet. It happened in Sylvia's place before I came here, it was just a misunderstanding between me and two wolves."

"What wolves?"

"The gamma couple of the royal pack."

"Did Zane do this, the fucking mongrel? I will have his head. Hurting my only true love."

Smoke was streaming out from his nose, and his eyes flickered between human and dragon. The acrid smoke burned Lillian's already irritated eyes. Lillian had no choice then to go up on her tippy toes and, kiss his cheek and speak with a soft voice.

"Stefan, I'm okay, and it was Darla. Everything is sorted I promise, it will heal soon. You really do need to get going to Morgana, Stefan. I only have a few hours left before I need to be back to her as well."

"You should hurry up as well. Last time I heard a word from the Black Forest, Ash and Sarah were in grave danger. I couldn't make it down there. I was occupied with other stuff."

"Do you need a lift down, my love?"

"Stefan, stop it, your parents will never agree with us. Why are you set on making this worse?"

"I don't care what they think. My feelings for you are true and deep; my dragon won't accept anyone else. When I think about it, Morgana is collecting the war team again then something is up. Jump up on my back; I will drop you off outside the Black Forest pack on my way down."

Lillian looked at him confused; she wasn't sure what to think about everything around them anymore. Then she saw him shifting back into his golden dragon. With a slow, deliberate movement, he lowered one of his massive wings to the ground, creating an easy path for her to climb onto his back. Lillian started to climb up as she felt it was of no use to argue with him or his dragon about this. As soon as Lillian was sitting, the dragon took off straight up in the sky, with powerful wing beats, going higher up between all the clouds. Wind rushed past her, sending her hair dancing wildly around her face. A laugh bubbled up from her chest—light, unrestrained. She had forgotten the feeling of sailing over banks of clouds. She knew her feelings for Stefan had never gone away from the depths of her heart. Yes, she was crushed, but she never lost the love for this man. During the flight Lillian lowered her upper body down against Stefan's dragon's neck and wrapped her arms around it, whispering words he never thought he would hear again from her.

"I never stopped loving you, you know, even though what happened broke my heart."

Then she laid a soft kiss on his scale and started to hum a melody to herself, but the dragon took in every single tone that left her throat. He knew the song very well; he had heard it many times coming from Lillian in her sleep and when they spent time together. Memories were

flashing in his mind from the first time they ever met to the day he lost
her.

185

A few hours away from Lillian and Stefan, in the territory of the Black Forest pack, several wolves were fighting, and more came spilling out from the forest edge. The smell of rotten flesh spread all around on the pack ground. At the forefront of the battle stood a majestic wolf adorned with a stunning coat of long, white fur. Its sleek physique was dappled with spots ranging in size and color, from shades of grey to hints of reddish hues. Intense black eyes burned with a mixture of hatred and sorrow, directed towards the invaders encroaching upon their sacred pack lands.

As the days wore on, the rogues seemed to grow stronger, their power escalating as if fueled by an unnatural force. Sensing the urgency of the situation, the wolf at the front line swiftly sent a telepathic message to its brother, desperately pleading for assistance.

"Ash, please, where are you? I can't hold them much longer; they are taking over the eastern border."

She never got an answer back before she saw a midnight black wolf jump in front of her between six rogue wolves, showing its teeth towards the invaders. Behind him, several pack warriors came in tow attacking every rogue on the field. The rogues stood out for their remarkable training, organization, and seamless teamwork, the rogues were undoubtedly a well-oiled machine. The question was, where the fuck were they coming from? As a burst of magical energy descended, the ground beneath them erupted with writhing tree roots, ensnaring the rogue wolves in shocking collars. Simultaneously, intense heat radiated, soothing the packs' weary muscles and warming their chilled skin. Ignoring their nudity, the wolves glanced upward and were relieved to witness a majestic golden dragon unleashing a fiery rain. To their delight, a dear friend of theirs sat confidently on the dragon's back. Eventually, the dragon landed next to them all, letting down its wing so Lillian could jump off. As soon as her feet landed on the ground, she ran to her dear friends.

"Ash, Sarah, why haven't you asked for help? We came here in the nick of time."

"Lillian, I'm so happy to see you, what a surprise as well. Unfortunately, we haven't had any time to send out a request for help for three weeks."

"Lillian this may be a dumb question. What are you going to do with the rogues in your trap spell."

"Ash, that's up to you, I do believe Stefan's dragon is hungry for a few assholes anyway."

The dragon looked at Lillian with panicked eyes, shook his head frantically, and shifted back to Stefan so he could speak for them both.

"Love, I wouldn't think so. Both me and my dragon kind of want to have a breath that at least smells like mint and not rotten assholes."

"Ash, Sarah, I hope the help here was okay without a prior invitation, but I need to take my leave. Lillian, I will tell Morgana that you are here and will need extra time. See you soon, my love."

Then Stefan shifted back to his dragon, and with a hard wing slap to the ground, he took off. Lillian stood and waved him off, then turned around to the two friends and gave a wicked smile away. With a single snap of her fingers, howls echoed around them. New roots and vines started to grow over them, slithering around them and slowly tightened up, constricting the rogues like a giant snake suffocating their prey. The sound of bones breaking slowly and popping out from their sockets making them shift back to humans, and their screams of agony could be heard. Blood pouring out from the compound fractures open wounds on the bodies, bones jutting out at bizarre angles, making it impossible for them to heal to save themselves from the sure death around them. Crying and screams began to quiet down as each rogue breath was extinguished by the weave of death until complete silence fell over the field like an oppressive blanket of snow. When there was no more movement from the rogues, the vines and roots started to retract themselves from the limp bodies, and return to under the ground. Lillian looked over the field when she heard Sarah's gasp and cry out for help.

"Lillian, come quickly, something is wrong with Ash."

Lillian ran back to Sarah and noticed that Ash started to shake and couldn't stand up straight when his legs buckled under his weight, and he fell heavy to the ground. The last thing Ash could hear before darkness took over was.

"Lillian, what is happening to him?"

Lillian's concern for her friend grew as she recalled their conversation about the ongoing fight they had been involved in for the past three weeks. Sensing something was amiss, Lillian inquired about how much sleep they have had, to which Sarah admitted they had only managed a few hours here and there. As Lillian pressed further, asking about the whereabouts of Alpha and Luna, she noticed a sudden change in Sarah's expression. Sarah hesitated before admitting, tears welled up in her eyes as she began to explain the devastating loss they had suffered. Alpha and Luna had tragically lost their lives two days ago, and their twins had been murdered a week prior.

The pack was now reduced to a mere handful of survivors.

"I'm so sorry Sarah, I don't know what to say. I need to contact Morgana about this."

"Lillian, can you help Ash? We can't just leave him on the ground. I don't have the strength to carry him by myself."

"Of course, I will help him. I can do an electric shock so he can walk back to the pack house. I urgently need to speak with the two of you as well. Then contact Morgana and explain."

Sarah looked at Lillian with a hopeful eye when Lillian let her hands trail over Ash's sleeping body, letting a soft light flow from her palms. Ash's body started to quiver and move slowly, and then he bolted up right into a sitting position, yelling out.

"Fuck Lillian, take it easy with the energy blast. I kind of want to keep my heart inside my body."

Sarah flew into his arms, crying and screaming.

"Don't you fucking dare scare me like that again? I thought I lost you as well."

Lillian giggled a little as Ash wrapped his arms around his crying sister, giving Lillian a grateful smile and mouthed a thank you. When he finally got loose from his sister's embrace, he looked at them both saying.

"Let's get to the back house; Lillian looks like she needs a cup of tea or maybe a whiskey."

"Well, I need to get in touch with my aunt first because I will be late away from here. Also, I need to talk to both of you about something important."

"Okay let's make our way, Ash you still need some extra rest. Lillian only helped you with her magic because none of us are strong enough to carry your fat ass."

After enduring three tough weeks, Ash began to laugh heartily, feeling happy for the first time. The walk was long and hard everywhere. Lillian looked lay body on body, all from old to even infant children. Throats ripped open, bellies carved up, tears rolling down on Lillian's face while she cried in her silence. She looked behind them and saw some of the warriors collecting the bodies of their loved ones to carry them to their final resting place. As Lillian looked behind her, she stumbled and lost her footing, falling down next to the Alpha of the pack. She screamed out in agony over the loss of one of her closest friends. He was barely recognisable. His face was clawed so deep that half the side was missing, letting the eyeball hang out from its socket, bobbing and twisting in the breeze.

The ground around him was soaked with blood, and coils of intestines lying beneath him like a knot of mating snakes. Maggots were crawling in his open wounds, eating his rotting flesh slowly, the smell of decomposition emitted from his limp body. Causing Lillian to gag. His right arm was stretched out above his head with barely any skin left, but Lillian followed the arm and saw Luna in the same shape as the Alpha. She couldn't bear it and crawled up to a ball between them crying out loud for the loss of them both. She could feel four arms hugging her tightly, trying to help her grief over what she just witnessed. When a burst of energy exploded within Lillian, making them fall back. When a lady came running a few minutes later towards them with a phone in her hand yelling.

"Ash, Sarah you need to take this phone call; I can't take being yelled at much more."

"Martha, who is it?"

"One very angry woman, and in the background, you can hear a man and a child screaming and yelling."

Ash took the phone from her hand and gulped down hard, as he kind of knew who the man and woman, would be. With a shaking hand, he took the phone to his ear and spoke.

"Ash speaking. Who am I speaking with?"

"Do you think it's funny, you fucking idiot? What is going on with Lillian?"

"She is fine, she just got bad news and witnessed something."

"Don't play fucking games with me, or I will let Jade and Stefan put your ass on fire while I'm holding you down."

"Morgana calm down. We have been fighting for three weeks, and she got to see the Alpha and Luna just a bit more than she needed to as she tripped on their bodies; we are here for her."

"What happened to Ben and Vivian? Why haven't you called for help, you stupid wolf."

"Morgana, can you calm the fuck down and stop with your insults, it's pissing me off. Lillian will stay here for a few hours, maybe a day. Then she will come back home. By the way, who is Jade?"

"Prepare seven beds for us. We will be coming to your place. Jade is a girl in need of yours and Sarah's help training. She is a special girl. Didn't Lillian tell you about why I needed your help?"

"Seven people, Morgana the pack house is half destroyed. Who are all these people you're bringing with you? No Lillian hasn't, as she and Stefan arrived to help us out in the nick of time with some rogues. So, she hasn't had time to talk to us about anything, and I think she isn't in that capacity to do it now either, so enlighten me, please."

"I will tell you when we are there. Get Lillian and yourself to the house and take some rest. You sound like you need it; we will be there soon. Oh, Stefan wants to talk to Lillian."

"Lillian baby, are you okay? Can you speak with me?"

Lillian couldn't hold back her tears, and it was like something was stuck in her throat making a new energy burst fly out from her, knocking Ash and Sarah to the ground as well. It was then Sarah took the phone.

"Stefan, I think you should hurry back up. I do believe Morgana felt that blast as well. It knocked us all to the ground. She is unstable due to grief."

"We will be there as soon as we can. All of us."

Then he hung up the phone. Sarah looked down and gave out a deep sign. Stood up and walked over to Lillian to take her arm over her head to help her walk. The sooner they got into the house so they could lay her down for a while the better. Ash helped his sister out, and he gave out orders as they were walking. He also told Martha to prepare the bedroom as best she could for the visitors that were coming. When they reached the house, they got into the Alpha's office to lay Lillian down on the sofa. As soon her back hit the soft material she closed her eyes and fell into a sleep. Sarah shifted into her wolf and laid down on the floor next to her head, and so did Ash but down at her feet. It didn't take long before both of them fell into a deep sleep.

Back at the Sturt stone desert, Morgana was pacing back and forth, yelling and screaming. Jade had the same effect, both of them were clearly unsettled, both not knowing what to make of the situation. Jade was a volcano on the verge of a pyroclastic eruption. She was still in somewhat control over her magic but she felt her control slipping from her grasp when she yelled out in pure panic.

"Move away, NOW!"

Purple mist washed over her body down to the ground, following a pattern as a slow-flowing river. Everyone jumped up on separate stone boulders, looking at Jade in amazement and shock. Morgana looked at her and asked Jade.

"Sweet child, are you okay?"

"I think so Morgana, I don't know what is going on but we need to leave."

"Okay everyone, let's pay attention to Jade's words. Her magic is acting up, and she appears to be quite anxious. I can sense that she's feeling Lillian's distress over her friend's death just as strongly as I am. Something alarming has occurred over there in the past three weeks with these strange rogue attacks, and they need our assistance before it's too late. Anyone who disagrees is free to leave," Morgana exclaimed.

The room fell silent as everyone began to gather around Jade, eager to hear more. Samantha, curious, approached Jade and asked her a question.

"When do you want to leave, baby?"

"Now. Morgana can you help out with the teleport spell? We are few more this time, I'm not sure if I want to risk doing it by myself this time."

"Sure, thing sweetheart. I can make the whole spell this time; you need to rest. That purple mist must take a lot out of you my dear."

"I'm fine. It's just weird that it has never happened before. It's something new."

"Princess, are Aria or Sapphire saying anything?"

"Nothing Dad. Last time they spoke was to tell me to stay calm, and help will come."

Jake looked at Morgana, she was standing in shock, she wasn't sure what was going on. Then again, she had never dealt with someone with three different souls before, well four souls in a few years, according to what the moon goddess had told Jade. Morgana felt the magic within both Jade and Lillian. Their magic had a strange, eerie quality about it, like the weight of earth on a coffin. An unshakable instinct told her they needed to leave—soon. She looked at everyone, nodded her head and saw that everyone present was united in their support to help Jade and go to the Black Forest pack. So, Morgana spoke up again.

"We will leave in half an hour, Samantha, Jake grab what you need from your stuff. We will come back here to collect the rest later."

"Morgana, we don't need to pack. Let's get going right away," Samantha said.

Morgana gave a smile to her and accepted what she saw in front of her. Then she gathered everyone together to open up a portal so everyone could walk in and appear at the Black Forest pack.

Chapter 17

They arrived at a field near the Packhouse in no time, but what they witnessed was beyond anyone's expectations. Samantha urgently called out to Jade, "Quick, put up the safety barrier!" Without hesitation, Jade swiftly erected the barrier around them and over the portal, barely having a moment to take in their surroundings. As Morgana emerged from the portal, she let out a gasp, covering her mouth with her hands. Before her lay a horrifying sight—a once lush green field now saturated with blood and scattered body parts. There was not a single patch of green left, as the field had been completely transformed.

"Jade darling, don't look. Princess, what kind of barrier did you bring up?"

"Just a normal one, but Dad it's too late. All this death for what?"

"The land, sweet child, nothing more," Morgana said in sadness.

Jade looked at Morgana and saw tears in her eyes, then Morgana said something she never thought she would hear.

"Everyone that can shift, do it now. We need to help defend the land. Jade, you stay in here."

All around Jade, she heard ripping sound and clothes flying all around her, even her own parents took part in this. Samantha linked to Jade and explained.

"We are helping out defending our friends and what is right. Please stay in the safety of the barrier for all of us. Jade, can you please open up a path so we all can get out? I really don't want to be burnt to a crisp."

Jade looked at her mother and nodded her head, shortly after Jade opened an orifice in the barrier just big enough to let the allies out to defend against the foul intruders. Jade found herself surrounded by a cacophony of growls, howls, and hissing, as the menacing sounds echoed all around her. Outside the protective barrier, Sylvia's panther, Sly, stood with blood-soaked fur, a chilling testament to the violence that had transpired. Aria, consumed by her insatiable thirst for blood, threatened to unleash her savage instincts. Thankfully, Sapphire, the voice of reason, maintained control over Aria, ensuring that she remained subdued within Jade's consciousness.

Amidst the chaos, Jade's parents, adorned with fiery feathers, were beset by a vampire lurking in the shadows. In a desperate plea for help, Jade's voice pierced through the air, shattering the tense atmosphere.

"Look out behind you."

Jake's phoenix turned around in the nick of time and severed the head from the vampire's body. Before Jade could tell Sly to move, she got hit on her head by the fallen vampire's head, and the corpse of the vampire's body landed on the barrier and slowly slid down from the top to the ground, sizzling as the limp carcass fell. Leaving a steaming trail of coagulated blood. Jade stood, hand covering her mouth to suppress a giggle directed at Sly. Annoyed, Sly glanced at Jade, shook her head, and hurried away to assist others. Lillian and Morgana stood back-to-back, casting powerful spells that caused the ground to tremble, ensnaring as many enemies as possible. Meanwhile, the warriors and Sly swiftly dispatched their trapped foes. However, a sense of unease began to creep over Jade, accompanied by a burning sensation in her skin.

Above, clouds gathered and darkened the sky, punctuated by flashes of lightning that illuminated the ongoing battle. Each bolt revealed a purple hue, casting an ethereal glow over the treetops. Thunder followed, echoing loudly across the battlefield. As the storm intensified, a mist emerged, gradually descending towards the ground. It seeped under Jade's protective barrier, slithering towards her feet and slowly creeping up her legs.

The mist infiltrated Jade's pores, causing her veins to glow with a pulsating purple light. The vibrant glow spread throughout her body, as Jade watched in horror, her hands trembling. Her scream pierced the air, causing the entire battlefield to freeze. Even the rogues, previously in motion, came to a standstill. Lillian's voice broke through the silence, cutting through the chaos.

"Morgana, what is going on with Jade?"

"I'm not sure Lillian, something isn't right."

"She got everyone to stop fighting."

"That's a good thing in one way."

Then a scream echoed out from the forest, and two vampires came out laughing at Jade's condition when one of them said, "What are you dirty things doing just standing there, kill the rest of the pack scum and their friends."

That broke the spell over the rogues, and they started to attack the still-stunned pack members. Screams throughout the field started to take place yet again. The rogues managed to get the upper hand and several of the pack members fell to their ruthless slaughter. The scene that evolved in front of Jade made her shake in fury, and she started to lose her control over the magic within her. The last straw was when she heard the two vampires laugh at the pack's destruction. It wasn't long before Jake, Samantha and Stefan had to create a firewall around their allies. The soil on the ground started to rumble as spears of stone and dirt shot up from every corner. The bolts intensified, sending waves of electricity pulsing through the jagged earth. A horrifying scream came out from the barrier when it fell down from around Jade. Everyone gasped when they looked at Jade, appalled at her appearance. Her feet had pierced out from her shoes, and the pants had slowly begun to rip apart and were being replaced with fur of gold.

The screaming increased emanating from Jade's vocal cords, and began getting hoarse. Slowly, Jade bent down on all fours, letting her back and legs bend in an inhuman position, breaking bones one by one, all two hundred six of them. Where her feet and hands once were, two giant fluffy paws emerged. Slowly Jade's legs enlarged, and muscle mass dramatically increased. Her spine got longer, and the last part of her to be changed was her head and face. Jade's nose and mouth turned into a snout, and the teeth grew larger into sharp canines. Last in her transformation, two fluffy ears with odd markings of the purest white on the very top of her ears. Shimmering in sharp contrast to the golden long fur, letting sparkles flow within the thick coat. Before Jade even got to open up her eyes again, she heard a voice within her head.

"Hello Jade. I'm Diamond. Let's make this battle a fair fight. Are you all with me?"

"Welcome into Jade's mind. Let's give them hell on earth," Sapphire spoke up.

"Let's burn them alive," Aria continued.

"Girls, I have a better idea. Lay back and enjoy the pain and suffering of others."

Jade's eyes, a mesmerizing combination of white diamonds with a faint ring of light blue, opened wide. A menacing growl escaped her mouth as she chose to retreat into her mind, surrendering control to her alter ego, Diamond. With a single step forward, Diamond raised her left front paw, causing a light purple mist to flow gracefully from her claws, like a veil drifting over the blood-soaked grass.

With each step Diamond took towards the firewall, the mist continued to emanate from her paws, unaffected by the flames. Serenely, she approached the wall, compelling it to part and create a passage for her to pass through. Leaving her newfound friends and parents behind the safety of the fire, Diamond closed the wall and proceeded towards a large rock.

As she settled down and began to sway her tail like a broom on the ground, a heart-wrenching howl escaped her, piercing the sky. Before the mournful sound faded, a burst of magic accompanied by a powerful purple mist billowed from her mouth, rising into the sky and spreading over the Black Forest Pack lands. Gradually, the mist descended, causing vampires and other living beings to fall helplessly to the ground.

One by one falling down to the ground coughing and twisting their bodies, the rogues started to shift back to their human form. Screams echoed out between the coughing. Diamond could see vampires making their way towards her on shaking legs, screaming at her.

"What have you done to us? You filthy mutt."

"Only what you deserve, you damn bloodsucker."

With that answer, Diamond's eyes glow brighter and with a visceral howl, the mist pulled all the rogues and vampires into a pile in front of her. Then she spoke again.

"Any last words?"

"All hail Queen Tanja," they yelled in unison.

The barking came faster, and the mist turned into a burning flame that no one could escape from. Then Diamond remembered what they all had said in unison and put out the flames over one female rogue that had gotten burnt with no hope of healing, yet she was still clinging to life. She was screaming in agony and begging for death by Diamond. She looked at the burning woman with an empty stare, not showing any care. While in the flames the screams of the others began to mercifully settle down until it was complete silence. Diamond howled again, and the flames turned into icy blue, flattening down onto the ground, and slithering towards the members of the Black Forest pack.

For every member of the pack on the ground, the flame made its way into their bodies through their open wounds. Slowly closing the wounds and making the corpse twitch like they were being electrocuted, one by one, Diamond could hear slowly the heartbeats taking form once more and a hard intake of air. New screams interrupted the silence on the field, and not long, four arms came across Diamond's neck in a tight hug. The familiar scent of her parents made its way into her nose. All of them were looking out over the field at all the pack members sitting up, gasping for air and touching their own bodies for the wounds. Soon the field changed again, and the gasps and screams shifted into cries of sorrow for their fallen families and friends. Sylvia looked at Diamond and asked, "How did you do this? And what's your name?"

"My name is Diamond. To be honest, I'm not completely sure. I only had rage building within me, and sorrow overwhelmed me, then the pressure burst out."

"You can talk?"

"We all can talk, Sylvia. I do think we should walk over to the pack house. I don't see Lillian anywhere."

Some of the pack members looked at the seven people standing up and began to walk away. When they started to remember everything from before, how they were killed, their last breath and their willingness to accept their own death. But now they are sitting here next to fallen friends and family and still alive. They saw the huge golden wolf walk away in the direction of the pack house, so some were trying to stand up and follow them. Their legs trembled, their bodies weak, but they pushed forward, following in staggering steps. Soon enough they got to see their Alpha and Luna sitting on the grass in shock looking at each other with sadness and love. Morgana noticed them both and began to take off in their direction while exclaiming.

"Thank the goddess, you are alive. Diamond, you have my respect in every way. I will forever be thankful towards you."

"Morgana you are here. How is this even possible? I felt my husband die; I felt our mate bond be destroyed. How is it possible that we are alive? Where are Ash and Sarah?"

"Calm down, Luna. We are here to help you all, and it's amazing seeing the two of you alive and well."

"Morgana, we died. What is going on? Who is that wolf?"

"That is Diamond; she saved you all. Well, most of your pack. Let me help you up. Stefan can you please help the Alpha to his feet?"

"Alpha, would you like me to help you up?" Stefan asked with a smile.

Diamond looked at the couple and gave out a wolf grin when she felt two pairs of hands on her back. So, she turned her head to both sides and noticed both Sylvia and Sylvestro scratching her back and whispered in a low tone to her.

"Diamond, thank you so much for saving our friends and family."

"You are one amazing wolf. We would be honoured and happy to start training you even though you can be a bit scary with those powers of yours."

"I don't want to hurt anyone," Diamond said quietly, her voice laced with regret. "But I don't know how to control this… How do I even begin to trust myself?"

Sylvia placed a hand gently on her arm, her touch warm and steady. "By letting others help you. We're a pack, Diamond. You don't have to do this alone." Her gaze softened, and she nodded toward the others who were slowly gathering, their murmurs quieting as they listened in. "We've all got our scars, our darkness. You're not the only one. But together, we can help you figure it out. No matter how scary your powers may seem, we'll face them as a family."

Diamond looked at them, twisting her head a little in confusion, but ended up nodding her head in understanding. She knew if she started to speak now, the Alpha and Luna wouldn't be able to handle any more surprises. She was listening to the conversation between themselves and Morgana. After a while, she began to walk away to let them all have some time alone. She also needed Jade to take back control and shift back to human but wasn't in any luck to get a connection with her —until Sapphire's voice broke through, ready to explain.

"Diamond, she passed out after your shift and she was holding back the magic earlier, and you came out five years too early."

"I know. I forced myself out to help her and both you and Aria."

"We are okay, and you are more than welcome out early as well Diamond. Jade's magic has been growing a little too fast for us to handle."

"Thank you, Aria. Well it seems we are needed over there again. Luna is walking our way."

Chapter 18

Diamond looked at Luna walking butt naked. Diamond shook her head and let magic float from her paws in a golden light until it reached Luna, a white summer dress materialised over Luna's bare skin. Luna's cotton V-neck top clung lightly to her shoulders, its cotton fabric soft against her skin. As she slowly made her way forward, the fabric flared out just below her hips, loose and free around her legs. It was comforting in its simplicity—nothing too tight, nothing too restricting. Her legs still wobbled slightly beneath her, each step a reminder of what she had gone through and how far she still had to go.

She paused for a moment, glancing at her reflection in the nearby window, the faint light of the afternoon casting a glow on her face. There was a strength in her that hadn't been there before, a quiet resolve. Her lips curved into a small, grateful smile as she thought of Diamond.

"Thank you, Diamond, for the lovely dress. Would it be okay if I bother you with a personal question?"

Diamond looked at the red-haired woman, her pale, full face covered in freckles and outstanding green eyes, and opened her mouth.

"What would your name be, *Luna*?*"

*(*Luna denotes the female title for dominant werewolf pairings.)*

Luna looked stunned that she just heard the wolf speak in human tongue; however, Luna recovered her composure fast and began to speak.

"Oh, I'm sorry for my bad manners. My name is Vivian."

"That's fine, Luna Vivian. What could I help you with?"

Then a voice, a little further away, broke through.

"Vivian… love, please understand that it's best to leave the wolf alone. We can't expect anything from her as she is an outsider and unfamiliar to us. Even if Morgana trusts her, I personally don't share the same trust. It would be wise for you to distance yourself from her.

Diamond responded immediately, "If you have any issues with my presence here, I would appreciate it if you could at least show some manners, like your mate, and express gratitude for being given another day to live. Whether you like me or not, my intention in coming here was to offer help and ensure Lillian's well-being is restored."

Diamond lost her temper with the alpha. Her hackles raised, she barked, bearing her gleaming white teeth towards him. At the same time, Luna Vivian was glaring at her own mate for his disrespect to their young saviour. Unable to hold back her ire she yelled back at him with a venomous tone laced with fury.

"How the fuck dare you Benjamin! We died… and are only still alive again thanks to this wolf. Because we both know damn fucking well that neither Morgana nor Lillian has that kind of power. So,

Diamond here, is a large golden wolf that towers over your own wolf. Your fragile male ego is pathetic; I suggest you start being an alpha, not a god-damned snowflake. Either keep your disrespectful mouth shut or open it when you decide to apologise and can show gratitude towards her."

After Luna Vivian's outburst, many pack members had been walking—or even crawling—toward her with their tails between their legs, nodding in respect while also thanking Diamond for saving them. Some even reached out, trying to touch her. Diamond started to back away from the crowd and signalled Sylvia and Sylvestro to follow her to the pack house. She had started to feel more anxious about Lillian and was very uncomfortable with all this attention on herself. However, barely anyone noticed the three of them removing themselves from the place, and Sylvia looked at Diamond and asked.

"How do you feel? When are you shifting back to your human form?"

"Jade is still unconscious in our mind, so I will stay like this until she wakes up. Jade is still fine, just exhausted from the shift and the immense amount of magical energy expended. I'm okay, just worried about Lillian and want to find her and make sure she is okay."

"It was very amazing to see what you did for this pack, even with Alpha Ben who can be stupid sometimes. Don't take his words to heart, okay, Diamond."

"Sylvestro, I never did; he was just very disrespectful. Then when all the pack members came up to me, it just got to be too much."

After that small conversation, it got quiet for a little while during their walk all the way to the pack house entrance stairs. As they surveyed the dilapidated house that had once exuded grandeur, its state was a stark reminder of its former glory. The remnants of red stones, reaching up to a height of four stories, still bore witness to its past magnificence. The house, with its unmistakable Victorian architecture, had suffered the ravages of time and war. The windows, once adorned with vibrant colored glass, now lay shattered, their fragments scattered on both sides of the window frames.

Amidst the gravel-covered ground, a grim sight greeted them. A haunting tableau of lifeless bodies. Some were still strewn across the stones, their forms partially concealed by a mixture of fresh and dried blood. It was evident that most of these casualties did not belong to the pack a testament to the ferocity of the recent battle. Soon they heard footsteps coming from behind them and noticed Luna Vivian walking angrily towards the house; before she even got one foot on the stairs, the door violently slammed open. Bolting out from the doorway was Ash and Sarah, holding their hands over their hearts. Shortly after, behind them popped out Lillian, who was running after them with a worried expression on her face. When both of them fell down on the porch at the top of the stairs, looking into Luna Vivian's eyes, making Sarah scream out.

"Who is doing this? Is this just a cruel trick!?"

"What is a trick? You don't make any sense, Sarah," Luna Vivian asked in a soft voice

"Luna, I think they don't believe that you are here. That a dark witch is pulling a trick over their minds. Try walking up to them and touching them instead. That could help them both to believe that you are really here."

Diamond started to explain to Luna Vivian and prompted her to walk with her up the stairs. She saw Lillian behind them with tears in her eyes, holding her hands in front of her mouth. Diamond noticed that Luna Vivian had a hard time walking on the stairs due to her weak, newly awakened legs and asked her.

"Luna, do you want to hold on to me while we walk up?"

"Would that be okay for you? It would help me a lot here."

"Of course, it's okay. Hang on to me, and we will do it together."

Luna Vivian took a hold around Diamond's neck just over her shoulders and got the support she needed to make her way up to her sister and brother. When they arrived on the porch, Luna Vivian let go of her hold over Diamond and sat down next to Sarah's shaking body. Putting her two arms around her whispering softly in her ear a secret between them that only she knew about. With tear-filled eyes and a shaking voice, Sarah looked at her big sister and spoke.

"I can't believe it's you… that you are back... How can this be possible?"

"Diamond here, she saved most of us on the field and close to our home. She came with Morgana, Stefan, Sylvestro, Sylvia and her parents."

"Diamond, I don't know how to thank you enough for giving me back my family."

"There is no need for thanks. Lillian, how do you feel? Jade has been worried sick about you."

Yet again, Ash and Sarah gasped at the knowledge that Diamond could communicate openly. Ash even bowed his head to her in gratitude over what she had done for them, and yet she didn't even owe it to the pack. Lillian looked at Diamond and spoke up.

"I'm fine, thank you for asking. I'm sorry if I have worried her too much when I lost my control. It was horrible to see those I see as my family laying dead on the ground like that. Thank you again for saving them all and giving the pack a second chance."

Diamond gave a wolfish grin and remembered that Luna Vivian wanted to ask her something.

"Luna Vivian, you had a personal question for me earlier; what was that?"

"Let's take that inside the office if that's okay."

Before they even got to stand up, they all could hear the alpha's voice booming out an alpha command.

"She stays outside. She is to leave my pack lands NOW. LEAVE before I get you killed ROGUE!"

Behind him, all his friends were running after him to calm him down before it was too late. Unfortunately, luck wasn't on his side that day. Two very angry phenoxies landed next to Diamond, leaving a trail of embers. Diamond was sick of his attitude and his audacity to try his Alpha command on her. Diamond raised her voice over them all.

"How dare you try to command me? Especially when I frickin' saved yours and your pack's lives, letting you have a second chance. If this is how you show gratitude? Then you can keep it, and good luck with that Tanya woman."

After that last word, Diamond jumped down the stairs, never dropping her intense gaze from the Alpha's eyes, letting Aria and Sapphire also be known to him. Then she walked past him while shoved her shoulder into his side, making the Alpha lose his balance and fall on his butt. Giggles interrupted all around him; the loudest of them was of his mate and her siblings. He glared at them, cursing under his breath, when Morgana walked up to him and spoke in a stern voice.

"Ben, have you lost your mind? How can you be so disrespectful to a child, a child that came here to help and seek help herself? Has old age made you that stupid and fragile, or has your ego grown so high that you cannot accept that *you* had to be protected by a little girl? Good fucking Christ, you are pathetic!"

Then she left him without a chance to defend himself. Morgana walked up the stairs to Lillian to check her over to make sure she was okay. She could see the confusion in her niece's eyes over what Alpha Ben had just said to Diamond. Both of them have always been close to the Alpha and Luna because of their friendship with Ash and Sarah, but after what they heard in that command. They lost all respect for him, Lillian asked Morgana, "Did I just hear that right? He called Diamond a rogue and then threatened to kill her?"

"I'm afraid so; we can only hope she doesn't hold grudges and is willing to come back. Her parents didn't look especially happy about this either, and they would be hard-pressed to let the Alpha come close to their daughter ever again."

They looked at Luna Vivian. She had started to limp down the stairs slowly, the anger from her was evidently clear. When she came to the last step, her mate came to hug her, but she slapped him hard across the face and reprimanded him.

"How dare you! Are you trying to get us all killed AGAIN? Was dying once not enough for you; it was for me. You are going to sleep on the floor like the pathetic dog you are. Don't you even dare try speaking to me before you have apologised to Diamond and her human, and don't forget her parents that you just set off? You are lucky they didn't fry your snowflake ass on the spot!"

Alpha Ben was holding his own cheek after that slap. It was still burning and had left a red mark showing how hard his own mate had slapped him. He began to feel more anger towards this golden wolf. After she showed up, everything went downhill for him. Even his closest friends and family showed him less respect than what he was used to. At this, he saw Stefan's dragon landing next to his mate Vivian and Sylvestro helping her up onto his back followed by Lillian and Morgana. That was when he asked his own mate.

"Where do you think you are going?"

"What do you think? I'm going to talk to Diamond and apologise for your lack of manners and your unwarranted hostility towards her. I don't care what you think about it. You are staying here to help the pack clean up so you do not cause any more problems from your fragile ego."

"Sylvestro and Sylvia will stay with you, Ash and Sarah. Maybe they can knock some sense back into you. Don't even think about linking with me, Benjamin."

Then Stefan's dragon took off up in the air in a burst of dust and debris, scanning the area for Diamond and the two Phoenixes. Stefan took notice of two firebirds a few miles away still squawking loudly and Diamond looking annoyed as well when he flew past them and landed a little bit away allowing the three to jump off him. It was harder for Luna Vivian with her weakened legs, and she unceremoniously fell off of him. Diamond came running at full speed and got to Luna just before she hit the ground, allowing Luna Vivian to land on top of her back.

"I'm so sorry Diamond, for everything. You may be a rogue in some eyes but you don't smell like one, and definitely don't act like one. You are one of us and belong to us. Please Diamond, stay with us."

"Luna, I don't think your mate will allow that to happen."

"Please, don't call me Luna. Just say my name, Vivian, from now on, and I'm asking you to please stay."

Diamond didn't know what to do or what to say; she looked towards her parents who just shifted back to humans for guidance. Again, all of them looked at Vivian. Her parents were about to say something when Vivian gasped and thrust her hand towards her heart, causing Diamond to jump. In concern, Diamond asked.

"Vivian, what's wrong?"

"I don't know; it's like a bond has been created within my heart. Do you have any clue what could be happening, Morgana?"

"Vivian, I don't know. Diamond, can you have some ideas about this?"

"First, how does it feel? Is it a normal pack bond, or is it stronger than that?"

"Strong, it's hard to take in a breath."

"I'm sorry for asking this. Did you and your mate have kids or other family members in the pack except Ash and Sarah?"

"Princess, what are you thinking it can be?" Jake asked, clearly worried for the woman on the ground.

"We had twins a few weeks before the attacks started. Why, what is wrong?"

"Mom, Dad put Luna Vivian on my back. Vivian, hold onto me tightly; this is going to go fast."

Jake and Samantha did what she asked; they saw the tears falling down on her face and looked at the other ones. All they could see was the same facial expression. Stefan shifted back to his dragon and let Morgana and Lillian climb up, and Samantha and Jake shifted as well. They took off into the air, following the golden wolf but could barely keep up with her speed. Vivian was holding on for dear life around Diamond's neck so she wouldn't fall off. All she could see of the trees was big blurs and smells from the soil and leaf bed. She turned her head to look back and noticed a trail of golden mist; in the mist, flowers started to grow. She must ask about the flowers as they were so beautiful.

"Diamond, what kind of flowers are those?"

"They are called Lilium Asiatic, also known as Forever Susan. The second one is called Lilium Asiatic Whistler. They are a symbol of life and happiness."

"They are beautiful."

"Indeed, they are. How do you feel? It's not too much farther; we will be there soon."

"I'm feeling better. What is going on? You never told me."

"You will be happy and surprised as well. I promise you."

Vivian nodded her head in Diamond's neck and enjoyed the rest of the ride, looking back at the beautiful flowers that were following them.

Chapter 19

Back at the pack house, Sylvia and Sylvestro tore the alpha a new one about his behaviour and tried to explain to him why they even came to the pack. It was Jade that wanted to go as fast as possible. When they noticed something fast running towards them, Sylvestro said.

"Looks like the Luna got Diamond to come back. It's time for you to apologise properly to Diamond and Jade otherwise, we will not be staying here to help with whomever this Tanya is. You already were killed without Diamond's help. Do you really think you would fare any better next time Tanya's lot attack?"

"You will treat Diamond with the utmost courtesy unless you want to jeopardise our friendship, Alpha Ben," Sylvia said in a stern voice.

He looked at them, knowing he was to blame; he knew he had treated this wolf wrong, but his pride had been hurt over being saved by one outsider wolf, nonetheless a little girl. That was embarrassing; even his own wolf had been screaming at him. As soon as Diamond returned with Luna Vivian on her back, his anger flared again. But a very angry look from Sylvestro got him to hold back. Alpha Ben made the choice to bow his head to Diamond and utter the words.

"Thank you, Diamond!" he said, barely holding in his sarcasm.

Diamond only looked at him and asked Luna Vivian to go towards the porch stairs and wait. Luna Vivian looked confused but did what Diamond asked her to do. Diamond walked with Luna Vivian standing close by to be a support, then asked Alpha Ben one question.

"Don't you feel a bond being created within your heart?"

"Yes, I do. It's strong, but I have no idea who or what this bond is with?"

"Please come here and stand by your mate."

He went and stood together with his mate, and not long after, the doors flung open again, and a screaming Omega came out, crawling on her hands and knees. No one could make sense of what she was screaming.

"Max... breathing Max... breathing. Lillith almost... Lillith... almost. Who is playing a game? Why... am I *alive*? How... is this possible?"

The poor omega screamed over and over until she lost her voice, with tears streaming down like waterfalls from her red-rimmed eyes. Diamond noticed the woman's distress and walked slowly to her and laid down beside her, breathing slow and steady, covering the frantic woman with a warming calm. Letting a soft huff leave her snout. The woman looked at Diamond and reached out her hand to get the feeling of the fur. When her hand took hold of the fur, she pushed herself into the neck, hugging and crying softly. Diamond started to chuckle a little, then started to speak.

"Are you feeling better? It must have been a scare for you; I'm sorry for that."

"You can talk?"

"Yes, I can talk like a human. Do you think you can stand up now?"

"I think so. I'm sorry for hugging you like that; you don't know me. Was that you that saved us?"

"Yes, that was me. So, Max is fine. What about Lillith? Could you take me and your Luna and Alpha to them?"

"Yes, miss. Would it be okay to hold on to you while we walk? My legs feel weak."

"No worries at all. I will walk with you."

Diamond stood up letting the woman take her time and lean on to her, when she began to speak towards the Alpha and Luna.

"Let's help her and follow her to Max and Lillith."

"They are alive?" gasped Alpha Ben.

"Yes, why do you think the poor woman was freaking out?"

"My babies. Love, let's help her."

Both of them rushed up to the Omega to help her back into the house. Diamond followed behind when they came into a large foyer. In the centre was a large staircase going up to the next level to each floor. Light beige marble flooring and the walls had wallpaper on them with flower patterns in different sizes. The Omega took them towards the kitchen into a secret door hidden behind the larger fridge. With a creak of the moving fridge, the doorway appeared. A strong, high-pitched screaming from a baby was evident as soon as the door opened. Luna took off down the stairs three at a time, her weak legs no longer an issue to her adrenaline-filled body. The screaming got louder but settled down fast when Luna's voice calmed the baby's distress. She came up walking with two bundles, one in dark blue and the second one in light purple. The boy was wide awake, giggling in his mother's arms, while the girl's skin lost all colour, turning a pale grey-blue again. Luna Vivian's eyes were tear-filled when she asked Diamond.

"Can you help Lillith? I know it's a lot to ask Diamond."

"Luna, I do not know. I'm sorry, let's take her somewhere else and I will try. I do not promise you anything, okay?"

"Of course, and I know it's much of me to ask."

"I'm sorry for asking this. How long ago was it when they died?"

"Almost two weeks, miss," the Omega answered.

"This can be hard. I'm surprised as well that they are alive."

"What do you mean, Diamond?" asked the Alpha.

"The spell should only be working on those that died within a week I'm sorry to say."

They all gasped when Luna showed Diamond into the sitting room and laid down Lillith on the floor next to Diamond's paws. Then Diamond asked one final question.

"May I be alone with her?"

"That's okay; we will walk out and try to help clean up the mess outside," the Alpha replied.

"Luna, could you go and pick two of each of the flowers for me? You know those that were growing up from run out to here, the Lilium Asiatic."

"I will be back as soon as I can, anything else? I will do anything to help you."

"No, nothing else. Thank you."

As Diamond and Lillith were left alone, Diamond sensed something that could potentially save the girl. However, she regretted sending Luna so quickly and realized she needed Vivian for a more urgent task.

Determined, Diamond curled up around Lillith, providing warmth and comfort while they awaited Luna's arrival. Occasionally, Diamond would gently blow warm air over Lillith's head, infusing her with healing magic and revitalizing her energy to sustain her heartbeat. Finally, after an hour, Luna Vivian hurriedly entered the room, bringing along four flowers and placing them next to Diamond as she had requested.

"Luna Vivian, would you be okay if I gave Lillith some of my blood? The wound on her neck is not healing."

"What did you need the flowers for then, Diamond?"

"To Help me to get more power only, my blood, aided by the flowers, will greatly enhance the chances of Lilliths survival. Now will you agree to my request?"

"Anything, as long as it helps her and maybe can give her a second chance, do it; you never had to ask my permission."

"Okay thank you, Luna. If you want, you can stay."

Diamond unwrapped herself from her position and took the flowers and ate them in a few bites. Luna Vivian could feel the stream of magic increasing around Diamond, and her white diamond eyes changed colours to gold and black. A golden mist slowly coalesced around both the wolf and the baby.

"Don't be afraid, Luna. Can you please turn her head a little to expose the wound? After some of my blood has covered the wound, I need you to open her mouth."

The Luna nodded her head and did what she was asked to do. Diamond sat down close to them both and bit down on her own paw, making a fresh wound appear, and the blood began to drop fast. Diamond lifted her paw over the neck of the child and let drop by drop land on her. As soon as the wound was covered, Luna opened her baby's mouth so the blood could drip into it and tilted her head gently back to allow the blood to slide down her throat. When she was done, Diamond stepped back and fell to the ground, exhausted. Her eyes fluttered shut as Vivian gasped in panic, calling for help.

"Someone quick, Diamond needs help. Please someone."

Morgana came running and saw Diamond on the ground and Vivian on her knees with Lillith in her arms, covered in blood, which was glowing with an aura of a rainbow's colours.

"Vivian, what happened?"

"She ate the four flowers she asked me to pick, and then she gave her blood to Lillith over her wound on the neck and then in her mouth. Then, the… then… Diamond… she just collapsed. Will she be okay? Did I kill her because I asked for too much?"

"What flowers? This is important."

"I think their name was *Lilium Asiatic, Forever Susan*. The second one is called *Lilium Asiatic Whistler*. What is going on?"

"Oh, my goddess. This girl *is* very special. There is nothing we can do for her at the moment, the only thing we can do is to hope that Lillith will survive."

"Morgana, what do you mean?"

"This is not going to be easy to say. Diamond is putting her own life at risk to save your daughter only because you asked her. You've shown her kindness, and she is willing to do anything to make you happy, even at the cost of her own health."

"Why didn't she tell me that? Oh no, I just killed her by being selfish. Will her parents ever forgive me?"

Vivian began to cry and regretted asking Diamond for so much, she would never have done it if she knew the full truth in this. When she heard the entrance door open again, her mate came in, noticing her distress, wrapping his arms around her when he noticed Diamond laying prone on the floor, barely breathing, nearly lifeless, when he asked.

"What happened? Whatever it is, I didn't do it"

"She is sacrificing herself for our daughter. I didn't know she was doing that. I just killed our saviour because I asked her to save our baby."

"Honey, you never forced her, you asked her. She did it of her own free will. Try to relax."

A loud snap broke through Luna's tears the sound of bones shifting, breaking apart, reforming. The golden fur was falling off in great hanks; white began to replace it. Morgana looked at Diamond and noticed she was shifting into Sapphire when the baby began to cry in Luna Vivian's arms. So, Morgana spoke up to break the tension.

"Well let me introduce Sapphire to the two of you."

Sapphire stood up and walked over to Lillith, blowing warm air over her head again, making her settle down fast. Then she looked into Vivian's eyes and spoke.

"Hi Vivian. Nice to finally meet you. And Diamond is fine, just very tired and weak. She took a huge risk for you and Lillith. Alpha Ben, you should show new people respect before you judge them. Next time, you may not be so lucky. Take that as a warning for the future. Not everyone is forgiving, especially Aria."

"Who is Aria?" asked Vivian as she was cradling Lillith in her arms.

"Oh, that is Jade's vampire soul. Jade is the witch within us all. So, we are one of a kind, as you noticed."

With that sentence Alpha Ben gulped down hard when he started to replay everything he said to Diamond in his head. He hung his head low and felt embarrassed over his own actions. When he questioned, "Do you think Diamond will ever forgive me for my behaviour?"

"Alpha Ben, she already has. Why do you think she was willing to die for your own flesh and blood?"

That made everyone look stunned at Sapphire, not knowing how to answer back on that. When the Alpha collected his thoughts and spoke again.

"Never call me Alpha again; only call me Ben. I will show more respect and Thank you Sapphire, for Diamond saving my children. I don't know how to thank all of you. Not even that is enough for what you have done for my family and pack. You will always have a home and protection here."

"As you wish Ben, the only thing you can do is show us the real you and stop feeling ashamed over small things. Everyone needs help sometimes in their life. By the way, where is everyone else?"

"Sarah and Ash took off into the forest, running in their wolf form. After they got to see us alive, it came as a hard shock for them both, but they will be back soon. Sylvestro, Stefan and Sylvia are outside and helping with the cleanup."

Sapphire looked at them and began to walk to the door when her back legs gave out from under her, and she fell down to the floor. Morgana noticed it and rushed over, followed by Vivian and Ben, hot on her heels.

"Sapphire, you should lay down and rest as well."

"Morgana, I'm fi…"

Then another huge SNAP echoed through the room. The sound of broken limbs and grinding bones began, and slowly, the brilliant white fur cascaded off, leaving bare skin in its place. Then, a naked young girl laid in Morgana's arms, crying. Between the sobs, Jade uttered words that barely anyone could understand. The words turned into a melody that began to calm not only her down but also everyone else in the room. When Morgana started to shake Jade harshly while harshly stating.

"Jade, you need to stop. Stop right now. Just stop."

"Morgana, what can we do to help?"

"Get me a bucket of ice-cold water. Hurry up."

Ben ran off as fast as he could meanwhile, Vivian tried to help Morgana wake up Jade. It didn't take long before Ben was back with the bucket. Asking what he is going to do with it.

"Throw it over Jade and me. We need to wake her up fast."

Ben didn't hesitate before he poured the water over them, and with a jolt, Jade screamed out in shock.

"Holy fucking goddess, are you fucking insane?"

"Thank the moon goddess, Jade. How do you feel?"

"I'm okay Morgana, just very scared, is everyone okay? Is the fight over?"

"Sweet child, don't you remember anything?"

"I remember I shifted nothing more after that. Who are these people that are hanging over us?"

"Jade, you and your wolf saved the pack. This man and woman's names are Ben and Vivian. Also known as Alpha and Luna of the Black Forest pack. The last deed you did for them was that you saved their daughter."

"Where are Mom and Dad?"

Just seconds after Jade requested their presence, the door was engulfed in flames as two majestic phoenixes burst into the room, fixating their fierce gazes on Alpha Ben. Hissing and arching their necks, they menacingly extended their beaks towards him. Sensing the danger, Jade reached out her hand, beckoning the phoenixes to come closer to her. Meanwhile, Samantha, in a state of panic, shouted at the top of her lungs.

"Are you out of your fucking mind? She could get sick! That man that calls itself an Alpha should be locked up!" Samantha exclaimed, her voice filled with concern for Jade's well-being.

"Calm down, Samantha," Morgana responded to the outburst, trying to pacify her friend. "I asked for the water. Jade was mumbling and then started humming one of the Queen's songs, and its power was amplifying."

"But it's just a song," Samantha protested. "It helps her to calm down. She's been doing it for years, both awake and asleep."

"That song is incredibly dangerous, especially when used by a witch," Morgana explained. "It can have calming effects, but it can also be deadly."

Turning her attention to Jade, Morgana asked, "Darling, are you feeling better now?"

Jade nodded her head stunned over what she had just learned about the melody she knew by heart and was always on her mind. Suddenly, a memory flashed through her mind, leaving her confused. Making her fall back into a deep sleep within herself. Aria noticed it and took over control of Jade's body so she could tell the parents and everyone else what just happened…

Chapter 20

Aria opened her eyes and Samantha got to see that they were blood red, and told everyone.

"Aria is present. Aria, is Jade fine?"

"She is fine, she is having a memory flashback within herself. Morgana, do you have the magic to invade someone's mind and memories?"

"I do Aria, but I don't feel comfortable doing that without Jade's consent. Well, does it help if I give you the consent? It's about the Queens song that you talked about earlier."

"Okay Aria, I will do this, but if Jade gets angry, you take that one on you."

"Fine by me, none of us can get into her memory at the moment, so just do it."

Morgana showed Aria down to the floor and started putting her hands on her temples then began to chant a spell. It was quiet all around them. The only sound you could make out of was heavy breathing and water dripping down the sink in the kitchen. It took a while for Morgana to come in and create a pass into Jade's memory circle. She pushed herself in and began to see a rocking chair and a woman sitting in it with a pink blanket in her arms while humming the melody slowly. Letting her feet rock slowly not wanting to disturb the boy playing next to her feet. Morgana looked around and saw Jade curled up in the corner of the room, crying. When she spoke in a soft, calm voice.

"Sweet child, what do you see?"

"Morgana, you are here! I don't know what I am seeing, but I do see a boy and a pink blanket, a white flowy, long dress and some black long hair. I can't see the face of the woman."

"Do you see the baby?"

"Yes, I don't know what that means."

"That baby is you, and the boy is probably your own brother."

"Morgana, who is this woman?"

"I'm not sure, sweet child. I do see very long black hair she is looking down on her baby. The face is covered."

"Why is she humming the melody? Wasn't that a dangerous song?"

"It is, but only if you don't know how to use it. I will explain more about the song later. Jade dear, do you feel safe to come back out with me?"

"I would love to stay here, the feeling I have is of warmth and love, the same I have from my parents back in my real life."

"Jade, please listen to me and try to recall the memory without getting too stuck in it. Remember the warmth and love surrounding you, both from new people and those you consider as family. I personally consider you as part of my family and will always be there for you in any way I can," Morgana assured Jade.

"I understand, Morgana. I will continue to follow you as long as I can keep this memory in mind," Jade replied.

"Thank you, my dear child," Morgana said, holding Jade's hand as they exited through the passageway she had created earlier. Meanwhile, outside in the realm of memories, Aria was fiercely confronting Alpha Ben, expressing her discontent with him.

"Do you think I would be friendly with you after everything you said to Diamond? After everything she did for you. Calling someone a rogue after saving your pathetic ass, well then you should go and have a mental health check or, better yet, get your sorry ass to the vet. You should be looking at yourself as lucky you have a mate that loves you, and correct your stupid mistakes. If it wasn't for Jade and Diamond nothing would be here left alive. Or even from your friends. We are here to get trained by Sylvestro, Sylvia, Stefan, Ash, Saraha, Lillian and Morgana. Don't come to me next time you have bloody problems if you can't show me that you are man enough to ask for help and show better remorse."

"Aria, I am truly sorry for how I acted; there are no words to correct my wrongdoings. I do know my amazing mate has saved me many times, but I will do anything to earn your respect, even train you myself in any form you want."

Then she looked at her mother, and her blood-red eyes slowly faded down into Jade's green eyes, a smile spread over her lips. Then Jade turned to Morgana to ask her.

"Do you know anyone named Tanya?"

"That is a name I haven't heard in a long time. Where did you learn about it?"

"I remembered something that one of the rogues said before Diamond killed them. They yelled out all hail, Queen Tanya."

"Ben, increase the guards on patrol. Jade, I need you and Lillian; we are going outside. This is not good, Jade, be careful showing your different spirits. Try to only shift into wolf form when you are out in the open. Tanya is a dark witch, and she has lost her mind, to be quite frank about it."

"How do you know about her?"

"A long time ago, she was a white witch and belonged to my coven, but she started to change after the great war. I had to kick her out of my home, and after that, she disappeared. Tanya was once a close friend of mine."

Alpha Ben's eyes had fogged over while he was telepathically linking his pack warriors about increasing border security. When he was done with his task, he looked at Jade and smiled. He saw she was hesitant towards him but tentatively wanted to get to know him as well, when he stretched out his arm to her.

"Let me help you up, Jade."

Jade looked at Morgana and her mother. They nodded their heads, and then she looked at her dad who was still in his form, but the flames around him showed calmness. So, she took a leap of fate and lifted her hand to place it in his, letting him help her up from the floor. When she finally was standing, Luna Vivian took her in her arms and hugged her in a motherly warm hug. Vivian's eyes fogged over, and she got trapped in a mind link, and as soon as the link was done, she spoke up.

"It seems that Ash found his mate out at the battlefield in a sedated state, and they are on their way back to the pack hospital."

"Okay that is great. I'm so happy for him. Let me borrow Jade and Lillian for a little while so I can have my task done and we will meet you there." Morgana said.

Jade broke free from Luna Vivian's arms and began to walk to the entrance charred opening where on the sides were the ashes of the lost door. Jade looked back at Morgana and nodded her head. Then passed to the opening and walked out in the sunlight again, where Lillian saw her and came walking to give her a hug. Jade told her about Morgana's request.

"Okay, well she is coming out now. Let's see what task we need to help out with."

"Lillian, Tanya is on the way up again."

"Tanya, I thought she had died years ago. This can't be good. How do you know, Aunt?"

"Jade asked about her. Apparently, the rogues were working for her. We need to create a barrier over the pack lands, where it can help the pack and keep everyone safe."

"Morgana, may I suggest one barrier?"

"Yes, what would that be, Jade?"

"Remember the barrier I made back in Australia? Where you put the invisibility part in, but we tweak it so pack members can go in and out of it without getting hurt."

"Jade, don't forget the animals and humans and those with good hearts."

Enthralled by the marvelous idea, Lillian and Jade wasted no time and immediately set off towards the open field. Once they reached the designated spot, they formed a circle, grasping each other's hands, ready to commence their task.

Morgana, with her immense power, allowed Jade to initiate the creation of the barrier. The sudden explosion surprised both Lillian and Morgana, who then channeled their energy through their hands, establishing a strong bond. Gradually, the barrier emerged from the center and ascended into the sky, transforming into a transparent dome that encompassed the pack area. Satisfied with the first step, Jade signaled her completion to the others, and Lillian took charge of the next phase. She began casting a purifying spell, ensuring that humans, animals, and kind-hearted shifters could enter without any harm while also granting pack members unrestricted access. Lastly, Morgana concealed the barrier, making it invisible to prying eyes. With the barrier successfully erected, the trio settled down on the grass, stained with blood, exhausted. As they caught their breath, Jade began crafting a new spell.

"Mar a bha e aon uair, dealraicheadh e a rìs anns a' ghlòir a bh' ann roimhe."

(As is it once was, let it shine again in the former glory)

Light blue dust spread fast out from her fingernails and out over all the pack lands. Little by little the grass turned green and well-kept again. Inch by inch, it covered more area, so it came to the pack house, where it steadily built up brick by brick back to its former pride and glory. After an hour Jade stood up and stretched her back and body out, and spoke happily.

"Well, should we go back to the others?"

"Jade, you will never stop surprising me with your powers. Let's go Lillian. Ash found his mate."

Morgana and Lillian stood up and began walking with Jade back towards the pack hospital. When Jade got an unsettling feeling within herself, she stopped walking mid-stride. Morgana curiously asked her.

"Jade, what is wrong?"

"I'm not sure, but I have a feeling I should shift into my wolf again. Something feels wrong, and we need to be careful."

"How do you mean Jade? Can you try to explain the feeling more?" Lillian asked.

"Can any of you message Vivian or Ben and ask if she has any purple mist around her?"

Lillian took out her phone from her back pocket and, texted Vivian and asked the peculiar question Jade had just asked. Diamond had woken up and had told Jade about the purple mist, and its purpose was to kill off the rogues that had been attacking the pack. They didn't have to wait long for a response. Lillian's phone lit up with a reply, and Lillian read the message for Jade.

"Yes, there appears to be a faint purple glow lingering around her."

Hearing this, Jade let Diamond take over control, and she shifted into the golden wolf again. Continuing to make their way to the pack hospital. Morgana looked at Lillian to ask a question.

"Would you mind telling us what is going on?"

"Ash's mate was with the rogues. So, she knows Tanya, probably as well. That purple mist was for taking down the rogues before I burned them. Just in case I don't want her to see Jade yet."

"That is not good. Diamond, do you or Jade have a mind-reading spell? If not, I will teach the two of you one. Because if she has been with Tanya my magic would be useless on her," Morgana said with a hint of worry in it.

"I know of one. I will use it if we are in need of that; let's give the girl a chance at least. She should be dead by now, but she probably has a good heart and ended up on the wrong path at some point."

They continued their walk back and not long the doors of the hospital were in reach. White brick house on two floors disinfected the smell all around, and the scent got stronger after Morgana opened up the doors. People were running around in confusion, and happiness spread from room to room. In one room, you could hear some crying, and it pulled on Diamond's heart; she knew she couldn't save every person in the pack, and it weighed heavy on her heart. Morgana went up to the front desk and asked, "In what room may we find Beta Ash?"

"The Beta would be in room 225, second floor, Miss Morgana."

"Thank you. Come on Lillian and Diamond, let's get to the second floor."

The both of them followed Morgana to the stairs for their search for room 225 when a loud scream boomed out.

"AAAAH! Help, someone please help. They are trying to abduct me. Get back."

"Morgana, Lillian, that doesn't sound good."

"You are right Diamond, and that noise is coming from the room we are going to. Let's play around a little Diamond, only nod your head and huff, pretend that you can't speak. In the meantime, you can go and read her mind at the same time."

Sarah and Luna Vivian came out walking and saw the two witches and Diamond, only to let out a sigh of relief.

"Thank the moon goddess that you're here, Morgana," Sarah and Luna Vivian exclaimed in relief as they spotted the two witches and Diamond. "Morgana, Ash's mate, woke up earlier and has been screaming at everyone, refusing to acknowledge their bond."

Curious, Luna asked, "Do we know if she's a shifter?"

"Yes, she's a raven shifter," Morgana confirmed.

"That's intriguing. We should go in and help her calm down," Diamond suggested, walking towards the door and signaling for assistance by scraping on it. Lillian quickly came to open the door, and as soon as she stepped inside, the room fell silent.

After a moment of calm, Ash's mate's voice, now composed, asked, "Please golden wolf, you have to let me go. I can't stay here; I will be in deep trouble if I do."

"My love, what possible trouble would you be in when you are with your mate?"

"I don't have a mate; I can't have a mate."

Diamond looked at her and saw a very scared woman in her early twenties with amazing corkscrew locks that looked tamed and well-kept. Light brown eyes that were filled with fear and hatred. An oval face with a small faint scar on her right cheek that looked like a small pentagram had been burnt into her skin. Within her veins glowed a small faint purple hint from Diamond's mist earlier that day, which also amazed her that this woman was still alive and looked well. It was then Diamond decided to invade her memories to find out the truth about what was going on as something or someone was terrifying her to the bones. Diamond started the spell fast and got a small glimpse, only for her to notice that they must let her go; it was between life and death.

Her purple mist was purifying her from the evil within, making her scared and lost at the same time. She knew Ash was her mate, but the weight of her past—everything she had done under Tanya's influence—made her fear disappointing him. She also found out that she had a brother and that she had been looking for Tanya for her revenge. Diamond made the choice to leave her mind and began to walk to the room door hoping that Alpha Ben would understand that she wanted out of the room. Luckily, Alpha Ben understood and opened up the door for her and she walked out, and as soon as the door was closed behind her, she turned to Morgana and began revealing everything she had learned.

"Morgana, we need to let her go. Before my mist has purified her completely, she is not an evil girl just consumed with revenge."

"We can't just let her go, Diamond; she is Ash's mate."

"I know that she knows that, but she is also marked with a burned pentacle. With that she is still connected with Tanya."

Morgan looked at Diamond, then walked to the door to call for both Ash and Alpha Ben.

"Beta Ash, Alpha Ben, can the two of you come out here? I have something urgent to discuss with the both of you."

"My love, I will be back soon. Don't go anywhere, I will be back."

The two of them walked out to see worried faces around them, and Luna Vivian walked up to her brother to take hold of his hand and then said something he never thought he would ever hear.

"Ash, we need to let your mate go for the moment, she is still connected with Tanya, and Diamond's purple mist is purifying her slowly. I know it's hard to hear, but we will get her back."

"You can't be serious about this, Sis. You know how long I have been waiting for my mate; I can't just let her go."

"Ash, we are twins. I know how you are feeling, but it's for the best, for your mate and us. I promise you I will personally look for her in one day."

"Ash, ask her if you can mark her," Diamond said in a stern voice.

"I beg your pardon. How the fuck can you speak?"

No one had noticed that Ash's mate had walked out behind them and also heard Diamond speak. Diamond took a small step towards her and looked her in the eyes and spoke again.

"Because I'm a hybrid, and you, my friend, can start by telling us your name."

"My… my… name is Sanna. I'm so sorry for all the trouble I have created in this pack. I was only just following orders."

"So Sanna, if we let you go back to that witch, would you agree that Ash marks you? Before you even think about lying about the mate bond, I know the truth already."

Sanna stepped back into the room and looked at everyone not knowing what to say or to do. She knew she couldn't lie anymore, but she knew she needed to get back again. She began to hesitate a little before she spoke.

"If I agree with this, will you let me go?"

"Yes, I have to. Can you tell me why you want to go back so bad?"

"I apologize for misleading you with my previous statement. The scar on my face seems to be a ticking time bomb, ready to explode. However, I want to assure you that I did not choose this fate willingly. I must confess that I lied about you not being my soulmate. I deeply regret deceiving you."

"My love, please understand that it's alright. I will leave a mark on you, symbolizing our connection and set you free. But I must emphasize that if you don't return within a week, I will come looking for you. And I won't be coming alone."

Sanna nodded, tilting her head to the side, giving him have full access to her neck. The marking went fast, and Sanna could feel his feelings towards her, and she loved every moment of it. Ash looked at her and spoke.

"Time to let you go. Love, remember my warning to you."

"I will. I will come back as soon as I can."

She placed her hand behind his neck and kissed him deeply on his lips before stepping away to walk towards the hospital doors.

Chapter 21

Sanna took one look back and saw Ash was looking at her, sending love through the telepathic link between them. Then she looked at the golden wolf and smiled. Diamond glanced at her and nodded her head back, sending a fast link to her.

"If you ever need us, think about me and make a mind link with me. We will come for you. Stay safe. Remember that you have a home here and people that will love you. Leave the hate and follow your heart."

Sanna, stunned by the encounter with the wolf, silently acknowledged its presence and swiftly transformed into her raven form, taking flight into the open sky. As she soared through the air, her mind was filled with thoughts of the enigmatic words spoken by the Golden wolf. Suddenly, a sharp pang of pain shot through her heart, a physical manifestation of the turmoil within her.

Leaving her mate behind was not the sole cause of this ache; there was something deeper at play. Sanna realized that she had never experienced such a profound sense of security in the presence of wolves, but with the Golden wolf, it was different. There was an inexplicable magnetic pull towards the she-wolf, drawing her closer.

Memories flooded her mind, particularly of the battlefield where the mist had descended, subduing everyone except for her. She vividly recalled the appearance of the Golden wolf amidst the chaos and how her presence had somehow shielded her from the mist's effects. The recollection of this event sent shivers down her spine.

The hospital scene haunted her thoughts as well. The fact that the Alpha and the Luna had inexplicably come back to life left her terrified. She pondered the existence of a power capable of such a feat, realizing that even Tanya, a powerful being herself, did not possess such abilities.

It did not take Sanna long to notice where she was. Slowly, she circled down for a landing, too afraid to make that awful walk back to Tanya's place. Her place was located in the middle of Feldberg, just on the southern border of the Black Forest pack. Sanna dreaded walking in that area due to the overwhelming stench of pure malevolence. The air was thick with the putrid odor of charred bodies decomposing, mingling with a pervasive sulfuric aroma that enveloped the surroundings like a misty cloud. Nevertheless, she embarked on her journey through the seemingly interminable forest, determined to reach the moss-covered stone stairs. Sadness filled her heart over all the dead trees laying around mixed in with long lost friends' skeletons that beaconed her forward.

Before she began climbing up the one hundred fifty-four steps, she had to pass a last obstacle with roots of the trees that were covered with a thick lingering mist. If you looked closely, you had the chance to make them out within the shadows. One wrong step could set off a spell made by the witch Tanya, and you would be trapped for eternity. Facing the moss-covered stairs, Sanna felt the weight of uncertainty pressing down on her as she prepared to climb into the unknown. Suppressing her fear, she kept her troubling memories hidden from Tanya. Sanna had always been the bearer of bad news whenever her rogue allies lost battles over the pack lands. The steps ahead seemed endless, filled with dread and fear. Finally reaching the top, Sanna's eyes fell upon a house, flanked by two old whiskey barrels. One barrel lay open, while the other had a lid with a small crack, from which a metallic smell leaked out, causing Sanna to cringe. She knew that Tanya's bad mood would lead to someone suffering the consequences of her wrath. Suddenly, a screeching, icy-cold voice erupted from inside the house.

"Sanna, don't you dare try to avoid me, you sneaky little rat. Get in here, you little imbecile and tell me everything before it's too late for you."

Dread filled Sanna, and all the colour drained from her face when she received a mind link from Diamond.

"Sanna, are you okay? Ash felt your fear but couldn't reach you."

"Tell him I'm okay, I just got back and Tanya is in a foul mood. Tell him I love him."

"Stay calm; I will be within the link with you, so keep it open. I will see you soon."

That made Sanna smile; it was a long time ago since she felt someone had her back, and this time, it was a new person in her life.

When the screeching voice broke into her mind, breaking her happy moment, and then the fear started up again.

"Did you not hear me, you stupid piece of shit? Don't you fucking dare make me come out there to get you!"

Then Diamond's voice interrupted again.

"Remember Sanna deep breaths. Deep in and let it out slowly. If it helps, think about your mate."

Sanna began to run up the wooden stairs, to the door and pushed it open, letting the door let out a squeak and followed with a bang when it hit the wall behind Sanna. She continued straight through the dank, dark hallway to knock on a glass door before opening it, to go inside and get down to her knees and then take both arms and stretch them out on the floor over her head, genuflecting to the lone occupant.

"I'm sorry, my Queen."

In front of Sanna sat a woman with dead grey eyes and long blond hair. The eyes didn't hold any light in them; the only thing left in them was hatred and rage. She sat in a chair that looked more like a throne. On the chair arms, she was tapping her knife-like fingernails, impatiently waiting for Sanna to tell her news about the battle that had recently happened. The frustration in her exploded out in the room, making every work jump on the empty walls.

"Well, do I have to do everything? Speak, you filthy thing."

"No ma'am. I do not have any news to report to you that can meet your high expectations."

The face of the woman darkened as she stood up from the chair and walked heavily towards Sanna, grabbing her around the neck and letting the nails dig deeply into the skin. Blood started to trickle down between her fingers, and the metallic smell of fresh blood spread in the room. A satisfying grin crept onto the woman's face when she saw the fear in Sanna's eyes and the colour draining from her face. It began to be harder for Sanna to breathe because the hold got stronger and stronger until the hands let go. With a shaking voice, Sanna spoke.

"Queen Tanya, I'm sorry for bringing bad news. Please spare my life."

"Spare your life? Why should I spare you? You can't even do a simple task. Let's see what your memory can provide for me before your doom."

Unbeknownst to Sanna, she had forgotten to close the mind link with Diamond, allowing her to overhear every conversation taking place. Diamond, always quick-witted, decided to pull a prank on Sanna by casting a reverse spell within her mind. Just as Tanya began to perform the truth image spell, Sanna let out a piercing scream, her eyes welling up with tears. Simultaneously, a small memory bubble appeared, displaying vivid pictures from her past. First of the memories was of her in her early teens, and you could see how her own parents held her down, and a man came up from behind her with a large erection. Thankfully there was no sound from the bubble. However, you couldn't take the pain and the fear from the images; her parents laughed together when the man violated her. The memory continued into the end, where he had used her in every part he could, blood was dripping slowly out both from her front and back, and Tanya couldn't stand anymore. Her arms and neck were covered in bruises and she was left on the floor all alone.

After a little while, a new memory started to flash through with her being a little older, and she was talking to a person with a wicked smile, giving her a card, and with that card Tanya gave her hand to him. She looked happy but also something had started to change within her. A few moons later, she meets up with the man again, but something was off. He had his arms around someone else, and Tanya fell to her knees pleading with him, tears falling down on her face, the agony as evident on her face and slowly turning her crushed heart into stone. The sad face contorted into pure hatred and determination. The light in her eye darkened and slowly took over her heart and soul.

The last episode was when she got kicked out from her home and family of Morgana's coven, Morgana's face was full of hurt and sorrow, grieving the loss of a friend and someone she saw as family. People had started to come into the room where everything was taking place, when someone suddenly yelled out.

"My Queen, Sanna's scent has changed."

"Indeed, and her loyalty as well."

Sanna's body stiffened up fast when she heard Diamond's voice again in her mind.

"Sanna, you need to leave NOW. Try to escape."

There was one thing Diamond forgot to think of when she mind-linked Sanna, that her eyes would fog over, making it harder for Sanna to escape. Three rogue wolves took hold of her arms, bending them cruelly behind her back, forcing her down onto her knees. When Tanya started to laugh out loud like a hyena spitting in her face and telling her.

"You sneaky little whore, did you really think you could come back here and stab me in the back? You found your mate and let him mark you. Do you even believe he could save you? You are just a pathetic little raven shifter; no one cares about a shifter like you."

It was then Sanna found her courage and venomously snapped back at Tanya.

"You are no Queen of mine, and you are wrong; my mate loves me and will come for me. Morgana and her coven will destroy all of you. You are a bitch with no real life or friends, hell you don't even have a family. Even the man you loved, hated you. You think people follow you because you pretend to be a queen. They follow you, awaiting a way to kill you off; that is how much your followers hate you!"

Consumed by her intense hatred towards Tanya, Sanna found herself oblivious to her surroundings. Suddenly, a piercing pain jolted her from her fixation, originating from the right side of her abdomen.

As the pain intensified, an icy sensation crept over her, and Sanna's clothes became drenched in a cold sweat. Her head grew heavy, and the room seemed to blur and spin as if time itself had slowed down. Struggling to grasp reality, Sanna mustered the strength to raise her gaze and lock eyes with Tanya. However, as her strength ebbed, Sanna's gaze lowered as she noticed something gripped tightly in Tanya's hand. A sickening realization crashed over Sanna. Tanya was holding her appendix. While laughing like a mad woman when she made a statement.

"Take this as a warning, everyone. Double cross me; this is what is going to happen to you as well."

The blood was dripping down onto the wooden floor and everything sounded so calm and still. The only sound Sanna could pick up was of her own blood, leaving her body draining her life with it. When she got the last mind-link to Diamond.

"Tell Ash I love him, and I'm sorry. I'm sorry Diamond, I will not be able to come back to my new family."

Then the link went quiet, and Sanna passed out from the loss of blood. It was then Tanya made her new move and told the people in the room.

"Wake that whore up, and have some fun with her body. I'm going to enjoy this."

Some went away to get water to make sure they had their turn with her. Even for a Raven shifter, she was a good-looking woman, and even if she had a mate, it didn't matter. There weren't many women in this place, and those that were present were already well-used by everyone. When the water came back into the room, they poured the bucket over Sanna's body, making her body jerk up and shake off the cold wetness that came in contact with her clothes and skin. Sanna started to feel hands on her, ripping her wet clothes off from her body. Then a sinister laugh started to echo out in the room; Tanya was looking down on Sanna while laughing and grinning from ear to ear. Sanna tried to protect her half-naked body, but it was to no use as she had no strength left in her body, and soon she felt two hands on her private areas and the only thing she could think of saying in a weak voice.

"Please stop, don't do this to me. I was your friend; I haven't betrayed anyone."

Her pleas went past her attackers, and soon she felt the pain of how she was penetrated and her hymen being taken away from her by force. The cries and screams that left her mouth never got acknowledged by anyone. The only thing she could recognise was the evil grins and lust-filled eyes on everyone's faces. All the rogues present took turns with Sanna's broken body. Loud voices of others demanding their turn echoed through Sanna's mind. Every time Sanna could muster up any strength in her body and tried to push them or herself away, they started to hit her. Harshly stabbing their dirty fingers into the already bleeding wound on her side, making her flinch in pain, allowing the merciful darkness to take her away again, only to get ice-cold water thrown over her so they could continue with their own sadistic pleasure.

Hours went by, and several men had their way with her, as Tanya was sitting on her chair, laughing and clapping her hands in pure enjoyment. When Tanya finally snapped her fingers, the ordeal suddenly stopped. She stood up and walked down towards Sanna, hunching down next to her badly beaten and used body, whispering something into Sanna's ear. Words—Sanna could not make out in her traumatised state. And then she felt her throat being sliced open vertically, the slicing never stopping until the blade slid down to her severely damaged lower abdomen. Sanna's heart rate plummeted lower, and she could barely hold her eyes open. The last thing she heard before blissfully being taken by death's cold hand was Tanya's repulsive voice.

"Throw her into the second barrel and leave this used whore to rot in her own blood and filth; we can feed the vultures the leftovers later."

Chapter 22

Even with everything that was going down at Tanya's house, Stefan and Sylvestro had taken Ash to a local pub in a human town. While they talked and laughed, both Sylvestro and Stefan listened to how happy Ash sounded. Ash started to feel pain on his side of the stomach and fell down from the bar chair down to the floor, crawling up in a foetal position. Screaming in pure agony until he passed out of the pain. Stefan and Sylvestro lifted him up and helped each other out to carry him to a car; worry etched on their faces. As soon as they were in the car, Stefan started it, threw it in gear and mashed the accelerator down to the floor. With a cloud of dust billowing behind, the tires spun and marked their departure, leaving a lingering gouged-out track as a reminder of their presence.

Emerging from the haze, a man stepped forward, his face etched with a stony expression as he watched the car vanish in a hurry, tail lights fading into the night. Determined, he turned back towards the pub, resolute in his quest for answers about the girl he had been tirelessly searching for. While inside the pub, he ordered a Bierstiefel "beer boot." He got the beer and walked to an empty table to sit down, and began thinking back on old memories. It's been two years since the last time I saw my sister, ever since we lost our parents in a horrible murder, she disappeared. The sorrow and grief took over within himself as tears formed in his cold eyes; just thinking what it did to his own sister made it harder.

Then one gloomy day, he heard a rumour about some dark witch who had started to assemble an army of all kinds of different shifters throughout the rest of Europe. As he sipped on his beer, a thought crossed his mind—could his own sister be a part of that army? With her rare ability to shift into a raven and her incredible eyesight from the air, not everyone was familiar with the existence of raven shifters. But what worried him the most was the possibility of her acting recklessly out of blindness for revenge.

Memories began flashing in his mind, taking him back to a time when their family of four was on vacation in Las Vegas. It was a happy time until a dark witch and a vampire approached them, hurling insults at his mother and sister. In a fit of rage, their father lost control and retaliated with insults of his own, which proved to be a terrible mistake.

The vampires, angered by their father's words, swiftly attacked, tearing open his throat and causing his blood to spray over both of his children. In the midst of their father's lifeless body falling to the ground, their mother let out a heart-wrenching scream, filled with agony and sorrow over the loss of her beloved husband and mate. As if reveling in their mother's misery, the witch standing before them laughed and began chanting a spell.

That made their mother fall down to her knees in pain, holding her head with both her hands, gradually blood poured out from her eyes and nose. Until her body gave up and fell down on the ground lifeless. Sanna got so scared of all the screaming and ran away. Unfortunately for the man he got trapped by the vampire in a controlling hypnosis, where he forced him to serve his clan as a blood bank. It took several attempts before he could escape the madness of his life with one goal in mind: finding his sister again.

Before he escaped, he managed to get a hold of some information about the dark witch that had accompanied the vampire and for months, he has been hunting for more information about her location, and hopefully his sister. After a while, he snapped his head out from his memories and began looking around to see if he could find someone drunk enough to tell stories while he was asking for information. Lucky for him, two guys walked in angry, spoke loud and were clearly pissed off over something. So he took the opportunity, leaned in slightly, listening carefully, waiting for the right moment to make his move.

"I'm telling you man, that freaking witch has gone insanely mad. She has lost her fucking mind. How could she even do that to her?"

"Hey man, scream louder if you can. I don't think the whole fucking pub could hear you. Keep it down; you never know who is listening in on us. Plus, there are still humans here as well, and don't forget those who are loyal to that bitch."

"I don't fucking care anymore. I only hope that someone can take her fat ass down before she can destroy everything nice in this world. I feel so sorry for what happened to Sanna. Her life had just been starting, she definitely didn't deserve that treatment from everyone. Considering all she had done for Tanya from the first day she came into the group. Sanna always had everyone's back."

"I know man, and I do feel the same as you. I do think it's time for us to escape that shit hole. We shouldn't go back there from here. I think we should leave the country to be safe, Canada maybe. What do you think?"

"We need to save her before it's too late, I can't leave her there like garbage. Think about the mate she found today."

"You know damn well what she will do to us if we even try that. I want to save her as well, but without backup, we are fucked. The pack will not help us if there is anyone left of them."

"You are right. There is nothing we can do to help her. She has probably already bled to death. I can't get the state of her out of my mind, it will haunt me forever."

"Shhh! Calm down, there's a man coming towards us."

The two quieted down and looked at the person walking in their direction, starting to get closer to them when he opened his mouth and spoke, "Hi guys I'm William. Could I offer you some beers?"

"Why do you want to give us beers? What is it that you really want?"

William looked at the guy with long black hair and said, "I understand that I may not belong to your group, but please hear me out.

I am desperate to find my sister, Sanna. She has distinct features: red curly hair, bright blue eyes, and a small button nose. The last time I saw her, she had a slim and well-trained body. I mention that she is a raven shifter just to clarify who I am searching for."

The other guy's response was filled with animosity, clearly displaying his hatred towards William or anyone not part of his group. He was a slightly chubby man with light brown short hair, emitting an unpleasant odor akin to that of a sweating pig. William, unfazed by the man's words and stench, casually waved his hand in front of his nose and continued speaking.

"Hey man, you need a shower badly."

"You don't have to be rude, I'm Ben, and this here is Ty. I do think you are too late, my friend, well if you don't know anyone that could heal or bring folks back from the dead."

"What do you mean Ben, do you know my sister?"

"Ben, be quiet. You don't know if he works for her."

"Well, if he so badly wants to know, why not just tell him? We will not be going back there anyway. If Sanna is his sister, he should know the truth."

Ben swallowed hard before he started to tell the story to William about what happened earlier that day to Sanna. Then he talked about the Black Forest pack that was close to the pub. William started to understand everything and continued to listen to the story Ben and Ty spun, he also noticed that both were remorseful and in deep regret over what they had done and witnessed. Ben continued telling William.

"This insane woman believes that she is a queen and she is the rightful ruler over all the shifters. So, if you think this girl is your sister, you should leave right away before it's too late to save her. Take her to the Black Forest pack, hopefully they can save her. There are two white witches there."

"Thank you for sharing all of this with me. I truly understand that it has been difficult for both of you. I encourage you to consider joining a pack and making a fresh start. I believe that you can improve your situation from now on."

"We are planning on doing that, we just need to leave this place and for that, we need to find work."

"I'm glad to hear that you are planning on taking that step. Finding work is indeed crucial in order to leave this place. As a gesture of gratitude for your help, please accept this sum of five hundred. It's not meant as charity, but rather as a token of appreciation for your assistance. Take care of yourselves and stay well."

After he put the money on the table, William sprinted out into the shadows to find his way to his long-lost sister. It wasn't hard for William to locate the area. It reeked of death and dark magic, corpses piled over each other on the ground, scattered hanging from the top of nearby dead trees. It was one of the gruesomest scenes William had ever witnessed. Some bodies were ripped apart as if animals had been

261

fighting over their entrails. The closer he got to the centre of the place he knew he had to mask his own smell, and the only way he could think of was to, well… roll around among the corpses to get the dead scent on himself. After he was done rolling with the dead, he had to force himself not to throw up, gagging on the smell around him and the thought of what he just had to do.

William kept to the shadows around the houses so he could locate the house he was looking for without being detected. In front of the stairs up to the entrance were the two barrels. Both of them had the lids on. He opened the first one, and out came a flood of rotten flesh and skeletons floating out, sliding down the small hill. He jumped over the contents and opened up the other one. In it there was a barely breathing girl laying in a foetal position. Blood was leaving her body from all the different wounds. William looked at her and spoke in a soft voice.

"I finally found you, little sis. Let me help you out and take you somewhere safe."

With a very weak voice, Sanna answered him in a bare whisper

"Brother, is that you? I'm so sorry. Leave me here, save yourself."

"I'm sorry, sis that is never going to happen again. I will keep you safe, but first I need to get you out of here."

Slowly he bent down and halfway crawled into the barrel. Took a gentle hold on her to slide her out slowly and gently, hoping that he didn't create more damage to her very fragile body as had already been done. Slowly and steadily, he got her out and laid her tight into his chest while holding her in his arms, cradling her. When William heard her weak voice again.

"William, can you please take me to Black Forest pack? My mate is there."

"Okay, hold on tight and don't you dare fall asleep on me. I don't want your drool on me as well."

A small giggle left Sanna's lips as she felt her brother start to run faster and as smoothly as he could. William had a hard time keeping his anger at bay, yet the worry for his beloved sister was unbearable to handle at the same time. A run that probably took only thirty minutes to run felt like hours had passed, when he finally saw the open field, a surge of strength took over within him and pushed the last of the way. It wasn't long before he reached it and could lay his sister down to see all the damage done to her. He slowly looked over her naked body, and not long after vibration started to make itself known, William knew that they had made it. They were back on pack lands.

"Sanna, I will be back soon. I need to find stuff to help you heal, and I don't think your mate would like to see me looking at you in this state. I will not be far away. You never told me your mate's name."

"Beta Ash of the Black Forest pack"

"Okay, he can definitely not see me looking over you. I will come back soon, I promise. I love you, little sister. Stay strong, don't fall asleep."

"I love you too, brother."

William stepped back into the darkness of the forest a few metres from his sister, looking over her with worry and sadness. Not long after William was between the trees, three wolves came running together. The first two had normal colours, but the third one was golden and enormous, even bigger than the alphas of the packs. The two first wolves shifted into human form, and the man ran to William's sister, screaming to the other woman while the golden wolf looked around and walked up to Sanna and the man. Then she opens her mouth.

"Ash, I'm so sorry I lost connection with her earlier when you came in all that pain."

"Diamond, you could not know this would happen to her, but that witch will pay for this. Sarah, tell the fucking doctor that we are coming in with my mate."

"Ash, I'm already on it. Diamond, don't put this on yourself. Remember, she wanted to go, and only you know what you saw in her mind. Diamond, is there any chance you could help her?"

"Yes, it is, and I will help her. I'm not sure she came here by herself. Jade will not come out here in the open, so give me a little time, and I will work on it."

William stepped a little closer when a smell wafted towards his nose, he never thought he ever would smell. When he looked at the three that were next to his sister, he noticed that the Sarah girl had stepped closer, and that scent came from her. She was his mate and she was the most beautiful girl he had ever seen before.

Chapter 23

Sarah and Ash looked at Diamond, hoping that she could help Sanna on the spot, and then Diamond spoke up again.

"We need to move her a little further in the territory; it feels like someone is keeping an eye on us."

Ash bent down to lift her up when Sarah yelled out.

"Ash, stop, this is not good. Don't move her. Diamond, look at her right side."

Diamond looked over and saw the gashing open wound and gasped in shock. She walked around Sanna's body, which was starting to lose its colour. She also noticed Ash's increasing worry and hatred growing within him for every second that passed. She laid down close to Sanna and Ash started to growl when she looked up and spoke.

"Do you want me to help her or not?"

"I'm sorry Diamond, I can't control it."

"Well, turn around and shield us then. Because I need to focus here."

"Come on, Ash. Let's turn around and keep an eye on the forest while she helps my new sister. Or don't you trust Diamond?"

"I trust her with my life, but you are right."

The both of them turned around to keep an eye open for anything out of the ordinary and let Diamond help out Sanna. Diamond began to tap into the magic and tried a new spell Jade had been practising in secret. Slowly, the wind started to pick up around the trees floating over the grass on the field, circling around Diamond and Sanna, making a wall around them.

"Thoir air leigheas òirleach air òirleach leig leis an fhuil sruthadh mar an abhainn a-steach don chuan, bheir an rud a tha e air a dhèanamh air falbh i fhèin. rach gu toiseach ùr."

(Make it heal inch by inch, let the blood flow like the river into the ocean, what it's done remove itself. Past be gone to a new beginning.)

Slowly, water began to appear around the wound on Sanna's stomach. Forming a protective layer over the wound, with a steady pace, new skin cells emerged, weaving together into the wound, bonding itself into one piece. Then it left that area to continue working on other areas of the skin. When it finally directed its way to the inside of her body, Sanna's body acted more and more in a way like she was having a seizure, her body writhing and jerking a marionette that had lost its way.

When the spell worked its way from the inside, the water slowly sluiced out from her vaginal area and mixed with a white sticky, gooey substance making Diamond gag. As soon as the water left Sanna, it sank down into the soil, leaving a black rose after itself and with that, the wind lifted up to the air, separating into small thin clouds. Diamond looked down at Sanna and saw her colour had started to reappear on rose rose-pink cheeks. Her eyes fluttered open and looked right into

Diamond's white eyes. She smiled and raised her arm up so she could touch Diamond. Then letting out a sigh of relief, she spoke to Diamond.

"Diamond, it's so nice to see you again, I knew I could count on you."

"Sanna, we found you here alone on the field. Do you have any memories of how you ended up here?"

"My brother came and rescued me. Diamond where is Ash?"

"I'm right here, love. You scared the piss out of me. Does anything hurt? Diamond, thank you so much; there are no words for me to say to you."

"That's okay. Sanna…"

Diamond jerked up, twitching her ears around listing and began to growl in the direction of the forest. Sanna got scared, and Sarah shifted instantly, while Ash held Sanna close to his chest, asking Diamond, "What's going on? What did you hear?"

"Something just moved in the shadows of the woods."

"Diamond, that could be my brother. He said he was going to be close."

"Your brother, what is he?"

"William is a shadow shifter. Almost like me as a raven, but he is more comfortable within the shadows."

Sanna sat up a little away from Ash's chest and looked into the forest, focusing her eyes after the blurry figure of her older brother. When she saw him, she yelled out.

"William, it's safe; they won't hurt you."

William took a step out from the comfort of the shadows, and at first, you could only make out a blur that, with time settled into the hard form of a man. The man grew taller, up to around six foot seven inches, the top of his head was short cropped hair of light red with green eyes staring back at them. Sarah felt drawn to him but couldn't see why he didn't have a mate aura around him, nor could she pick up. His eyes held so much hurt and sadness but also love and hate. William never took one step more to cross the borderline, but Diamond knew he could pass; he had already done it when his voice boomed out.

"Beta Ash, may I have permission to step inside?"

"How do you know my name?"

"My sister, the one in your arms, told me before I walked away. I knew I passed into your pack lands and didn't want to create any more unnecessary problems for any of us."

"Why was she this bad? How could you leave her like this?"

"Beta, I felt the vibration from the three of you running. Sanna knew I wouldn't go far away. I just found her again."

"Where did you find her?"

"In a freaking barrel not too far away. In a rogue campsite. I came across two rogues in the pub in town. That one you were in earlier. By the way, how are you feeling that pain didn't look nice or fun to handle?"

Diamond looked at them both talking back and forth, but when she had enough, she interrupted.

"Well don't just stand there; come in here to your sister. She is fine, just a little weak. Nothing food wouldn't help her with. I just linked the Luna to our new guest here as well."

William looked at the golden wolf and, nodded his head and walked straight to his sister, looking her over for any wounds. He wasn't sure what he was looking for anymore. She was fully healed, but then he noticed the black rose on the ground and looked at it funny. He pointed at it, and Diamond told him.

"Don't touch it. I will summon Morgana here."

Lillian looked at it, and her face paled and screamed.

"Get it away from me."

Diamond gazed at Morgana, her eyes burning with fire and ice as she summoned her through her magical flames. The intense heat filled the air, only to gradually dissipate. In the center of the circle, Morgana stood, arms crossed and glaring at Diamond, demanding an explanation.

"Diamond, what on earth are you doing?" Morgana questioned, her tone laced with frustration.

"Morgana, we've encountered a peculiar black rose that appeared after I saved Sanna's life. Can you shed some light on this?" Diamond inquired, seeking Morgana's wisdom.

Morgana's expression softened with concern as she turned her attention to Sanna. She knelt down and gently asked, "Sanna, I hope you don't mind, but could you share what happened before this rose emerged?"

Sanna hesitated for a moment before responding, "Well… after I was healed by Diamond, a strange thing occurred. Her water left my body, and it was followed by a significant amount of sticky white substances."

Morgana's eyes widened in understanding as she processed the information.

"Sanna, what happened to you at the rogue place? Because I know some of it from what Diamond has just told me."

Sanna started to shake and cry, holding on to Ash, not wanting to look at anyone. Morgana looked at Diamond while Diamond looked at Sanna, worried and confused. Morgana put her hand on Sanna's shoulder and whispered.

"I can remove those memories if you want."

Sanna only nodded her head; she didn't want to look into Ash's eyes knowing what had happened to her; she wasn't pure anymore for him. The fear of rejection, or worse, his hatred, gripped her. She was so afraid he would reject her or, even worse, hate her only to make her pay for it for the rest of her life. Morgana laid her hand on top of Sanna's head to reach into her mind for the most recent memory, she saw the last hours before she ended up on this field. Making her look over to Diamond and giving a small smile, she removed the bad and created some new happy ones of being on a field running around with Ash. Holding their hands together at dinner parties and time with her brother. After Morgana was done, she asked Diamond.

"Diamond, can you burn that flower for me and then come for a walk with me? I need to talk to you."

Diamond twisted her head to the side but did what she was asked to do. Within seconds, the black rose was incinerated, and dark smoke rose up towards the sky, and then the flower dissipated with the smoke. After the task of the flower was complete, Diamond stood up, and walked away with Morgana asking her.

"What is it you wanted to talk to me about?"

"Tell me how you can mind link people without sharing a bond or a pack? I know what you did with a counter spell on Tanya; it was smart but evil. I do know you tried to keep her safe as well, giving Sanna a chance to escape before anything could happen to her."

"I can mind link with anyone that gives me their name or touches me. I'm not sure why, but it was great in that situation. I didn't mean for Sanna to get hurt by it. I heard everything through the link, and she never blocked me out."

"I know I saw and heard everything. I must say you are a girl with a lot of potential and have one devious side in you. I know we are going to have fun training you."

"Morgana, one more thing. Jade can read minds; they are like an open book for her, and they are nothing she has ever had control over. She is very good at ignoring everything, well at least most of the time."

"That is interesting indeed, well the training is not going to be fun anymore because no one will be able to surprise her."

With that, Morgana started to laugh so hard that she started to have tears running down her face.

"Morgana, one more thing. I believe that the William guy is hiding something."

"Diamond, what makes you think that?"

"First he is hiding his scent, both with corpse smell and also blocking it from us. It's like he could smell more like a human than a shifter."

"That is indeed interesting. I do smell the foul smell from him but not the other part; that is good to know. So, Diamond, do you think we should take everyone back to the pack house, letting them travel in Diamond Express."

"Morgana, sometimes it can be fun with just a run."

"I'm too old to run, and you did summon me here. Either we travel Diamond Express or I will piggyback ride on you all the way back."

Diamond looked at Morgana, giving away a huge huff of irritation, but gave in. They both walked back to the group, and Diamond said out loud.

"Let's get back to the pack house, like Morgana so eloquently said, via the Diamond Express, because I'm not a horse for Morgana."

That last sentence made everyone laugh so hard that they had to sit down to hold their bellies, which made Diamond even more irritated, letting out an indignant huff at them all. So, Diamond started the teleportation spell around them all while they couldn't contain their laughter. William noticed what Diamond was doing and jumped a little but didn't move away from them all. One second, they were at the field, next, they all appeared in Alpha Ben's office still laughing, and the Alpha looked at them, then at Diamond's irritated face. He made up his mind not to even ask what had happened. Alpha Ben stretched out his arm to Diamond. She took notice of it and walked to him when he asked, "You wouldn't mind if I petted you for a little while, as they go on with their laughter?"

Diamond shook her head and leaned in for a much-needed head and neck massage. Making Alpha Ben chuckle but didn't say a word when Diamond lost her temper about William still hiding his scent and barked out.

"Willian, when in the hell of this earth are you going to unblock your scent? Is it that you don't trust us, or is it me you are afraid of?"

That bark made the whole room quiet, and Alpha Ben's eyes darted to the newcomer in the room and raised an eyebrow, waiting for an answer. When William slammed his facepalm onto his forehead, he started to explain.

"I'm so sorry. I completely forgot I put it on after my swim with the dead half-rotten corpses to hide it even more from Tanya."

"Well, that would explain the dead smell on you, go and get a shower. It's the second door, right."

Alpha Ben pointed to the door, letting William take a much-needed shower.

Then he looked at Sanna and gave her a smile.

"Welcome home, Sanna. We all hope you will stay for good now. You are one of our family now; do not ever believe you can't talk to us about anything."

After half an hour, William walked out with a worried expression on his face, clenching his hands several times, Diamond took note of it and started to listen into his mind to see if she could help him. The only thing she could catch up in his mind was.

"What if she rejects me? I never claimed her, she smells so good."

The rant went on and on over and over again until Diamond got fed up.

"William, please just stop it. You're acting like a child. No one in their right mind would reject their goddess-given mate."

"Diamond, how did you know?"

"Let's just say it's a girl's intuition about it. How is your mate?"

Sanna looked at her brother and walked up to him, taking his hand to give him support and comfort. Nodding to him, making sure it's safe to make his scent known to everyone. She also followed his eyes and noticed he was looking at Sarah all the time with regret over what he had done and a glint of hope at the same time. Sarah looked back at him with curious eyes, trying to figure out why she was drawn to him. When the scent hit her at the same time that he took down his scent blocker. Sarah could only smell sandalwood mixed with a hint of vanilla. Her jaw dropped, and the only thing her own wolf was screaming was *Mate* in her mind, giving her an intense headache at the same time. Sarah looked at him with the eyes of a puppy, asking him.

"Why would I reject you?"

"Because I never revealed to you who I was from the beginning, and it's wrong, and who wants a shadow shifter as a mate?"

"I want you, and you are coming with me right now. Because I'm going to mark you and bond you to myself until the day we die."

That made William's jaw drop to the floor when his brain finally caught up, replacing his shock with a goofy grin. He walked up to Sarah so he could take her and start to walk out of the room. As soon as they left, Ash stood up and lifted up Sanna in his arms to carry her away. He told everyone else.

"See you all in a few days. Sanna and I will be out of reach for a while. I do believe it's going to be the same with Sarah. Diamond, have some fun with your training because when I'm back, it's on."

With that, he walked out, slammed the door after himself, and the rest of them shook their heads. They all looked at Diamond when she stood up and spoke up.

"I will go home to my parents for some well-needed rest. Night everyone."

"Good night, Diamond. See you tomorrow."

Chapter 24

After five days, Ash and Sarah entered the training arena, their faces beaming with smiles. In the center, Jade stood, deflecting a fiery attack from Stefan's Dragon while effortlessly holding Sylvestro and Sylvia in the air. Morgana and Lillian were desperately attempting to free them from Jade's grasp.

Taking in the scene, Ash and Sara transformed into their wolf forms, launching a diversionary assault on Jade. As the sounds of tearing clothes and bones breaking filled the air, Jade smirked and released Sylvestro and Sylvia, sending them flying toward Morgana and Lillian. They landed safely on top of the two as a wall of flooring and dirt rose around Jade and Stefan's dragon.

Growing bored, Jade yawned, provoking an enraged response from the dragon. It spread its wings and soared into the air, positioning itself as high as possible under the roof. With all its might, the dragon unleashed a torrent of flames and fury. However, Jade quickly summoned water and directed it towards the dragon, extinguishing his flame, causing it to cough and descend to the ground, expelling steaming water when Stefan hit the ground with a whoosh.

Lillian rushed to check on the dragon's well-being, prompting him to revert back to its human form, still coughing. It took a while before the coughing calmed down for Stefan, but between the coughing, he was laughing, eventually he started to talk to everyone.

"We all can say she is one hell of a cookie to beat. Love, are you okay?"

"Yes, we are all fine. Jade, how did you know what Ash and Sarah were about to do?"

"Uhm. I heard their thoughts."

"Oh, that is so not fair. That's called cheating, Jade."

Morgana laughed at everything and shook her head. Then spoke up.

"Jade, in just five days, you can single-handedly take all of us, even with a surprise event as well. You also have more control over your magic than you think. I'm very impressed with what you have accomplished in a very short time. What do you think, Lillian?"

"You are one amazing girl, and the control you are showing is amazing; that took me years to do. The power in you is extraordinary. I can't wait to see what you do in your adult life."

While Lillian talked, Ash got a mind link from Sanna asking where the golden wolf was and how Morgana was.

"Ash, where are you, or do you know where Morgana is? I have been looking for the golden wolf, but she is nowhere to be found."

"Oh, sweetheart, she is in the training area with me and the others and beating the crap out of us. By the way she has shifted back to human, and her name is Jade, and your brother just came in here as well, to try to train Jade."

"Tell him to be careful; I just got him back in my life. I will be there soon."

"Okay, love."

Sanna rushed towards the training arena, easily finding her way by asking people in the pack house. Upon reaching the hall, she heard a loud crash and noticed a door with a wolf-shaped dent. Gasping for air, Sanna quickly opened the door to find a black panther leaping across the training area. The panther gracefully landed on its feet, accompanied by a vampire. They both headed towards a small girl who was manipulating a shadow in a whirlwind by controlling strong gusts of wind, keeping the shadow contained.

In a state of panic, Sanna screamed for her brother and the girl being attacked. The piercing scream caught everyone's attention. Jade, who had been holding William captive, released the spell. Sylvia and Sylvestro, who were sprinting towards the girl, froze in their tracks and collapsed to the floor.

Jade, noticing Sanna, approached her with a wide smile, extending her arm and speaking up.

"Hi Sanna. My name is Jade; it is so nice to finally be able to meet you. Well, I hope Ash has taken good care of you for the last five days."

"So, you are the golden wolf. It's nice to meet the human part of you. I must say I'm surprised by how young you are and how big your wolf is. I hope I'm not overstepping, but are the vampire and panther bullying you?"

"Oh, goddess no, they are training me. You just came in when everyone got frustrated with me because they couldn't beat me in human form. I'm sorry if it scared you. I promise your brother is fine; no harm done to him."

"Oh, sorry I interrupted your training, but I want to talk to you and explain my story. Thank you for saving my pathetic life."

"Well, your life is worthy of saving. You belong in the family whether you want it or not. You are Ash's mate, and William is Sarah's mate and they are close friends with Morgana. As she sees them as family, you are our family as well."

"About my life, what happened? I know everyone here wants to know about it. I do think it's important to tell my part in everything that happened."

The group came walking together with yoga mats under their arms, folding them out on the floor to sit on. Ash had grabbed two of them so his mate would sit comfortably as well. As Sanna placed her yoga mat beside Ash, she allowed him to wrap his arm around her waist, seeking solace in their mate bond. Their mate bond was a silent source of comfort, a reminder that she wasn't alone. With a small smile, she mustered the courage to share her story with the others. Recounting the tragic events that unfolded in Las Vegas, she revealed the heart-wrenching loss of their parents at the hands of a ruthless witch and vampire. The impact of that fateful day was evident in her eyes and on her face, weighing heavily on her heart. The very fabric of their family bond had been torn apart in an instant, leaving Sanna adrift in a sea of despair.

In the aftermath of their parents' brutal murder, Sanna found herself lost and broken. It took several months for her to rediscover a sense of purpose, a flicker of hope in the darkness. During this time, she tirelessly searched for her brother, longing to reunite with him. Yet, despite her relentless efforts, he seemed to have vanished without a trace, as if swallowed by the earth itself.

By chance I found a pub named Claw. It was there I met Tanya; she reminded me of that witch that killed our mother. Curiosity got the better of me, so I walked up to her and struck up a conversation. The more we talked, the more I noticed her insane personality breaking through. She did invite me to her home so I could have a bed for the night. I gratefully accepted her generosity. However, I never left. It became my new home. I had a new purpose in my life. Day by day, her behaviour changed to the day she declared herself Queen of all shifters of the world. The worst part was that everyone there agreed with her. Even I got sucked into it and believed that even deep inside me, it was wrong. For every new person joining us, her power grew more, and she was a toxic vacuum sucking up all the questionable folk around the area. However, some of the older members began to go missing, only to appear dead, scattered around in the nearby woods. Till one day, one of my closest friends was half beaten to the brink of death outside my door, fighting for her life. She had the same injuries that I had before, but she was lucky at least she could die outside of that awful barrel. She begged me to run for my life before it was too late for me. Next time, it could be me laying in front of someone's door, or even worse, no one would ever find me or be able to recognise me. She died in my arms not long after her pleading. Her blood ran down my arms and legs that day, the metallic scent filling my nostrils. It was that day I lost the very little humanity I had left within me, and it turned me into a robot. I followed every order that was given to me. Tanya trusted me, and turned me into a spy. I'm so sorry for everything I created. I'm the one that organised that last attack with planning and execution, but I also supervised the attack on your pack here. I asked Tanya about all of them, to increase their strength, speed and tolerance against the Betas of the pack. You two were standing the whole time, even after all the heartbreak during the three weeks. Tanya's mission was to get Ash and Sarah to join her and help her take over the real kingdom and then the world. She knew if she got them both to join her, her allies would follow them. The thing is I'm not sure how she would get either of you to change sides and join the darkness. She even asked me to lure Ash out in the woods. I never tried that; I did still have some integrity within myself and everyone should have a choice of what side they pick. With the last attack, she would have gotten her will if it wasn't for you Jade. When I saw that golden wolf, it felt like my heart began to beat, and I slowly got my life back. With that I knew I had to escape with my life. I was living in hell, trying to find a new purpose, and Ash found me, and we were mates. I was scared when I woke up at the hospital. When your wolf Jade let me go back, you never left me, I could still feel your presence in my head and your mind links, and I do thank you for that. Well, that is my story for you. Ash, I do understand if you reject me over this, I do love you and these past five days have been heaven for me. I do understand if Alpha doesn't want me in his pack anymore or anyone else for that matter. Thank you… all for everything… especially helping me escape out of hell."

After finishing telling her story Sanna started to stand up with tears falling down from her eyes. The regret in her was shown clearly. When Sanna almost was on her two feet, a growl left Ash lips, followed by everyone else in the room. Ash stood up and spoke between the growls.

"Where the fuck do you think you are doing. You are not leaving me one more time?"

"I'm leaving the pack lands. I don't think anyone wants me here after everything I have done, so I will leave and never come back. If you want Ash, I can start the rejection for you if that would make it easier."

After the last word left her lips, a new voice broke through Jade's mouth and everyone looked at her and got met by a pair of blood-red furious eyes staring daggers at Sanna. Slowly but steadily, the hair changed, but Aria never shifted fully out, but it was clear as day the hatred over Sanna's words triggered her. Aria opens her mouth and hissed out.

"Why the fuck would you leave for something that has happened? Everyone here is fine, and Ash is your mate. Are you stupid or just dumb? You and him are marked, have fully completed the mate bond, you are family, so stop with your bloody nonsense and grow the fuck up, or we will have a big problem."

The training area got quiet, and everyone looked shocked at Aria in Jade's body, so Morgana spoke up and told Sanna who she was.

"Sanna, this is Aria. She is Jade's less than eloquent vampire soul, and you are the first one dragging her out to play with us. Do you think everyone would hate you for that? Take that thought out of your mind. As for Tanya, she will be dealt with when the time comes; we will be prepared for that. So Sanna please stay; I don't think the Alpha has anything against you. Right Alpha Ben?"

"Of course, not Morgana, she is Ash's mate. She is to stay. No matter what has happened."

Alpha Ben smiled at Sanna, stood up and walked over to her with open his arms, pulling her into a hug and said in her ear.

"Welcome to the family, Sanna. Please stay."

Sanna broke down, bowing her head, tears flowing down her pale cheeks and began thanking him.

"Thank… you, Alpha. I… promise to make you… proud," Sanna said between racking sobs.

"In our family, I'm only Ben, not Alpha. Let's get back to training again. My bruises are all healed again, and I'm prepared for another beating."

That made the room relax again, and everyone stood up, walking into position for a new beating of their lives.

Chapter 25

Jade started to grow into the pack and became a part of it, creating a new bond with young adults like herself. She also started school for the second time in her life and was a bright student. She always made sure to have good grades and be a helpful person towards every pack member. Jake and Samantha saw how happy she was and they themselves had grown comfortable in the pack life. They both got a job in the security part of the pack and did regular patrol duties. Jade finished school one year earlier than the other pupils her age, and she also started to help other students with their academics. The bond between the Alpha and Luna increased every day with Jade, and she blossomed under their wing, taking every opportunity to have a chance to learn more about the outside world and laws around the shifters community. Jade had also tried to find memories about her past with the help of Morgana and Lillian, but they always came to a mental block no one could break past. Despite the brutal nature of the training, Jade remained undefeated. Sanna occasionally worried that they pushed her too far, but she was always amazed by Jade's abilities. Ash often returned from training with bruises and broken bones, prompting Sanna to console him while teasingly laughing at his puppy dog eyes. Stefan had learned the hard way not to unleash his full firepower on Jade, as it only resulted in him coughing up water for hours after losing his temper.

287

Sylvia trained Jade in speed and agility, showing how to use the trees and roots as help if she was out scouting or just playing hide and seek with the younger children. Jade received a question from Luna Vivian (if Jade would like to be the godmother of her children), which Jade accepted and was so thrilled about. She had fallen in love with them both and always played in human form, but she would also give them piggyback rides on Diamond. There had been a big change in the pack after Jade and her parents joined. Most were happy with life changing for them. Ash and Sarah had two kids together; both kids inherited two shifting skills and gave Ash a run for his money. There were many times Ash had to get Jade to help him because they both had shifted into ravens and were out of reach for him to grab them. Every time Jade came, she tried to hold in her laughter and helped him put the two small devils to bed, humming her favourite song, but this time, she knew how to control it and turned it into a lullaby for every child within the pack. This day, the pack was bustling in preparation for a very special day that was to come. Everyone was helping out and refused Jade to help out in any way or form, only because her birthday was coming up and it was her sixteenth. It's also the day she would be able to find her own mate, and that was a big thing for every wolf. Jade had begun to feel on edge, so she looked for Morgana to see if she wanted to go for a walk and ask her about something.

"Oh, there you are Morgana. Would you like to go for a walk with me? I need to talk to you for a bit."

"No worries, Jade, let's walk for a little bit, and of course, you can always come to me for a chat."

Jade and Morgana left and went for a walk in the forest when Jade started to talk openly about her feelings.

"Morgana, I'm scared about finding my mate after everything the moon goddess said so many years ago."

"I understand Jade, but you do have the knowledge about everything beforehand. Use that to your advantage. Give it a chance; he could have changed as well over the years, perhaps gotten on to the right path."

"I do know that as well. It's just that I can't shake off the feeling growing in me."

"Jade, you can mind-link us all whenever you feel insecure. No one knows all that, only your closest friends and family. You have worked very hard to keep yourself and everyone else safe. You are strong and powerful, don't think a mate could change that, and if he tried well then set his ass on fire."

With that, Jade started to laugh, looked behind them, and saw an Omega running towards them, screaming.

"Morgana, Jade you both are needed at the southern border."

"Okay, Jade will teleport us there?"

"You should take a hold of my hand. Mentor."

Within a nanosecond, Morgana and Jade disappeared in front of the Omega while she linked Ash back that they were on their way. Jade felt a bit nervous that nothing had happened around the pack in the last five years, and she always wondered what could be so important this time.

Jade and Morgana appeared next to Ash and Sanna, when Jade saw Sanna shaking like an autumn leaf falling from the tree tops to the ground. Without thinking about it, Aria took over Jade's body and fully shifted for the very first time. A gasp was heard all around her, and Ash boomed out.

"Holy shit, this can't be good, Morgana, look at Jade. She is turning into one scary mother fucker. Holy fuck!"

Morgana looked next to her and noticed Jade's appearance had changed to a new, complete form. Where Jade stood was a tall woman with silver/white hair, blood-red eyes, a sharp nose and full red lips. Her nails grew longer, forming the shape of hunter's knives. The whole body filled up and simulated a more grown adult woman in her early twenties. Creating a perfect illusion and seductive figure, all for making it easier to trap her new victims in lust and love. Morgana opened her mouth and before she even could speak, Aria spoke.

"Listen and watch."

Everyone got quiet and was listening in for whatever Aria had noticed when a weak, small howl interrupted the silence around them all. It was then Aria smirked and spoke up sarcastically.

"Do they have all your full attention now?"

Slowly, eyes upon eyes started to let themself be known in between the trees of the forest. Aria lifted her nose up to the sky and began to laugh. When she settled down in her laughter, she uttered some words under her breath.

"Did it really take that bitch five years to get an army together? Such pathetic piece of a witch."

Morgana looked back at Sanna and saw her pale face and she said in a stern voice to Ash, "Get her out of here, keep her safe."

"Morgana, we can fight."

It was then Aria looked at him with murderous eyes.

"Don't be fucking stupid, pup. Do as you are told, put your mate and family first. Stupid ass, or I will make you run for your life."

"Morgana, is that little bitch on the bear back Tanya?"

"Yes, it is. She has aged and is not doing well. I do wonder what happened to her."

"Oh, I can answer that question; he left her for someone else. Diamond put a spell over Sanna's mind that spilled the beans on her meaningless life. I must say he made the right choice there."

With that Aria started to laugh again and walked up towards the barrier so she could make contact with her new little bitch toy. When she reached the end of the barrier, her laughter stopped, and she yelled out.

"Hey you! Yeah you, the scrawny old witch on the bear's back. Why don't you take your boney ass off that poor thing? He is not yours to ride. How about you? Use your chicken legs and try walking instead."

"Who do you think you are, scum?"

"I'm the mother fucking queen going over your brainless head, so you should do as your told vermin."

"How dare you? You are nothing compared to my powers."

"Wanna bet? Let's have a fight, just you and me then stupid. By the way, your former mate saved his ass from you, go him!"

Tanya looked at Aria with hatred fuming from her eyes while tears slowly left the corner of them both. Morgana looked at Aria, wondering what she was doing. No one had ever dealt with the full Aria before, and she was surprised by how she acted. Nothing like Jade would do, but Morgana prepared for a battle of the lifetime yet again against hundreds of outcast shifters. Jade looked back at Morgana and Lillian and spoke up.

"Let's move this barrier around us and these misfits out there. I feel like I need to make them feel cosy when they are welcomed by death. Who feels up for playing with some new toys before they get all tarnished?"

Lillian and Morgana gazed at each other, giving away a wicked smile, and with help from Aria, moved the barrier, shrinking it down bit by bit. Set and done, the team shifted, and Sylvestro walked up to Aria and spoke.

"Little one, why are you antagonising her more? She is already beyond repair?"

"Don't you see the funny faces she is making? Just wait for it, big brother, give it a few seconds."

"Oh, I get to be a big brother; I'm so proud of myself. Honey, did you just hear that I'm her big brother? That is topping anything for today."

Sylvia's panther just looked at her childish mate and shook her head in embarrassment, walking behind Morgana with her tail between her legs. Making Lillian and Morgana giggle at this behaviour. When Lillian said in a soft voice.

"Come on Sylvia, you know Sylvestro is an overgrown toddler who will probably never grow up."

Before any more was spoken between the friends, a shrieking voice interrupted them, yelling.

"I will rip your throat out; you mean nothing. You are a disgusting worthless flea, a waste of space in this world. I will end you and everyone that you care about; let you hear them scream in agony while everyone on my followers has their way with them, and it will start with that bitch Sanna. It was such a mistake not to drain her life essence."

Aria's eyebrow twisted up, and an evil, wicked smile left her lips when she looked at Sylvestro and spoke.

"See brother you only had to wait a few seconds before she would tell us everything that's not going to happen. She is just brainless; it is amazing that she is still alive, and she can even call herself a witch. You think she would have used some of that power to upgrade her looks and give herself some manners. Poor little thing."

Sylvestro began laughing so hard he had to sit down while pointing towards Tanya and her face. For every laugh that left him, everyone else started cracking up as well, and Tanya's face turned even redder when she screamed out.

"Kill them all, have your way with them, let no one escape. They will suffer for what they have done."

"Oh Tanya, don't forget about yourself. They can have you as well. Your body is already well-used for years now. You must have started young anyway."

Now that was it: Aria hit a nerve, making Tanya jump off the bear and start running towards Aria, screeching so loud that everyone's ears started to hurt, and you could hear whining from all the shifters. Aria looked at the running chicken legs as she lost her footing and fell face-first into the dirt, still screeching only to collect soil and grass in her open mouth. Aria crouched down with mock concern to say.

"Are you okay, Queen chicken legs? I don't think they can carry you. You were probably safer on the bear's back, to be honest. Do you need help getting up, or are you trying to be a donkey as well?"

Aria stood up again, looked at Sylvestro and saw him just grinning from ear to ear. She turned her back towards Tanya, letting her have a chance to stand on her weak legs, but Aria was still focusing on the sounds around her. When she heard words leaving Tanya's mouth, a sizzling sound burst out after the words, and a whistling swept through the air towards Aria. She turned around at the last second, lifted her hand and grabbed the small electric ball with her right hand. So she could walk back towards Tanya and start to speak.

"Is this the best you've got for me? I think this belongs to you, and I'm willing to give it back as well. I was always taught not to accept unwanted gifts from a stranger or was it from someone that looks strange. Oh well, either way works!"

Then she slammed her closed fist down on the side of Tanya's face, letting her own spell reflect right into its caster's own body. The spell made her scream in pain every time a new electricity pulsated within her. Aria walked away yawning, it seemed there was a lack of creativity and strength in her new enemy. When Sylvestro spoke to Aria, "Little sis, I'm getting sick of this boring game. I have had enough empty threats towards our family and friends. Plus, I'm getting hungry as well, you know I don't eat breakfast. So can we please deal with this now so we can get on with attending your celebrations?"

"You are so right, and I shouldn't have delayed you in having a nice light snack when it was so delightful of it to walk to us. It really is a great delivery service though. Please bro, pick whatever flavour you want, but leave chicken legs for me. I need light protein today. I don't want to look fat on my big day, right?"

"Oh, good thank you. I have a taste for bear steak. I need to put on a bit of fat for one day. You can keep your chicken legs, well honestly, I would say she is more like a fish on dry land at the moment. She was supposed to be Queen? What a joke."

Sylvestro started to happily skip away towards the crowd of different shifters. In their eyes the shock was still lingering until they noticed Sylvestro happily skipping towards them. Then reality kicked in, and everyone tried to escape from the area, leaving Tanya alone to defend herself on the field. Not one shifter realized the true nature of their adversary, a force far more formidable than a mere pack of wolves. Sylvestro's drinking came to an abrupt halt as he erupted into a fit of contemptuous laughter. His voice echoed through the air, desperately attempting to halt the fleeing figure. "You cannot escape me! I crave your flesh, just a taste, a harmless nibble, nothing more!" But his pleas fell on deaf ears, as nobody paid him any heed.

Frustration fueled his undead speed, propelling him towards the fleeing bear and igniting a fierce confrontation between the two. Meanwhile, Tanya, seething with anger, rose from the ground. With a wave of her hand, she cast a spell, enveloping her allies in a torrent of fury and strength. The effects of the enchantment rippled through the other shifters, transforming them into formidable warriors.

As the chaos unfolded, Morgana observed the spell's impact on the shifters and cast a knowing smirk towards Tanya. Raising her voice above the commotion, she yelled back, adding fuel to the fire of the escalating conflict.

"I would love to see how you defend yourself against dark magic."

"Oh my dear, you have never learned at all, nothing during the years with us either; you are such a great disappointment."

Aria didn't move and looked over after Sylvestro, who was chasing the bear shifter, yelling and screaming.

"Come back here. You are my snack; you can't really let a starving vampire go hungry for real right. Stop running from me."

Chapter 26

The bear quivered in dread, the whites of its eyes clearly visible, its breath coming in racking gasps, fighting the enormous panic that threatened to overwhelm it. As Tanya's spell took effect, the rest of the people felt a surge of power, except for those who pretended to be furious but were actually consumed by fear. Some attempted to escape, but each time they encountered the barrier, a sharp pang of writhing pain shot through their bodies, forcing them to retreat closer to their doom. Reluctant to take the first step towards Aria, who was growing impatient, they watched as she nonchalantly blew on her fingernails.

Growing weary of the waiting game, Aria decided to take matters into her own hands. With a dismissive remark, she singled out a wolf from the crowd of shifters. "Well, it seems I'll start with you then. Waiting for you lazy buggers to attack is becoming unbearably boring." With a swift motion, she slashed her nails across the left side of the wolf's enraged face. A loud whine accompanied by a growl escaped the wolf as deep cuts marked its flesh, causing blood to trickle out slowly. The wolf's left eye hanging by the optic nerve as Aria withdrew her claws. Aria's eyes darkened at the sight of the blood, her thirst intensifying.

The wolf, now defending itself against Aria, only succeeded in amusing her. Chuckling, she taunted, "Oh, did I upset the puppy? Don't worry; soon you won't be feeling anything at all."

As she rushed in and grabbed the wolf by the throat heaving it up over her head twisting around, at the last seconded body slamming it down at her knees. Crouching down next to the wolf, she knew she had broken the spine. As the air left the wolf's lungs, Aria joyously dug her fangs deep down into the carotid artery and began drinking while savouring the sweet taste of her prey. During her drink, she used her nails to rip open the wolf's torso, letting the remaining blood bleed through the open wounds. The wolf's entrails spilling out onto the grass like a steaming pit of mating snakes. Little by little the life of the wolf slipped away, and Aria looked down on the wolf and turned it to the side, fascinated at how all the different organs were sliding out onto the ground, the heart now twitching like a bag full of maggots. It was then Aria bent down and took the purply green, ten-metre-long intestines, yanked it away from the body and, threw it over towards Sylvestro and yelled.

"Big bro, I have a dessert for you here, catch."

With a big grin, Sylvestro took off what Aria had thrown at him and caught it before it touched the ground again, yelling back.

"Sis, you forgot the heart; that's the best part."

"Fine, hold on, you are such a fucking picky eater."

Aria turned back around and bent down to the body again, stuck her hand in the open wound and took hold of the still quivering heart, ripping it out with a loud squelch, then mockingly yelled out to Sylvestro again.

"Here you go, you bastard. Next time, fix your own bloody breakfast."

Shortly after Aria's actions, the battle commenced, and Lillian began her spell to create a platform for herself. She used her magic to ensnare the intruders one by one, while William aided her by eliminating them with his knife and sword. However, without any warning, Lillian felt a sharp pain in her abdomen. Looking down, she discovered a silver arrow embedded in her side, causing excruciating agony. Unable to bear the pain, she fell to her knees, tears streaming down her face. Despite her suffering, she attempted to reach for the arrow, but each movement only intensified the torment. Witnessing Lillian's anguish, Stefan was overcome with fury. He took to the air, searching for the archer responsible. Spotting his target, Stefan swiftly descended upon him, clamping his powerful jaws around the man, causing him to scream in terror, but the scream was short-lived. With a forceful bite, Stefan tore the archer's body into three pieces, dropping them to the ground below. Meanwhile, William continued to defend Sarah, but suddenly, a severed body part landed in front of him. The resulting explosion of blood and flesh engulfed them, leaving them drenched in the remains of the fallen archer that had taken out Lillian. As the battle raged on, the killing intensified, covering the ground with blood and viscera; pieces of flesh and matted fur clung to trees like morbid Christmas decorations. All the blood and dead bodies were not the worst, though. You could hear the moaning screams of dying shifters mixed with the agonising cries of the misled human fighters. Sarah was frantically running, slicing throat after throat. She was completely covered with blood; on her back were dangling remains of the insides of the victims she had killed. Sarah was standing in a fight against a vampire when a rogue wolf snuck back behind her to grab hold of one of her back legs, trying to hamstring her. She noticed the wolf too late and didn't have time to react fast enough. A high howl of pain left her throat before she acted and spun around. While doing that she ripped her back leg out from its hold, damaging it gravely. While spinning loose, she launched her jaws at the offending wolf and got a hold of the rogue's neck, twisting it with everything she had to the side, into which she felt the body go limp before she ripped the head off with a loud snap of broken vertebrae to spit it out to the ground. Turning to handle the vampire next, she saw her mate with his head in his hands, grinning and blowing her a kiss before running off to do some more damage on the field. Sarah was trying to limp away as well, but to her horror, she was badly hurt. Her back legs and hamstring was severely damaged, causing a debilitating limp. The head Sarah had let go of had begun rolling towards Morgana's feet. When it touched her, she looked down to shake her head. She gave away a large smile and kicked it away like a wretched soccer and yelled out.

"Next one. Don't let it hit the ground."

A pain ripped through Morgana's body within the bond she had with Lillian. In a haste, she pulled up a barrier around her niece and looked for Stefan. She noticed his fire filled with fury, burning away corpses and humans alike. In all the pain Morgana felt, she lost her concentration for a few seconds. When she gathered herself, a rogue jumped towards her. A black mist of short fur flying in front of her, grabbing the rogue by the neck. Morgana took a deep breath of air and relaxed when her mind reflected that it was Sylvia who came to her rescue. Sylvia knew she looked horrible. Blood matted her fur, and all she could smell was metallic and dead wet dog. She managed to kill off the larger rogue by ripping out his larynx, Adam's apple falling out of her mouth. The rogue wolf shifted back to a human and was weakly coughing up blood through his missing larynx, while attempting to hold his throat together. As his breathing faded, he fell to his knees, struggling for air and was suffocating from his own blood that was welling out of the gaping wound. Sylvia took a small moment, catching her breath, and began looking around. The only thing she could see was a pure blood bath all around them. In the middle, she could see Aria, ripping limb after limb off of bodies. Aria was covered in both blood and an assortment of visceral organs. Her skin steamed from the bloody covering, her pale skin now a deep red hue. Her silver/white hair didn't have a single strand of its natural colour. You couldn't see one spot on her without someone's blood. Then a head flew towards Sylvia, hitting her right on her forehead. Stars danced in her eyes; with a grunt, she lost her balance and stumbled a little before she looked at Morgana and growled at her silliness. It wasn't long before most of the enemies had fallen by them all, and Sylvia shifted back to her human form, walked to Morgana and started to speak with her before Morgana butted in with

"Tag! You're it, Sylvia!"

"When are you going to stop playing soccer with heads?"

"Come on Sylvia, don't be like that. It's fun and keeps us focused as well."

"That's true. Morgana, I think we trained Jade a little too well. Look at Aria, she is scary angry. I have never seen Jade this angry."

"Aria, loves her friends and family. No one threatens them without consequences. She pushed Tanya as far as she could to make her blinded with hatred, most of it directed at herself."

"I hope she never loses her cool with us because she is deadly. We created a war machine in that girl."

In the middle of all this, Tanya had crawled away from everyone, and Morgana had taken notice of it and mind-linked Aria.

"Tanya is crawling away."

"I know I already laid a trap on that path for her, I'm just waiting until she falls into it."

Morgana started to chuckle and shook her head when she and everyone else heard Aria's voice booming over everything. Making the last shifter stop in mid-fight, causing a new choice over what they just had heard to be made.

"Stop trying to run away from me. You are just a dead little bitch trying to delay her own death."

"Leave me alone, you freak."

"I wish I could, but what's the fun in that? Keep your eyes open."

The few shifters that had survived the massacre put their hands over their head and went down on their knees, pleading for mercy.

"Please spare us; we were misled in all this. Our deepest apology."

"That's not up to me. If it was up to me, you would be killed. I wouldn't spare any vermin like you."

The shifters on the ground bowed their heads and looked around at the fallen ones that were barely recognisable, surrounded by the overpowering miasma of death. They knew their own mistake and mourned the loss in silence. Aria's gaze remained fixed on Tanya amidst the blood that dripped before her eyes. Occasionally, she licked her own lips, moistening them from the slowly coagulating blood. It didn't take long for a horrifying noise to shatter the silence. In a bald patch of grass, a large beach of fine sand lay undisturbed, except for Tanya, who found herself trapped in its center, screaming in desperation. Each futile attempt to move only caused her to sink further into her impending doom. Tanya's cries for mercy and pleas for help went unanswered, echoing in the empty air. Aria looked over to Sylvestro, gave way to a grin and spoke.

"Well, look at that, I trapped a rat."

"It looks like it. What are you going to do about that?"

"I'm going to have fun. Is anyone up for a barbecue with rat as the choice meat? I hear it tastes like chicken drumsticks!"

Everyone except Sylvestro wildly nodded their heads no, while Sylvestro only nodded with a big shit-eating grin, rubbing his belly happily. After that, Aria purposely walks at a normal human pace towards her trap and Tanya. Behind, Tanya could make out the sound of footsteps getting closer, her whole body shivering in fear. Eventually, the steps came to a stop in front of her. Tanya looked up and was met with a pair of red eyes peering down. It was then she noticed the field had gone completely hushed, silence so deep you could cut it with a knife. There was no growling or whining, not even a footstep for her. It was as if time had stopped yet again in her life. When she remembered that day her mate left her, tears started to creep down from her eyes, and then a voice broke the silence and her thoughts were broken.

"What the fuck are you crying for, rats don't cry!"

Tanya looked at Aria and shrunk away, trying to escape Aria's intense red-eyed stare. Forgetting the predicament she was in; her efforts caused her to sink down even more. The lower part of her body had disappeared in the quagmire. The only visible part left was up from her flat, boyish chest. Aria couldn't hold her laughter anymore; looking at the scared Tanya, Aria sat down in front of her, reaching out her hand gently, almost tenderly, towards Tanya's face. Letting one of her nails scrap a line from the hairline next to the ear to follow along the high cheekbones all the way to her lip philtrum. Pitiful screams erupted out of Tanya's throat as blood slowly flowed out of her wounded face, and the grin on Aria's face grew larger, more sadistic, to the point that her fangs were showing. Aria licked her fangs menacingly while at the same time looking at Tanya to ask her, "Do you want to know what it feels like being a blood bag?"

"Sis, may I have that honour? I don't want you to have bad blood in your system, and she stinks of it."

"Brother, I would never deny you that, and she isn't my type anyway. What girl wants to have the breath of rotten scum? Even cough syrup would taste better."

"Sis, we do need to talk about that last part very soon."

"You two can't do this to me; I'm a Queen."

Burst Tanya's voice out, interrupting Aria and Sylvestro's talk, making their heads snap towards her and laugh. Between everything Aria got out

"You... a... Queen? Ha! A queen of what, Turd Island, so that makes you queen Shit. At least you smell the part. You are a weasel, in fact, no you are weasel shit and with that, nothing. You have no one in your corner."

Tanya hung her head low, but then she felt the hatred boiling deep in her heart over everything that had happened to her. With the raging hatred inside her she was able to muster up enough courage to yell at Aria.

"Let me go, you fucking bitch. I will kill you when I get out and hang your head on my wall, showing everyone what would happen to them if they cross me."

"Are you for real? Making threats against my sister. Look what she has done to your companions. There are none left to protect you. You just throw them into the lion's den as fodder. You are one funny dead witch," Sylvestro scolded.

Aria stared at her quizzically, tapping her finger with her mouth. She blinked twice and asked Tanya.

"Do you want a painful death, or would you like to have it quick? My vote goes for painful, but out of professional courtesy, I will give you a choice"

Tanya refused to answer or even look at either of them. Aria took this as a sign; she looked at Sylvestro and smiled.

"Painful it is then, damn she takes way too long to make a decision. I'm not surprised, though we had to wait five years before this attack. So be it, have some fun brother. I'm going over to the others."

Sylvestro swiftly stood up and extended a helping hand to Aria, assisting her to her feet. With a beaming smile, he released her, turning his attention towards Tanya. Now, as he looked down at Tanya, trapped helpless in the magical quagmire, he realized that this wasn't just his victory; it was a testament to the power of teamwork and collaboration. Each person in the group had played a part in making this moment possible. Sylvestro shifted his focus back to the task at hand, leaning down to whisper something into Tanya's ear.

"Now, when it's just you and me, I'm going to have my way with you."

A large gasp came out, and as soon it left Tanya's mouth, it turned into a scream of pain. Sylvestro ripped off the ear from its attachment on her head, leaving an open hole directly into her skull and brain. He let his nail grow longer and began to push it inside the new wound he had created, wiggling it slowly, making the blood slowly leave its vessel drop by drop. Sylvestro pulled out his nail and finger, looked at it, and made a face before he could even speak up.

"You are really one hell of a dirty whore. I think I need to clean out your brain before anything else; I could get a disease from you."

Tanya wasn't sure what was going on anymore; the only thing she could feel was pain, and her whole body was paralysed after what just happened. She tried to speak, but nothing came out from inside of her. She was screaming in her own silence. Sylvestro walked around her and took hold of her hair, pulling it back and, on the hairline, he used the nail he just had in her ear. Steady but slowly scraped open the hairline from the face, letting the blood sliding down over her face inch by inch. When it began to loosen up more, he could take the part he had just separated and flipped it back, letting the skull be on display for everyone. Sylvestro looked proud over his handy work when he looked up and saw William walking down to him and asked him, "Do you need a knife or two? That bone looks a bit thick."

"Oh William, just what I need. Do you want the honour to crack it open? Maybe it will be like a Kinder Egg surprise, but a rotting one."

"You, my friend, are one sick bastard!"

Who have followed the journey of Jade. This book is based on pure fantasy mixed in with some personal experience as well. The journey with this writing has shown me all different ways, from scammers to the struggle to complete a full book. It's been hard to get all the words right well because English is my second languish, but it also has helped me grow more within it. My journey started mostly by reading all kinds of shifter books on different reading apps when I one day wanted to share my wired mind with the world. I sincerely hope everyone enjoyed this first book of many to come.

The first book is The Secret Within.

The second book is New Secrets Revealed.

I hope to see you all again in the next book about Jade and her life.

Warm hugs, and keep dreaming high, all of you out there!

C.J. Mellberg

www.ingramcontent.com/pod-product-compliance
Lightning Source LLC
Chambersburg PA
CBHW051110300726
48981CB00001B/73